It's true, she thought, it's loving that makes all the difference, and I love him. I think I have always loved him. She let him take the sweetness of her mouth, she held both mouth and body against him with no thought of resistance, for this was a rapture outside her experience, beyond even her imaginings.

At last he raised his head. 'Gentian, why do you run away from me?'

'Because . . . I must'

'No! You know I want you, and now I know you want me.'

'No!'

'Don't deny it. You are ready for love—you would still like to come to me.'

He kissed her again, quick teasing kisses.

'And I say you *are* a little witch!' He smiled. 'Haven't I seen you transform yourself? First you're disguised as a downtrodden slavey, next you're a prim serving-maid —now you're a capable bourgeoise, but one glowing with passion—what next?'

Evelyn Stewart Armstrong was educated in Bath. In 1941 she joined the BBC Engineering Division and worked at Bush House, London on technical control of the European Services, handling news broadcasts and code messages. In 1946 she went to British European Airways as an air stewardess and flew until 1951, when she married Charles Armstrong, a customs officer.

They moved to a village above the Romney Marsh, where Evelyn began to write novels. Five years ago they retired to the south of Spain, where they bought and renovated an old Andalusian farmhouse. She now does her writing at a window overlooking cork woods and the peaks of the Sierra Blanquilla.

Evelyn Stewart Armstrong's most recent novels include *Madam Satan*, *The Keepsake* and *A Winter Love*.

THE WARLOCK'S WENCH

Evelyn Stewart Armstrong

MILLS & BOON LIMITED
ETON HOUSE 18–24 PARADISE ROAD
RICHMOND SURREY TW9 1SR

First published in Great Britain 1988
by Mills & Boon Limited

© Evelyn Stewart Armstrong 1988

Australian copyright 1988

ISBN 0 263 11714 6

100 729728

Set in 10 on 11 pt Linotron Times
08–0188–73,000

Photoset by Rowland Phototypesetting Limited
Bury St Edmunds, Suffolk
Made and printed in Great Britain by
William Clowes Limited, Beccles and London

CHAPTER ONE

IT WAS THE SMELL of bread that saved her.

It came out of the darkness, a smell so sweet, so redolent of nourishment, that her empty stomach retched and a wave of nausea swept over her. She had been walking for nearly three days, following the winding marsh roads blindly, not knowing where they were leading, aware only that she must keep moving through the snow and the bitter wind—or die. Now her body was utterly exhausted, numb with cold and yet aching everywhere with a grinding, unrelenting pain; her feet felt as if they were encased in lead and that each step must be the last of which she was capable. If she fell, she would not have the strength to get up. It would be the easiest thing in the world to stop struggling, to give in, to drift into unconsciousness in the cold, to end everything by dying. What was the point of going on?

The night was moonless; she could see nothing but the eerie reflection from the snow all about her and the strip of darkness that was the hedge-bottom. But then she smelt bread, and at the same moment something more solid than the darkness loomed up in front of her. Then she saw a faint yellow glow. A house—a half-open door—there must be someone standing there, and at any moment they would shut the door again.

She summoned up her last remaining strength, dragging the freezing air into her lungs and crying out, 'In God's name . . . help me!'

If only her father had been alive, nothing would have been as bad as this.

Even when times had been hard, they had been happy together. They had been all in all to each other, for Gentian's mother had died at her birth. When her father travelled in his quest for knowledge, she went with him. In his company she had been to France, to Germany, to Italy, but the Continent was in turmoil. On their last journey they had made their way back by difficult and dangerous means, finally buying a passage across the Channel on a fishing-boat that was probably engaged in smuggling. They had been landed on a deserted beach and had walked to the nearest town, which turned out to be New Romney. They had so little money that John Summerlee had thought it best to stay there and to endeavour to earn enough to build a small reserve before moving on, he hoped, to London. His scholarship would not be wanted in this backward area, but he was a skilled herbalist, and since doctors were rare here and their methods crude, he stood a good chance of success.

They found a furnished room in a respectable home, and at first all went well. His services were in demand, and with Gentian's help he was able to start a practice. But then the rumours began—how or why, they never knew. Gentian had her suspicions; one man owed them a large sum of money and seemed unwilling to pay; she felt he was at the bottom of their trouble. In a community which was both suspicious and superstitious, one word was enough, and the word was—'warlock'. They began to hear it whispered, the demand for healing brews and ointments dropped, and worse, far worse, people came asking for charms, for love-potions and aphrodisiacs. They were turned away, and resentment was added to fear.

'We must show them we are honest herbalists, and live down these rumours of witchcraft,' John Summerlee said, and they struggled on through autumn. Then came winter, and human nature became as wild and dark as the weather.

There were bitter frosts that gripped like iron and cut like a knife, the ditches froze, ice was washed up on the seashore. The snow when it came brought no improvement. People were ill with chills and fevers, in many cases too ill for John Summerlee to cure them. 'Warlock . . . Witch . . .'—the whispers were everywhere they went. Then John Summerlee himself fell ill. Gentian, distracted with anxiety, did all she could, spending their last money on fuel for his fire and broth to revive his failing strength, but she could not save him, and she trudged through a foot of snow to see him buried in a pauper's grave.

They were waiting for her outside the churchyard—a knot of people with wild eyes, bitter looks and rough voices, and they followed her back to her lodging, shouting, 'Warlock's wench! Witch! Warlock's wench!'

'I'm sorry, you'll have to go,' said the woman who owned the house. 'You must see I daren't keep you. I'll have my windows broken any minute, and that will only be the start.'

Gentian gathered up a small bundle of belongings—a book or two, a few scraps of clothing; nearly everything else had been sold during her father's illness—and with most of her clothes on her back and her father's cloak pulled around her, she had gone out into the grey light of the winter afternoon.

It could have been worse: the steady gaze of her deep blue eyes seemed to keep them at their distance. They hustled her out of town, contenting themselves with shouts and gestures, ribald and scurrilous remarks, hurling stones with their abuse. As the light faded, she trudged through the snow and ice that lay thick on the deep-rutted road which led, she guessed, across the marsh, to heaven-knew-where.

After two days she knew she was near to dying. She had tried to beg food and shelter from isolated farms but had been driven away, as strangers were always regarded with suspicion, and the mood of the country-folk that winter was evil. Apart from a handful of sour vegetable scraps she had filched from a pig-trough, she had eaten nothing since leaving New Romney, and her shelter had been a sheep-fold the first night, a burnt-out barn the second. Across the marsh, the snow lay in great drifts. She had stumbled along the narrow track unable to see its pitfalls; sometimes the ice in the deep ruts held, sometimes her feet plunged through into muddy water that chilled to the bone. There was no help for her anywhere, and without help there was no hope.

Her spirit still rebelled. Had she been born for nothing better than to die in a ditch, when she was not yet seventeen and knew that life could hold better things?

Then came the smell of bread . . .

At first there was no answer to her wavering cry. Then a rough male voice said, 'Who is it? What d'you want?'

'Help me . . . Give me a crust! Let me sleep in your shed . . .'

The man was just a broad outline against the faint lamplight behind him. 'Be off—we don't want beggars here!' He turned, said to someone inside, 'There's no sign of him,' and made as if to shut the door.

'For pity's sake—I'll work!' she cried.

A voice called, 'What is it, William? Come in and shut the door!'

She fell against the house wall, leaning her weight on it, not knowing how she kept her feet.

'Please! Please . . .'

The man's hand went out and pushed the shawl back from her head. There was a long silence while he considered what he saw. Then he spoke again. 'You're young . . . Right, come in.'

With a sob she stumbled over the threshold and collapsed on to a bench just inside the door. For some moments she sat there, leaning against the wall, her eyes shut, her body slumped in utter exhaustion and pain. She was only aware that at last she did not have to force her legs to move, that the air around her held some warmth which registered on the bare skin of her face and hands, although it did not penetrate her snow-sodden clothes and ice-filled shoes. Voices went on talking; she heard the words, but could not bring her remaining scrap of consciousness to make sense of them.

'What have you got there? She looks like a dead rat!'

'Walked some way, I shouldn't wonder. Wanted shelter. I was sending her on, then I thought, with old Sarah no use to us at present . . .'

'She'll be no use neither. Look at her!'

'She's young. Rest and a bit of food—she'll do a turn. It's worth trying. If she can't work, we'll pack her off tomorrow.'

'Waste of a meal.'

'She can have some bread and a bit of Adam's stew. *He* won't miss that.'

'No sign of Adam, you say?'

'No. Stuck in a drift somewheres, shouldn't wonder.'

'Hope not. We need the cart.'

The voices were blurring together . . . She felt herself slipping off to sleep, but she was falling off the bench, and it jerked her back to something near consciousness.

'Shall I give her something?'

It was the first voice speaking; the second, elder, voice answered indifferently, 'If you like.'

She heard movement; a few moments later a faintly savoury smell reached her, and she dragged her eyes open to see a hand holding a pewter plate on which lay a crust of bread swimming in some greyish liquor.

'Here—take it.'

With infinite care she balanced it on her numb hand, and with frozen fingers brought the crust to her lips. Eating was extraordinarily difficult, but when she had mumbled her way through the crust, mopping up with it all the onion-flavoured liquid, she felt capable of raising her head and looking about her.

She was in a fair-sized room, sparsely furnished with a table and chairs, a couple of benches and a cupboard or two. The furniture was old and plain but substantial. In a large brick fireplace a wood fire was burning, and standing on a trivet beside the flames was a cooking-pot, presumably the one from which the thin broth had been ladled. The table bore some pewter plates, half a loaf of bread and a hunk of cheese, scattered anyhow across the board in a litter of crumbs. The two men, it seemed, had already eaten. She looked at them, too ill and tired to be curious, merely registering their presence.

They bore a distinct likeness to each other, and by their ages could be father and son. The older, who had not stirred from his seat by the fire, was like the other of stocky build, with a round face, small deepset eyes and a short broad nose. His hair was of a sandy colour, going grey; 'William', who looked to be in his mid-twenties, was ginger. The father's wide mouth was thin-lipped, compressed, the mouth of a mean and secretive man; William's was full and loose. The men wore rough breeches and coarse shirts, grubby and sweat-stained, topped with leather waistcoats. In normal times she would have found them an unattractive pair, but now her relief at being given a night's shelter wiped out all criticism.

The combined light of the fire and the oil lamp on the table was not enough to reach into the corners of the room, but she suspected it was dusty and uncared-for;

the parts of the brick floor that she could see were dirty and clotted with mud. There seemed no woman about the house, which would explain much.

Outside, there was a distant creaking and rattling. The two men looked at each other.

'That'll be him.'

Slowly the sounds grew nearer and resolved themselves into those of a horse and cart being driven up the rough track. Neither man moved. The sounds went round the house, presumably towards a stable, and then ceased. Some time later she heard footsteps coming from the back of the house, an inner door opened and a third man came into the room. The other two grunted a greeting.

'Had a job to get through,' said the newcomer. 'Snow's drifted deep.' Then his eyes fell on Gentian where she sat huddled on the bench near the door. 'What's this?'

'Come off the marsh begging shelter,' William volunteered. 'Thought she'd do a turn while old Sarah's away.'

He came across and stood looking down at her. He was taller, leaner of build than the other men, his face had finer features and his hair was a light brown, cut short and curling over his forehead.

'She looks half-starved,' he said.

'She's all right. Gave her a bit of bread and gravy.'

'When did you eat before that?' he asked her.

'Three days ago,' she whispered.

'Where have you come from?'

'The coast,' she said, even in that moment trying to cover her origins in case the rumours spread.

'You walked all the way—in this?' She nodded. 'Poor little devil!'

He took a couple of plates from the table over to the hearth and ladled the contents of the cooking-pot into them. When he had put them back on the table, he made a gesture with his head and said to her, 'Come on,' much as if he were calling a dog.

'You're a fool, Adam, going short for her,' said the older man indifferently.

'People are like horses,' Adam replied. 'If you want them to work, you've got to feed them.'

He cut a hunk of bread and pushed it across the table to her. She thanked him, and they ate in silence. The stew consisted of the thin greasy liquid she had had before, with pieces of vegetables and a few bits of gristly meat. Now she had overcome her nausea, and was grateful for it.

When he had finished his stew, Adam got up and filled two pewter mugs from a jug on the sideboard. He was about to hand her one when he thought better of it, and going over to the fire he pulled out the poker and plunged its glowing end into the mug. When the hissing and the steam had stopped, he set the mug before her. As he moved away, he looked down, and checked. He was gazing at her feet and ankles, at the broken shoes and the dried blood and dark bruises which splotched her legs.

'What happened to you?' he asked.

'At some of the farms they set the dogs on me,' she replied.

'They would.'

When he had finished his beer and cheese, he yawned, said, 'I'm off,' took a candle from the sideboard and lit it at the fire. No one answered as he left them by the steep staircase that ran from the far corner of the room against the back wall.

'We'd best get started,' said the older man, and hoisted himself from his chair. As he lifted up the lamp, he said to her, 'You can stretch out here.'

With that, they left her.

There was still some fire, and enough light to see by as she took off her shoes and her father's cloak and spread them on the hearth to dry. The floor was very dirty, so she lay down on the bench against the wall. Too tired to think about the strange household or her own situation, she closed her eyes and fell asleep.

She was aroused by the toe of a man's boot in her back.

'Come on!' a voice shouted. 'We want breakfast!'

Her feet were cut and bruised, and it was agony to thrust them into her shoes, which had dried stiff and hard. Stifling a cry of pain she followed the man—it was the older one—into a kitchen. It was still dark, not even the greyish pre-dawn light was visible outside the small bare windows, and she needed the lamp he had brought to see her way about the room. In a daze she did what he told her, kindled a fire and made a rough breakfast. She cleared the litter of the last night's meal from the other room while the two men ate. There was no sign of the one they called Adam. She went back to the kitchen.

'Here, you! What are you called?'

'Gen—Jenny,' she said.

'Right, Jenny. You can work here a few days. Our woman's sick with the marsh ague. Give us a proper day's work, and you can stay here till she comes back —for your keep.'

'Thank you. Oh, thank you!'

She would do anything, she thought, to avoid starvation and persecution and the need to trudge through the snow and ice hour after hour.

'I'm Master Bartlett,' he went on. 'That's my son, Master William. We're the bakers of Markinge. We'll need you in the bakehouse soon. Get busy in here until we call you.'

And so her servitude began. It was indeed virtual slavery, for they worked her unmercifully for all the hours they chose and paid her no wages. But she had food and shelter, and however hard the work it was preferable to the alternative—taking the road again. The weather did not break, and the thought of the snowbound countryside, depopulated and hostile, appalled her.

She soon discovered the routine of the house. The two Bartletts went into the bakehouse in the late evening to prepare the dough. A wood fire had to be laid and lit in the huge oven, and while the dough was proving and the oven heating, the men had their supper. Then they returned to the great bread-troughs. Later the fire was raked out of the heated oven, and the bread, now shaped into loaves, was put to bake. While it baked they breakfasted, and when they had taken the bread from the oven they slept.

The man called Adam took no part in the baking. He breakfasted alone, after the bakers, then went to the stables, attended to the horse and harnessed it to the cart. He loaded the cart with freshly baked bread and set off, being away most of the day and returning, the bread sold, with a varied load. Sometimes it would be sacks of flour from the mill, sometimes it was household necessities such as meat, salt, perhaps a sugar-loaf or a new bucket. Gentian was at a loss to know his position in the household. The Bartletts spoke to him as if he were a servant, yet he did not behave like one. They were hard-natured, boorish and uncouth in the extreme but she soon found that Adam was kinder and better-mannered, as if some natural instinct made him avoid giving offence. The Bartletts lost no opportunity of jeering at him if he showed any consideration or niceness of manner. He ignored them.

She had been at the bakehouse for several days when she had the occasion to ask him a question, and called him 'Master Adam', in the Bartletts' presence. William gave a coarse laugh, and Bartlett shouted at her.

'You don't "master" him! He be nobbut Adam—Adam Brenzett, my bastard!'

'His mother were a serving-wench!' William added with an unpleasant grin. 'He be lucky to know his father!'

Adam answered the question she had put to him and walked out of the room without another word, while William jeered, '*Master* Adam! That be rich!'

A week passed, and the daughter of the old woman Sarah came to say that she was still not fit for work.

'She lives with me,' she told Gentian. 'She likes to help with the few pence she can earn, and I be glad of it, but the marsh ague's got her. The trouble be, when it's got you, it don't leave. Keeps coming back. I reckon it'll finish her afore long.'

'Don't say that. She'll be better when the summer comes.'

'Will she? Maybe, if she sees summer . . .'

So Gentian stayed.

When the weather broke, conditions were little better, for the snow and bitter cold were replaced by rain which deluged down and turned all the tracks and paths and yards to mud, mud formed from the thick heavy clay, mud that sucked and dragged at every step and could not be kept out of the house or off shoes and garments.

It was February, when the rains had eased a little, that the redcoats came.

CHAPTER TWO

THE BRISK RASPING of the birch broom on the brick floor
had masked the sounds from outside, and it was not until
Gentian paused in her sweeping that she realised the
noise was that of several horsemen coming along the
narrow road. By that time they had nearly reached the
house, and when she looked out of the small window,
she caught a glimpse of scarlet. A troop of soldiers was
coming to a halt, and she gazed at them, thinking how
splendid they looked in full uniform with accoutrements
gleaming. Their officer, who sat erect on his horse with a
casual grace in his attitude, was truly magnificent; as
different from the labourers in the village as if he had
come from another world. She had almost forgotten
such people existed. She heard Master Bartlett's voice
shouting her name, and hurried obediently to the back
of the house. Slowness to respond earned at best a curse
and more often a blow.

Charles Claverton sat his great chestnut horse and
gazed about him with a distaste that verged on disgust.
In the thin light of early February the Romney Marsh
was a dismal prospect. In God's name, he thought, why
should I be here? A leg wound, long healed, was not
enough reason to keep him from active service. He
should be fighting Napoleon. And as for the new defensive canal, so laboriously cut, which he was policing,
he was sure that the brains and effort expended in
making it would have been better used in checking
Napoleon in his own country.

His keen dark eyes roved across the landscape. Grey
mist still lingered over the marsh levels, where the tired

16

winter grass was criss-crossed with bare hedges and dotted here and there with skeleton trees. In the foreground the red coats of his men were the only colour, a singing scarlet against greys and browns. The road beneath their horses' hooves was thick yellow-brown mud; the couple of cottages, little more than hovels, beside which they had stopped, were greyish plaster and dark thatch; the larger cottage opposite, big enough to be dignified by calling it a house, was pink and grey chequered brick, with a tiled roof splotched with yellow lichen. It had two storeys, and its rambling length carried two groups of chimneys, one central, one set to the side, where a huddle of outbuildings made a semi-enclosed yard of a stretch of trampled clay.

From a door giving on to the yard his sergeant reappeared, came over and saluted. 'It is the bakehouse, sir, and they have bread for sale.'

The one does not necessarily follow from the other, thought Claverton wryly, once more cursing the inefficient quartermaster who had sent them out inadequately provisioned. He held out a half-sovereign. 'Pay them in cash, Sergeant Hoskins.'

The sergeant took two men and went inside again. They came out carrying baskets of loaves, and a girl was following them, similarly laden; when she had stowed the bread in the provision wagon and was going back with her empty basket, Claverton was curious enough —or bored enough—to call her over. Unlike the average country girl, she was tall and slim and had a graceful way of moving.

'Girl! Come here!'

Obediently she approached him and looked up questioningly. She was wearing a coarse dark dress with a thin apron, old and broken shoes, no stockings; yet above this crude country garb rose a slender neck and a pale face with delicate features. The face had an air of refinement, a shower of light gold hair fell about her shoulders, and the eyes which gazed into his were an incredibly deep and brilliant blue.

Like a flower in the mud, he thought, and for a moment was too surprised to speak. Then he said the first thing that came into his head. 'Is the bread fresh?'

'It was baked early this morning,' she answered gravely, and he noticed the absence of the broad Kentish accent in the pleasant voice. She spoke without awkwardness, and had not given him the customary curtsy nor addressed him with any title. He was curious enough to keep her talking.

'Is it good bread?'

She paused before answering. 'That depends on your taste,' she replied. 'I have eaten better—and I have eaten worse. Sir,' she added, and made a little bob, both word and action coming so late as to be almost impudent, though she did not look as if she intended to be so, merely that until that moment she had forgotten their necessity.

'And who are you?' he asked. 'The baker's daughter?'

'No. The servant, sir.'

An odd servant for these parts, he considered, and noticed that the hands holding the rough basket were cracked and sore, yet small and well-shaped. She was well-shaped altogether, he noticed: not buxom, but delicately curved in hip and bosom with a slim waist, and her slender arms promised that her legs would be long and shapely under the baggy skirt. She did not fit in this God-forsaken countryside.

'Have you always lived here?'

She seemed to answer reluctantly. 'No, sir.'

'Then where do you come from?'

'From . . . the coast.'

That was not very informative.

'And what are you called?'

Before she could answer, a rough male voice shouted, 'Jenny! *Jenny!*'

'Excuse me, sir,' she said, and hurried back into the bakehouse.

Gentian thought she had never seen so fine-looking a man. Her drudgery was now lightened by the memory of him, erect on his great chestnut horse. She held a picture of him in her mind, seeing the lean-featured brown face, the flashing dark eyes, the gleam of even white teeth when he spoke. She recalled the deep rich timbre of his voice. Compared with the country-folk with whom she now mixed, he was like a being from another world.

It seemed like a miracle to her when the redcoats came again. She carried out the bread to the provision wagon, and he was there, walking his horse up and down near by, and she shot him a glance or two, when he appeared not to be looking, to refresh her memory of him. She had been right in every feature; he was just as handsome as she remembered, and the air of authority which sat so easily on him made him almost godlike. She longed for an excuse to go over to him, but she had none, and this time he did not speak to her.

After the first night, Gentian had been given a room to sleep in, little more than a cupboard between the kitchen and the bakery, but it was somewhere where she could have a little privacy. It was Adam who had found her a pallet bed and a couple of blankets. In this tiny room she tucked away the contents of the bundle that she had tied to her waist during her flight from New Romney and had refused to abandon. She thanked heaven she had managed to save it, for it contained her father's herbal. She promised herself that when the weather was better and the roads hard, she would move inland and try to earn a living, or to supplement a servant's wages, as a herbalist.

She saw few people. Markinge was no more than a scattered hamlet and most of the Bartletts' bread was sold abroad by Adam from the cart; only a handful of villagers came in for bread. It was such a poor community that they often paid in kind, usually with eggs or vegetables. The folk that came gave her curious glances, but said no more than to pass the time of day. Life was nothing but hard work, short commons, exhaustion and brief sleep, but at least, Gentian told herself, she was not starving, nor was she in terror of her life. But, one day, fear returned.

She had heard a horse clatter into the yard, and a man's voice calling, 'Joe! William!'

It was mid-day, and the bakers were upstairs sleeping, but as she looked out into the yard, Master Bartlett stuck his head out of a window and called,

'Is that Harry? I'll be down in a minute. Go inside.'

A short swarthy man shouldered his way into the kitchen and walked through to the living-room, paying no attention to Gentian as she stood in the shadow of the door.

A few minutes later Bartlett shouted to her to bring bread and cheese and beer. She loaded up a tray as quickly as she could and carried it in. The two Bartletts and the newcomer were sitting round the table, and appeared to be discussing something of interest to all of them. As she reached the door, Harry was saying,

'It'll soon be fair enough weather at sea and on land.'

William replied, as she came in, 'We can be ready for the stuff anytime.'

She set the food and drink on the table, aware that the stranger was eyeing her, and suspicion became a certainty. Not only had she seen him before, she could now remember when and where. She was about to leave the room when the man's hand shot out and seized her wrist.

'You be new here. Let's have a look at you!' he said.

Her heart was thumping. She said a prayer that he

would not recognise her. She knew him. He had been on the fishing-boat that had brought her and her father from France, and she had seen him several times in the streets of New Romney. But that was months ago.

A mouthful of blackened teeth showed as a grin spread across the man's face. 'Well, I'll be blowed!' he said, and still keeping a tight hold on her wrist, he turned to Bartlett. 'Do you know what you've got here?'

The baker shook his head. 'Don't care—so long as she works.'

The sailor laughed. 'It's the warlock's wench!'

Gentian tried to struggle free. 'No—it's not true!' she cried. 'He was no warlock!'

'That's what they called him.'

'He was never that! He was a herbalist—he made only healing draughts—he was the best man that ever lived!'

'But he's dead now. Did the devil claim him, I wonder?'

'No! No! Let me go!'

The two Bartletts were saying nothing, but they were looking at her, and she had been unable to hide her distress. What would they do? What would happen if they too drove her out?

'You're not bad looking,' Harry said. 'Reckon you're not too dangerous.'

'Dangerous! She can't even kill a cockroach!' said Bartlett. 'Let her go.'

She caught her breath on a sob, and hurried from the room.

From that time the Bartletts took to looking at her strangely, so she redoubled her efforts to please them, fearful that they might turn her out because of the reputation their friend had given her. To be adrift again without resources was a grim prospect.

The only break in the monotony of her life was when the redcoats came through. Sometimes they stopped for bread, sometimes not. When they did, the Bartletts were grudgingly glad of their custom, when they did not, the two men grumbled together and cursed them.

'They can't even help decent folk earn a living! No, they must go poke-nosing about instead, trying to stop us making a coin or two! . . . Exercises by the Military Canal! Looking for owlers, more like! Damn their eyes!'

'Owler,' she now knew, was the Marsh term for smuggler.

Then, one day, the soldiers stopped for bread, and the officer spoke to her again. 'Jenny, if that's your name!' he called to her. 'Have you got a small loaf that will go into my saddlebag?'

'Yes, sir.'

She hurried back into the bakehouse and came out with one. He gave her a coin.

'I'll get change.'

'No, keep it.' As he took the loaf, he smiled down at her. 'You were right. It's not the best bread, but it will do. Have you worked here long?'

'Since last December, sir.'

Not long. And where was she before that? Charles Claverton admitted to himself that he was intrigued by the servant-girl. She had nothing of the coarsened, blowsy look of the country servants; there was still a freshness and an innocence about her. Claverton, a man of experience, was sated, even repelled, by artificial beauties, and equally disillusioned by whores who gave all for payment and teases who gave nothing and still expected a price. A highly unsatisfactory marriage had driven him to seek consolation elsewhere, but he had found none—or none that lasted. Now this girl, wretchedly humble as she was, had the promise of a charm that was new and fresh and unlike anything he had experienced before. He smiled wryly to himself. Charles Claverton had fallen so low that he was considering a country drudge, a marsh mud-hopper! But gazing into the deep blue eyes, he knew that there was something different about her.

'You work hard here?'

She did not answer, but her look said: That is a foolish question!

'Have you ever thought of changing?'

'Changing? Changing what?' She did not hide her surprise.

'You must have opportunities. I should think, for instance, that life would be easier following the drum.'

'Following the drum?' She repeated his words as if she did not understand them.

'Yes. With the army. Oh, not indiscriminately with the men, you're too good for that. But you could come with me.'

'*With you?*'

'Yes. Don't look so surprised. I'd have you.'

'I don't understand. What should I do?'

'Do? You'd stay with me; no one would think it unusual. Men need women, and I've no woman with me.'

'But what should I do?' she persisted.

Could she really be so innocent? No, she had learnt to use those blue eyes, she had found that wide, candid look was attractive to men.

'You would be my woman, of course—in every respect. Oh, let me introduce myself: Charles Claverton, Captain of Foot.' Still she gazed at him and did not answer. 'You would make yourself useful to me in a number of ways, no doubt. You'd learn to please me . . . In fact, I think we should please each other.'

She looked at him gravely, thoughtfully, but he could see a pulse beating in the base of her throat. She is not really so calm, he thought. She has emotions.

'I don't know . . .'

'What don't you know? You don't have to know anything—we shall get on well as long as you remember you're my woman. No question of sharing favours.'

He let his gaze rest on her approvingly, and as he did so a flush mounted from the edge of her bodice until it stained her face with a hot rosy glow. The women he knew had to buy that colour for their cheeks! Then the deep blue eyes flashed—was it in sudden understanding, defiance, fear?—he didn't know—and then she lifted her head to gaze squarely at him.

'I am nobody's woman, Captain Claverton,' she said quietly, and went back into the bakery.

Calm as she looked, her heart was beating fast. What had she done? She had refused an opportunity to escape, and she was not likely to get another. But escape to what? She had no very clear idea of what the Captain had meant, and had to apply her only yardstick of behaviour: What would her father have thought? She knew he would not have approved of her going off as the Captain's 'woman'—whether as a servant, as she had at first supposed, to care for his uniform and cook his meals, or as something far more intimate. If that was it, it was something her father had always protected her from. The Captain had not looked at her as if he were seeking a servant. Something personal in his gaze had made her blush. But would it be so terrible to be his woman? The bakehouse was dreadful; it would break her father's heart if he could see her now. Had she been a fool to refuse? She admitted to herself that she had turned him down not so much from uncertainty but because he had so obviously assumed that she would accept.

If the sailor's recognition of Gentian had altered the Bartletts' attitude to her, it seemed to have affected William more than his father. He often struck her now, with even less provocation than before, and cursed her as a witch. Until she and her father had arrived in this wild corner of Kent, she had not thought that people still believed in witches, but here the old ways died hard; William probably had some lurking fear which he was venting on her. She told herself she must bear it until the weather improved, then she would take any opportunity to slip away and walk to the nearest town, which was Ashford. There might be a chance of finding work there, where she was unknown.

Because she could not bear to live in filth and disorder, she did her best to make the house clean and tidy. She got no thanks for that. Even keeping herself clean was so difficult and uncomfortable that there were times when she was tempted to become as dirty and slovenly as the Bartletts, but she reminded herself how horrified her father would have been, and told herself she would find a way to escape before long. And an escape, in secret, it would have to be, she knew that now; the Bartletts had found themselves an efficient servant at no cost, and intended to keep her. And then something happened which made them more determined not to let her go.

That night she had gone to bed, exhausted as usual, and had fallen into a heavy sleep. Then, for no apparent reason, she awoke. She guessed she had been asleep for little more than a couple of hours—by the position of the sliver of moon which showed through the small square window it must be not much past two o'clock. She settled down again, and then realised what had woken her. There were faint sounds of movement outside the house. She lay on her pallet, straining her ears, trying to distinguish them. Little dull thuds, a brief murmur of voices, a slight jingling—could there be horses in the yard? She went on listening. Yes, it could be, but if they were, their hooves were muffled in some way. Then she heard a voice, a little louder, almost under her window.

'That's enough for here. We'll take the rest to the church.'

Low as it was, she recognised the voice as Joseph Bartlett's. The *church*? What were they doing? Curiosity was too much for her, so she scrambled to her feet and peeped out of the window. It was too dark to see much more than the movement of shadows, of something more tangible than the general gloom, but it seemed to her that horses and men were filing cautiously out of the yard. In a few moments, the house was silent.

All at once she realised that this could be her opportunity. Joseph Bartlett had certainly gone with the men. If William too had left, she could slip out unnoticed, and by walking through the dark she could put some distance between herself and Markinge by morning light. They would not look for her in the house until they were ready for breakfast. As fast as she could she huddled herself into her clothes, and with the candle-end she had lit well shielded from the window, she tied her few possessions into a bundle. Then, with her heart in her mouth, she cautiously crept towards the kitchen.

When the door creaked, she thought her heart would stop beating. She waited in terror, listening for any movement, but there was none. With his father away, young Bartlett might be dozing in the bakehouse. She crept foot by foot to the dividing door. Once level with it, she could see into the bakehouse. The dough was mixed and proving in the troughs, but the room was empty. She sped to the outer door, lifted the latch, pulled it open, and slipped outside.

As she crept stealthily forward, something moved in the patch of blackness beside the door. The next moment she was seized, held in a cruel grip, and William's voice said hoarsely in her ear,

'And what are you up to, warlock's wench?'

CHAPTER THREE

GENTIAN STRUGGLED DESPERATELY in William's grasp.

'*Well?* What are you doing?'

'I heard people outside—I thought something might be wrong,' she gasped.

'You little liar! You knew we would be in the bakery, so no need for you to get up. You were spying! Here —what's this?' His arm had touched the bundle she was still holding.

'It's mine!'

He dragged her into the kitchen, threw her to the floor, kicked the door shut and bolted it, and pulled open the knot securing the bundle. Her few pitiful possessions were scattered on the floor.

'So you were running away! Is that it? Or were you finding out all you could first, to go . . .' His eyes narrowed with rage as another thought struck him. 'I've seen you speaking to the redcoat officer. Were you running to him to tell him about the owlers?' He began to unbuckle his thick leather belt. 'All right, I'll beat the truth out of you!'

He raised the strap and brought it down with all his strength across her back. She gave a shriek of pain and cowered away.

'No, no! It wasn't that! I just wanted to leave . . .'

Another blow, and another. William Bartlett was paying no attention to the words that broke from her between her screams. He was grinning, enjoying the steady inexorable rhythm he gave to the swinging strap, the slap of leather on thinly covered flesh, the cries of pain.

27

'Warlock's wench! Spy!'

'No, no! I just wanted to get away!'

'*What*—do you *know*—about the *owlers*?' With steady strokes of the strap, he accented the words.

'*Nothing*! I know nothing . . . I've seen nothing . . . I just wanted to go . . .'

He paused, and stood staring at her as she crouched upon the floor. He ran the belt through his fingers, and grinned again. 'So we be not good enough for you here? Going to tell tales to the redcoats, eh?'

'No! How could I? I've nothing to tell.'

'Be you sure?' He raised the strap again.

'*Yes*—I'm sure. Oh, please . . .'

'Then *that's* to keep you sure!' He continued to beat her, shouting a phrase between each stroke. 'Don't ever do that again! No spying, no running away! We'll not have you telling about our business to outsiders! You're here until we choose to get rid of you. Do you understand?'

'Yes! Yes . . .'

How much longer would it be before she became unconscious?

'Try to run away again, and I'll *really* beat you! You won't run . . . You won't even walk!'

Through a daze of pain, she heard the latch lift and the door rattle against the bolt. Reluctantly William lowered his arm and unbolted the door. It was not his father but Adam who came in.

He stopped short on the threshold and looked from one to the other. 'Christ! What have you been doing to her?'

Blood was seeping through Gentian's dress from the cuts on her back. She could feel it, and he could see it as she crouched on the floor with her hands over her head for protection. William, with deliberate casualness, was rebuckling his belt.

'I've been teaching the witch a lesson. She's been spying, and was going to run away. I've put paid to that.'

'You've *what*? You stinking brute!'

William turned on him with a snarl. 'Mind your words, bastard, or I'll start on you!'

Adam spoke to her, but his eyes did not leave William's face. 'Go to bed, Jenny.'

As she scrabbled the contents of her bundle together, the door opened again to admit Joseph.

'What the devil's going on here?' he growled.

'William has been beating Jenny,' said Adam through his teeth.

'Yes. She's been spying, and trying to run away. But I've taught her a lesson. She won't do it again.'

Joseph gave a noisy yawn. 'Is that all? Get out of here, you silly wench! You asked for it. Well, William, you've made your point. Adam, any brawling with William, and I'll sling you out, to fend for yourself like the bastard you are. Well, the job's done, and I'm going to get some rest. And I want a quiet house, d'you understand?'

Gentian, creeping to her tiny room, heard no more. Bruised and bleeding, she collapsed on her mattress, her head reeling, aware of nothing but pain.

The next day every movement was agony. She tried to clean her wounds, and used up the last remaining smears of some precious ointment she had kept till then. There was no knowing when she would be able to make any more. As she crawled about doing her work, she saw Adam's eyes upon her, but he did not speak. They both knew that any word between them raised the Bartletts' rage. For days she suffered the pain of her bruised body and the affront of William's gloating, leering looks.

It was nearly a week before Adam was able to talk to her alone. The Bartletts were both in the bakehouse, and she was helping him to load the cart. He looked at her and said quietly, 'Jenny, I'd help you if I could.'

'I know.'

'I was too late to stop him. If he touches you when I'm here, I'll kill him! Jenny, try not to anger him . . .'

'I do try.'

He went on packing in the loaves. 'I'd get you out of here if I could. Come summer, perhaps I'll think of a way.'

'Thank you, Adam.'

'*Jenny!*'

At the coarse shout, she ran back into the house.

There's nothing Adam can do, she thought. I'm at the Bartletts' mercy. She remembered Charles Claverton, and wondered if she should have gone with him. It couldn't be as bad as this. But she had refused, and he would never ask her again.

'I'll want a good meal on Sunday, wench,' Joseph told her. 'Parson's coming to dinner.'

She had been in the bakery for more than two months, and in all that time no service had been held in Markinge church. Adam had told her that the rector held several livings and never visited his remote marsh churches, but lived where he could enjoy the society of his patron and other acquaintances among the gentry, and indulge his liking for hunting and similar pursuits. He had a curate, who occasionally appeared to take a service or to perform weddings, christenings and burials. It was this curate, a Mr Bolton, who was coming to take a morning service and would afterwards dine with them.

'You clean up the place afore parson come,' Joseph told her. 'Then you cook a good meal. I'll find you a nice piece of meat, and we'll have a suet pudding to start with. With meat and vegetables and then some cheese and winter apples, we'll do all right. You'll wait at table—you know how to do that proper? You do it right, and cook that meal proper, too, or I'll take my belt to you.'

Adam looked up from his plate. 'If you want to impress parson,' he remarked, 'you'd best find Jenny a gown and a pair of shoes.'

Joseph said nothing, but turned a scowling look on Gentian and eyed her up and down. Then, 'I'd thought of that,' he grunted. 'I'll see about it.'

To her amazement, he came down from the bedrooms a few hours later and pushed into her hands a plain gown and a pair of stout shoes, neither of them new but in far better condition than those she was wearing.

'You keep them for best, mind,' he said.

Both were somewhat large for her, but she stuffed the toes of the shoes with pieces of rag, and when she tied her apron over the dress, it sat well enough.

Gentian had, for no reason, expected the curate to be young, but on seeing him she guessed Mr Bolton to be a man nearer forty than thirty. He was of medium height, inclined to stoutness; above his clerical bands was a suspicion of a double chin. He did not give the impression of kindliness that Gentian expected from a man of God: his grey eyes were cold, his pursed-up mouth had the look of disapproval—almost, she thought, of discontent. So much Gentian observed as she made her curtsy and took the hat from his outstretched hand. His eyes rested on her for a moment, then Joseph Bartlett ushered him into the living-room where the table was laid for the meal.

Gentian had been used to her father keeping servants, and knew how a servant should behave; now that she was obliged to be such herself she decided to be a good one, from personal pride, not from fear of Joseph Bartlett's belt. She had cooked a good dinner—the pudding was light, the pork succulent—now she waited at table quickly and deftly, with none of the clumsiness of a country kitchenmaid unaccustomed to handling dishes. While she was in the room the four men said little, but she noticed that when she left it, conversation quickened behind the closed door. She did not guess that some of it concerned her.

The curate left on horseback soon after dinner, but it was not until hours later, as she was serving supper, that Joseph himself gave her news of her deliverance.

'You can pack your bundle tonight,' he said to her roughly. 'You be leaving tomorrow.'

In her bewilderment, she could only repeat his word, 'Leaving?'

'Yes, leaving,' he said. 'You be going to parson as his servant. Adam will take you in the cart tomorrow.'

She could hardly believe her good fortune.

'She'd best take that gown,' said Adam. 'You don't want parson thinking you be short of pence.'

Joseph gave a grunt which could have been agreement, and Adam went on, 'And I'll give her another. She needs it.'

'Christ! You'll do no such thing!' he shouted.

Adam looked at him levelly. 'They were my mother's gowns. You didn't buy them, and since you never married her, you've no right to them. They be mine, and I say she shall have them.'

Joseph's face went red and he gripped the edge of the table. William looked from one to the other, smiling, as if he anticipated a fight. Then, 'Oh, suit yourself!' Joseph snarled, and kicking his chair aside, went off into the bakehouse.

Adam not only found her another gown, he gave her a clothes-basket to put her few possessions in. True, it was old and battered, nevertheless it looked better than having her belongings tied up in a bundle. She half expected William to protest at her going, and Joseph to change his mind, for it hardly seemed possible that she should get away so easily. But shortly after breakfast Adam swung her basket into the back of the cart with the loaves and helped her up to sit beside him. He shook the reins, clucked to the horse, and they were off.

He looked sideways down at her. 'You all right?'

'Yes, Adam. I can't believe it—why did they let me go?'

'The old man owes parson a favour, that's why. Parson's maid has to go, and he can't find another to suit him. When I heard that, I dropped the word to parson that we had a good maid. And he liked the way you waited at table.'

'All the same, I didn't think . . .'

'That the old man'd part with you so easy? Ah, but you see, he has to keep the parson sweet.'

'But why?'

'On account of the owling, of course.'

'Owling? Oh, you mean the smuggling?'

'Surely.'

'But parson doesn't *know*?'

Adam gave one of his rare bursts of laughter. 'Know! Course he knows! He's in it as deep as the rest of us—only he don't do nothing that shows! He keeps out of the way when we're using the church, and . . .'

Gentian's curiosity was roused. 'And what?'

Adam looked at her keenly. 'Whatever I say to you goes no further, mind. It's dangerous knowledge for a lass.'

'I understand.'

'If I thought you a flibbertigibbet and a chatterer, like most maids, I'd say nothing. But you bain't, and you've a head on your shoulders that'd work out a lot without telling, I reckon.'

'Thank you, Adam.'

'Parson tells us what we want to know, see? Such as when the Excisemen are around, and if the military are with them—things like that. Without him, we'd likely run into trouble sometime.'

'And you're in it as deep as the others? Oh, Adam, it's against the law!'

He grinned. 'You'll find none who cares about that round here! Everyone who can is an owler. If they politicians didn't want owlers, they shouldn't pass laws and taxes that bear so heavy on folk. We can't live by them, Jenny.'

'But it's dangerous, Adam.'

'A bit of danger, yes. But it bain't dull. And I reckon the other side's in worse danger than we be—there's fewer of them, for a start, and we allus knows where they be. It's as well for them we can avoid them.'

'What do you mean?'

'I mean that some of us—like the old man, and William—wouldn't think twice about cracking a man's skull if he was likely to be able to bear witness against them.'

'But not *you*, Adam?'

'I hope not. Reckon another man's life's as sweet to him as mine be to me.'

They drove on in silence for a while. Then she asked, 'Where are we going? I don't even know where parson lives.'

'It be about seven miles from here—place called Losely, on the way to Farrenden.' He broke off and pointed with his whip. 'See, Jenny, how they've cut that big ditch here! I've heard tell that it goes from the coast at Hythe to the coast at Rye, circling round the marsh. Can't see a ha'porth of sense in it myself, unless it drains some of the water off the land. I reckon that 'ud do good to us, but no harm to Boney!'

Gentian was not interested in the big ditch. 'You know the parson's house, then? What is it like? Is it big? And what sort of person is his wife?'

'Wife? He bain't married, Jenny. His mother lives with him—and she be a haughty, pernickety old lady, by all accounts. A big house? No—sort of middling, I'd say, but handsome enough.' His look became serious. 'I did what I could for you, Jenny. Parson wanting a maid—it seemed a good thing for you. So I put it into his head, saying how good our maid was. And since the parson asked the old man, *he* couldn't be suspicious of me, could he? It's safer for us both this way.'

'I understand. And thank you, Adam.' She looked at him with a sad smile. 'I'll miss you. You're the only one who has been kind to me. I won't forget you.'

'You'll be better off with parson. And if you be a good girl, you'll find a man to marry you.'

'I don't think I want to get married.'

'Don't say that. You'll need it, Jenny. A woman needs protection. All men bain't like William and the old man. There's a sweet side to marriage if man and maid agree.'

'You mean, being companions?'

'More than that, Jenny—being man and wife. You be a pure maid, so you've not—not found out about that. But it be true, as I could show you. I've got fond of you, Jenny. You bain't like any girl I know, and I'd marry you, if things were easier. I'd be good to you.'

His face had reddened, and he was staring straight ahead. She thought about his words.

'It's kind of you, Adam, but I know it's not possible.'

'No. The old man gives me no money, and I can make little enough besides, even with the owling. I could make some sort of a living if I hired myself out, but I won't go. Some day he'll pay for the way he treated my mother. Some day I'll make him give me a share of the bakery. It's my right, and I'll have it. So I'm biding my time. He suspects I want it, so he and William keep me out, they don't even let me know the mystery of baking. But someday I'll beat the both of them.'

Gentian had never heard Adam say so much. It was as if the pent-up words, the expression of years of brooding and resentment, had breached a dam and poured out unchecked at last.

With consciousness of new-found friendship and confidences, they rattled their way along the country track between the leafless hedgerows until at last Adam pointed ahead and said, 'There be Losely.' He turned and gave her a quick kiss on the cheek. 'I don't deliver hereabouts, but I'll come when I can and see you be all right.'

They came upon the parsonage quite suddenly, so that she had hardly time to appreciate the pleasant-looking house before she was climbing down at the back door with Adam placing her basket on the ground beside her.

The kitchen door was opened but Gentian did not even have time to speak to the plump girl with a cross, dispirited expression before another door at the far end of the kitchen swung back.

'Thank you, Brenzett,' came a crisp voice, and a grey-haired lady, finely dressed and leaning on a stick, came towards them.

'You know where Betty is to go, and I will not keep you. So this is the new girl.'

In no time at all Adam had taken the other girl's box, she had climbed up beside him, and the cart had rattled off, leaving Gentian face to face with her new mistress.

CHAPTER FOUR

GENTIAN SOON FOUND she would be working just as hard at Losely as she did at Marleinge. Although there was no bakehouse to see to, Mrs Bolton's standards of housekeeping were immeasurably higher than the Bartletts'. It was a larger house to care for, and the Boltons employed surprisingly few servants. There was no indoor manservant, and no odd-job boy. But the surroundings were so much more pleasant than the bakery, and she was not in constant fear of a beating. Her room was a little attic, furnished with a bed, a chest, a washstand and a chair, but small and bare as it was, it was heaven compared with the cupboard room at the bakery. She had reconciled herself to the fact that she must accept a menial position in order to survive, and considered herself lucky to have exchanged the baker of Markinge for the Losely curate as master.

She saw little of Mr Bolton, except at morning prayers —when she knelt at the prescribed distance from the Boltons—and at mealtimes, when she served under the steely gaze of Mrs Bolton, who never missed a spot of gravy on the tablecloth or a fork out of alignment. Gentian rose in the dark of early morning, worked with scarcely a break, and rarely reached her bed before midnight, but her food (though different from the Boltons') was adequate, she was to receive sixpence a week, and she considered her situation vastly improved. Why, at the bakery she had been revolted by the cockroaches that infested the whole of the ground floor of the house and came out in swarms when darkness fell. Here there were only a few, which confined their activities to the

37

kitchen, and she felt capable of dealing with them with the fire-irons.

The Boltons led a quiet life. Gentian supposed there were very few people of sufficient quality in the neighbourhood for them to meet on equal terms. Mrs Bolton gave her plenty of criticism and scant praise, but when after a few weeks she let slip that she was an improvement on the last girl, she thought she could consider herself in no danger of dismissal.

One morning after breakfast, Mrs Bolton said, 'I want you to prepare the guest-room, Jenny. A gentleman will be coming to stay for a few days.'

One more room to attend, she thought, and more elaborate meals, no doubt; but it would be a change to have someone else in the house.

Now the guest was due. Gentian heard horses in the drive and went to the hall ready to open the door. Even so, Mr Bolton appeared as soon as she, and as she swung the door back, he went forward in greeting.

'Captain Claverton! I am indeed glad you could come.'

The hall was suddenly filled with the dazzle of scarlet and gold.

Perhaps he would not remember her. Gentry took no notice of servants. He would not expect to see her here, and she was better dressed, with her bright hair hidden under a cap. She could not forget that he had suggested she might be his woman, and it would embarrass her so much to be recognised.

His dark eyes swept casually over her, and in them she saw no recognition. The tightness in her chest relaxed, and she breathed more normally. So far, so good. She must keep out of his way as much as possible and hope for the best.

A soldier who had arrived with the Captain carried his bags upstairs: a portmanteau and a couple of smaller cases. Jane Tozer—the 'help' from the village—told her that it was not the first time Captain Claverton had stayed there. He came when his troop was in the district; the men were billeted in a barn in the village, and one of them acted as the Captain's personal servant.

'You'll find he'll be here for breakfast, and he'll attend to the Captain's clothes and suchlike. You'll only have the room to clean.'

At dinner Captain Claverton appeared out of uniform, most elegantly dressed in a cutaway coat, knee breeches, silk stockings and pumps, and Gentian, eyeing him covertly as she served, could still find no fault in his looks. He had a fine figure; his face, not classically handsome, had strong and striking features; his hands were lean and brown, unlike Mr Bolton's, which were white and plump. She was clearing the dessert plates, and was able to see the easy grace with which he got up and opened the door for Mrs Bolton as she indicated her withdrawal.

'Don't deprive me of the Captain's company for too long, my son.'

'No, Mama. We shall not sit over our brandy.' He was already pouring out two glasses.

Claverton took his glass, passed it under his nose, sipped, and rolled the liquid appreciatively around his tongue. 'May I congratulate you, Mr Bolton. A most excellent cognac.'

'A small luxury I allow myself, to compensate for living in these uncivilised parts.'

And I can guess how you come by it! thought Gentian, as she left the room with a tray of plates.

The next morning, as soon as she had served breakfast and hurriedly eaten her own, Gentian made her way upstairs. She would not risk Mrs Bolton's displeasure by being late in attending to the bedrooms. She went from room to room, stripping beds, emptying slops, cleaning washbasins, putting hot-water cans on the landing ready to take them back to the kitchen. Next she made the beds. In the guest-room Captain Claverton had left a certain amount of disorder; clothes and boots lying about, a handsome leather toilet-case open and displaying silver-mounted bottles and toilet articles, silver-backed brushes abandoned on the dressing-table, an open razor by the crumpled towel on the washstand top.

She had made the bed and was smoothing the coverlet over it, when heavy footsteps came up the back stairs and someone entered the room. She looked up in surprise, and then recognised the soldier she had seen the previous day.

''Morning!' he said to her, a grin creasing his red cheeks. 'Both of us on duty, I see, attending to the gentry! What would they do without us?'

'They'd find someone else, I shouldn't wonder,' said Gentian flatly in reply.

'Right enough. But as it is, it's you and me.' Still grinning, he eyed her up and down. 'And I see no reason why we shouldn't agree.' He began picking up and folding clothes. 'You're new here, ain't you?'

'Yes.'

She would leave him to do his work, and see to the other bedrooms, coming back to clean when he had finished and the room was tidy. As she turned away from the bed, he crossed the room towards her.

'You're a pretty little wench,' he said with familiarity. 'Reckon I wouldn't mind getting acquainted with you.'

His arm came out and encircled her waist. He pulled her towards him and grinned down at her. Before she realised his intention, his mouth was pressed to hers, and one hand fumbled over her shoulder and down to her breast. She wrenched herself away from him, sick with revulsion, but he laughed, and saying, 'Come, you're not so shy!' he tried to thrust his hand inside her bodice.

Frightened and horrified, she struggled to free herself, but he still held her. With one hand she groped behind her, then raised it in desperation and held it near his face. The Captain's open razor was clenched in her fingers. '*Let me go!*'

His hands dropped away and he started back, looking dumbfounded. 'Christ! You've no call for that! I meant no harm!'

'Don't come near me—*ever*!'

'By God, I won't! I've lost interest!'

She walked to the door, and when she reached it, she turned and tossed the razor back into the room. She was glad to get rid of it.

A little while later they both happened to go out into the passage at the same moment. He pointedly made way for her, saying, 'I'll not come near you! Spitfires I can manage, and like them, but you're a different sort of wench entirely!'

'I only ask that you remember it.'

'Oh, I'll not forget seeing you with cold steel in your hand.'

Unnoticed by them, someone had come up the stairs. Now they both saw Captain Claverton, who had either overheard them or guessed that something was wrong, for he stood and looked from one to the other. 'What's the matter, Bates?' he asked.

The man looked shamefaced and began to mutter something non-committal. Gentian did not wait but took to her heels, and scooping up the hot-water cans she fled along the passage and down the back staircase.

Wet or fine, Gentian had to collect milk from the farm. Most of the days since her arrival there had been rain or the threat of it, but the next day was clear, with a pale weak sun struggling through the mist. She had found a pair of clogs in the scullery, and with these on her feet she would plunge through the mud of road and farm track, to return with the can heavy on her arm past hedges whose wet and shining twigs still held no hint of green. But, this morning, there was just a faint promise that winter might be ending. She squelched down the track carrying the milk can, back to the narrow rutted road, the ground mist swirling about her, and wondered how long she would stay at Losely. Her life there was arduous, but she was safe; she could do far worse. She heard a horse trotting down the road behind her and drew close into the hedge to avoid if possible the spurts of mud that would be thrown up by its hooves. When it slackened as it reached her, she looked up, expecting to see a stranger who wanted to ask the way. But the rider was Charles Claverton.

He dismounted and stood facing her, his gaze cold and critical. 'Now, girl,' he said crisply, 'what do you mean by drawing a razor on one of my men?'

'He told you?' she said in amazement.

'I insisted. I won't have trouble between my men and any of the servants where I stay.'

She faced him defiantly, the position of master and servant forgotten. 'Then perhaps he told you I was defending myself?'

'*Defending* yourself? With an open razor—when all he wanted was a kiss?' Claverton retorted ironically.

Was that really all? If so, right was still on her side. 'I was not to know that.'

'Good God, you have a tongue! You can say no!'

'I had no chance! He was . . . He was trying . . .' She could not bring herself to describe the man's handling of her.

Suddenly Charles Claverton laughed. 'You're not telling me you thought he wanted to rape you on the bedroom floor? That's ridiculous!'

Shame at the mention of the subject battled with fury. Fury won. 'Whatever he wanted, it was horrible! Why should I let him paw me, slobber over me, and do anything he liked? How could I know . . .'

The contemptuous smile had gone, and he considered her thoughtfully. He took her chin in one hand and held it so that she could not turn her face away from him.

'I find it hard to credit you're so innocent. The country folk you've mixed with on the Marsh are a coarse lot—worse than any I've met, and I've had some experience! You couldn't still be a virgin . . .'

'That is none of your business!'

'Not at present, no.'

She jerked her head away from the lean strong fingers and began to walk on, but he detained her with a hand on her arm.

'Wait. I haven't finished talking to you. Put down that confounded can.' He looked down at her shrewdly. 'You were not brought up to be a servant, were you?' She said nothing. 'When you are angry, you forget all about calling me "sir". You are not used to it, are you?' Reluctantly she shook her head. 'Then why are you a servant?'

Her gaze met his, clear and steady. 'I have no alternative. I am alone in the world.'

'Even so . . .'

'That too is my business.'

'What a touchy little creature you are! When I first saw you, you seemed so alien to your surroundings that you interested me. On an impulse, I made you an offer. I admit I was wrong to think you would do anything to improve your situation. But you still interest me, and I find you, in some strange way, attractive.'

'Should I be grateful for that?'

'No, but you can profit by it. I'll repeat my offer, in a way you may feel you can accept. You can come with me and look after my creature comforts, but I'll not make love to you. Not until you are ready. If we bore each other, or we have to part company for some other reason, I'll find you a good place. You will not suffer.'

He had released her arm, and they stood a pace apart as she stared at him with mounting indignation.

'You amaze me! Do you think women exist to suit your fancy—that we have no feelings, no pride?'

'I think you see very clearly what is to your advantage. In my experience, a woman is always weighing up how best a man can serve her. Did you expect a show of gallantry now? I told you I would not seduce you until you were ready, so I did not think it necessary.' He smiled, and moved a little closer. She stumbled back a pace, and put up a hand as if to ward him off. 'You're frightened! There's no need—I'll not hurt you. And surely, at your age, you have learnt to handle men?'

To add to her discomfiture, her eyes began to fill with tears. She felt weak and very vulnerable before his male strength. 'I know nothing about men,' she whispered.

'So . . . you have kept your virtue. With difficulty, I imagine. And you are reluctant to lose it.'

'Yes!' she said, with a flash of her previous defiance.

'Then I can only advise you to do what all virtuous women practise,' he said, his voice heavy with cynicism. 'You must learn to promise a little, and give nothing.'

She looked at him, bewildered.

'Oh, yes, you must play a man like a fish on a line. You are pretty enough to succeed if you learn how to do it.'

'I should not like that. It does not seem fair.'

'Fair? Who ever heard of fairness between amorous man and virtuous woman?' She noticed he put a sarcastic accent on the word 'virtuous'. 'No, a man gets better justice from a whore.' He laughed at her shocked expression. 'It's true! Virtue gives nothing in spite of promises; a whore gives everything she's asked for, but makes sure of good payment before she does so. If you're making your way in the world, that is your choice.'

'It's horrible! I can't—I won't . . .'

'Then you are in poor case, for sooner or later a man will force you or trick you. But at least we understand each other, so you could do worse than come to me. You run the risk of seduction, but I'll not force you, that I promise.' He smiled again. 'Has it never occurred to you that you might enjoy being seduced?'

Enjoy? She had never thought of it. Everything he said to her seemed to wake new ideas. She looked at him, and the expression in his dark eyes made her feel she was leaving her body, shedding her coarse clothes, her mud-caked clogs, and floating towards him like a piece of thistledown on a summer breeze. She felt buoyant, weightless. Perhaps she really floated; or perhaps he moved, for his face swam nearer, his eyes, a dark greenish hazel, were shining; his lips were smiling. Then his face went out of focus and she felt his mouth on hers. As it touched hers gently, the lips were surprisingly soft and shifted in a kind of roving movement that gave a sudden sensitivity to her mouth and sent strange tremors running through her. Her muscles, which had been tense with suspicion, relaxed as these sensations, wholly delightful, swept over her. Then she felt his arm against her back, warm through her gown and shawl. His lips pressed hers more strongly, and beside their softness there was a slight roughness from his cheek, while the faint odours of his hair and skin gave her an impression of maleness that made her heart leap. She was aware of her body again, for all her pulses were throbbing.

He released her, and she looked at him in wonder.

'So, you are not an unnatural woman, just a frightened one,' he said softly. 'Well, you may learn in time, Jenny. That is your name?'

'My real name is Gentian,' she whispered.

'Gentian! How strange, and charming.'

'But, please, you must not call me that!' Everything about her situation had come flooding back to her. 'It's not a servant's name—I'm known as Jenny.'

'I will remember. Now, you did not find that kiss unpleasant, did you?'

'No. With you it was . . . different.'

'Good. We make progress. Then you find me agreeable?'

'Yes . . .' What was it about him that drew the truth out of her?

'Then in that case you can make a choice. Do you prefer working for that pompous curate and his martinet mother to working for me?'

'Oh, no! I should so like to be with you, now you understand . . .'

'In that case, we'll seal the bargain.'

She felt his arms round her again, the warmth of his body seeming to enfold her as his lips pressed hers once more. His hand that caressed her hair was both strong and gentle. She gave her mouth willingly, and her heart lightened, her spirit flowed out to him.

'When will you come?' he asked softly.

'I don't know . . . I don't see how I can.'

'I will arrange it. Not now, that would be too sudden. But the next time I come I will tell Bolton that I have a place for you with the wife of another officer, and you wish to go. I'll get him to release you. How will that do?'

The prospect was too dazzling to resist. 'Yes, I will come. When will it be?'

'I can't say exactly. About three weeks, perhaps four. Just wait. I won't forget you.'

'Nor I you.' She smiled up at him, her face suddenly radiant. 'I'll wait.'

'Then it's a promise.'

She moved, and felt the milk can cold against her

ankles. It woke her to reality. 'Oh, heavens, I must go! The milk . . . I shall be punished for taking so long.'

'I'll carry it for you.'

'No! That would never do! If Mrs Bolton saw me with you . . . Please ride on.'

'Very well, if it will save you trouble. But remember our agreement.'

With that, he mounted his horse and rode off ahead of her between the bare hedges. She lifted the can in her cold stiff hand and stumbled after him up the road. But now she felt she could endure whatever harshness she had from the Boltons, for soon she would be free. Charles Claverton would take her away.

She would be happy with him; whatever he asked of her she would do willingly. It was madness, because she did not know him at all. She guessed that he was cynical but not cruel, worldly yet chivalrous; that he was a complex, mystifying man. He might have many faults, but she could bear them. She would do everything, give him everything, because she loved him.

CHAPTER FIVE

THE DAY AFTER Charles Claverton's departure, Gentian opened the kitchen door to a knock and found Adam Brenzett standing on the doorstep. He returned her warm greeting with an eager smile, but seemed to be groping for words.

'I'm sorry I can't ask you in, Adam,' she said quickly. 'Mrs Bolton doesn't allow it.'

'I understand,' he said. 'I only came to see you—to ask you if you be all right.'

'Oh, yes! As you see, Adam, I'm very well.'

'I wanted to be sure they're treating you right.'

'There's plenty of work, but that's to be expected. Yes, they're treating me well.'

He ran his hand awkwardly through his hair. 'I be glad about that, Jenny. If there was any—trouble—you'd let me know? I'd help if I could.'

'What trouble could there be?' she asked.

'Nothing, I suppose . . . Well, it be good to see you.'

'And how are you, Adam?'

'Me? Oh, everything's the same with me. I be all right.'

Gentian heard a door open behind her, and then a stick tapped on the kitchen floor. She turned to see Mrs Bolton.

'Who is that with you, Jenny?' the old lady questioned sharply.

'It's Adam Brenzett, madam. He called—only to see how I was. He's just going.' She turned back to Adam. 'Goodbye, Adam. Thank you for calling.'

48

'Goodbye, Jenny.' Then he added, 'I'll come again when I can.'

She closed the door. Mrs Bolton, with lips tightly compressed, looked at her accusingly.

'Jenny, you know you are not allowed followers.'

'I know, madam. But he's not—he's not a follower. He simply came to ask me if I was settling well. It was just his kindness of heart.'

'Then see that his kindness of heart does not bring him here often.'

When Mrs Bolton had gone, Jane Tozer—it was her day for helping with the laundry—looked up from stirring the steaming copper. 'That Adam Brenzett—he be a nice fellow! Be he your follower?'

'No, he's just a friend. He's a kind person. I suppose he was passing, and thought to call to see how I was.'

'Mistress Bolton's very strict about followers,' said Jane. 'That last girl—I don't know how she managed it.'

'Managed what?' asked Gentian.

'Well, she left here carrying someone's bastard in her belly, and she only went out of the house to get the milk each morning, except for when she went to see her mother for a day. It would have been then she did it, I reckon—it could hardly have been at the farm. And she was an ungrateful little slut! Mistress Bolton did the best she could for her—found her a place in a home where she could work and have the baby. She couldn't expect to be kept on here, could she? Yet when I tried to talk to her about it, she started telling me a load of lies—just trying to make trouble, I reckon.'

'What sort of lies?'

'Oh, I wouldn't repeat them! It was a load of nasty scandal. Must have been her spite.'

Gentian tentatively tried another question, but Jane Tozer was not to be drawn. With lips firmly closed, she merely shook her head and returned to her washtub.

It was Mrs Bolton's custom to retire for the night before her son, and as soon as she was in bed, her bell would be jangling. By then Gentian must have a posset prepared, and this she had to take upstairs to Mrs Bolton's room. Sitting up in bed, her grey hair straggling in a thin plait over one shoulder and crowned by a large white nightcap, her mistress would receive the cup with a brief nod and the words, 'Good night, Jenny.

Gentian would then return to the kitchen and assemble Mr Bolton's tray, placing on it a lemon, spice, sugar and the necessary articles which she would carry with a small kettle of hot water to the study, where he would make for himself a glass of negus.

That evening Mrs Bolton, who had been feeling unwell all day, retired to bed early. When Gentian had taken up the posset and had been told that her mistress required nothing more, she went to the parson and asked him at what time she should bring his tray.

'I may as well have it now,' was the reply.

The water was hot upon the kitchen fire, so Gentian set the tray, filled the little kettle and took both to the study. Mr Bolton was sitting in an armchair, a Bible open on his knee. Having put the tray on the side table and the kettle on the hob, she made her curtsy and was about to leave the room when he looked up and spoke to her.

'I suppose, Jenny, you cannot read?'

The unexpected question surprised her into the plain truth. 'Yes, sir, I can.' And then, remembering what an unusual accomplishment it was for a poor servant-girl, she added lamely, 'A little.'

'And can you write a little, too?'

'Yes, sir.'

'No more than your name, I suppose.'

She kept silent. Let him think that. It would never do to admit the truth—that she wrote an accomplished hand and could read fluently, not only English, but also French and Latin.

'Who taught you?' Mr Bolton asked.

'My father, sir. He had some learning, and I was his only child. He thought to pass it on to me.'

'I see. Well, Jenny, I think you are an intelligent girl, and as your master and your minister I feel it is my duty to help you. You will benefit by being able to read well enough to follow the instruction of the Bible, so I propose to give you lessons in reading.'

'Lessons, sir?'

Once again she was taken by surprise, and could hardly tell him that lessons were unnecessary. She recovered herself and added, 'Why, thank you, sir. That is very kind.'

'Then we will start tonight. Do what you have to do in the kitchen, then come back here.'

In the kitchen, Gentian thought this over. It was a somewhat disconcerting situation. She would have to pretend to be much more ignorant than she was; and the end of the day, when she was tired out and longing for bed, was not the best time for reading. But it would be good to exercise her brain even in so simple a manner, and she was grateful. Mr Bolton might consider it his duty, but it showed a kinder side to his nature, one that she had not thought he possessed. She remembered the look of relief on Adam Brenzett's face when she told him she was being treated well. What would he say to this, she wondered.

She quickly tidied the kitchen and returned to the study. Mr Bolton at once motioned her to a chair at the table where a large Bible lay open. A branch of candles stood beside it, illuminating the pages; the corners of the room were almost in darkness, and when he resumed his seat in the armchair by the fire, his face was only half lit by the flickering flames.

'Now, Jenny,' he said. 'Let us see what you can do. Begin with those large words at the top of the page.'

Obediently she read, as slowly as she could bring herself, *'The First Book of Moses, called Genesis.'*

'Good. Now you may miss the words under the words "Chapter one" and begin with the first verse.'

'In the beginning,' Gentian read, *'God created the heaven and the earth.'*

'Good. Go on reading as long as you can.'

So she continued in a flat voice, slowly, as if too much concerned with making out the words to put any expression or sense into them, and allowing herself to stumble over the longer words like 'firmament'.

After a while he said, 'I am pleased with you, Jenny. It seems you have mastered the rudiments; what you need is practice. You may be familiar with Genesis, for you must have heard it read many times. Let us try something you may not know so well.' He turned the pages. 'There, let us attempt Deuteronomy. Chapter eighteen —begin there.'

Quite unsuspectingly, Gentian began, *'The priests, the Levites, and all the tribe of Levi, shall have no part nor inheritance with Israel . . .'*

'Go on.'

He got up from his seat and began to mix his negus. She continued reading, thinking it was rather boring, and paused at the end of the eight verse. Mr Bolton turned his head to her.

'Continue—and think what you are reading.'

Another verse, the steady clinking of the silver spoon in the glass making a background to her low voice. And then—but it must have been a coincidence that he should select this passage—why was he looking at her so fixedly? In her voice there was a slight tremor which she could not control as she went on.

'There shall not be found among you any one that

maketh his son or his daughter to pass through the fire, or that useth divination, or an observer of times, or an enchanter, or a witch, or a charmer, or a consulter with familiar spirits, or a wizard, or a necromancer.'

'Well, Jenny, what is the matter?'

'Nothing, sir.'

'I think there is. That passage disturbs you, does it not?'

'No, sir.'

'Don't lie to me, Jenny! Your looks give you away. Besides, I happen to know that you have been accused of being a witch. "Warlock's wench"—that was what you were called, wasn't it?'

He took a sip from his glass, then continued to stand and gaze at her. She clutched the edge of the table, and said to herself: He can't believe it!

'It's not true, sir. My father was a herbalist—he never did anything wrong—you must know, sir, it's all superstition . . . *You* can't believe in witches!'

In contrast to her jerky phrases and the nervous tight pitch of her voice, Mr Bolton's words were soft and smooth, his tones low and positively silky. 'Think what you are saying, Jenny. You have just been reading from the Bible. It speaks of witches, wizards and necromancers. Are you denying the truth of the Bible? If the Bible condemns such people, then they must exist.'

Was it a trap, the first of a series that might be laid for her? Already she felt confused.

'No, I would not deny the Bible, but that was long ago. There are none now—not here.'

'Bible truths are for all time. Now, Jenny, I have been told by someone who considered I ought to know, that in New Romney you were thought to be a witch. If I ever had cause to believe that, what should I have to do?'

'I don't know, sir,' she whispered.

'Read the last verse—aloud.'

She did so. *'For all that do these things are an abomin-
ation unto the Lord: and because of these abominations
the Lord thy God doth drive them out from before
thee.'*

'You see? I should have to drive you out. But I don't
want to do that, so you must never give me cause.'

'Indeed, sir, I won't. I'm not a witch!'

'Good. But if you were—do you know the fate of
witches?' She said nothing. He rhythmically stirred his
negus. 'Turn back to Leviticus. Chapter twenty.'

She tried to check the feeling of panic that for no
reason was growing within her. She fumbled with the
pages, and all the time he stood in front of her, waiting.

'Read the last verse to me.'

Her throat felt so tight that she could hardly speak.
She had to force the words out. *'A man also or woman
that hath a familiar spirit, or that is a wizard, shall surely
be put to death: they shall stone them with stones: their
blood shall be upon them.'* Her mouth and lips were dry.
The pounding of her heart seemed almost to stop her
breathing.

'I wish you to be quite clear about your position,
Jenny. It is my duty to point out to you the risks you run.'

'Do you mean, sir, that they still kill witches?'

'There has not been a hanging for many years, but I
believe it is still possible. And sometimes people take
justice into their own hands.'

She remembered her flight across the Marsh. No, not
again, she prayed. Words came in a forced whisper. 'I
. . . am not . . . a witch!'

'No, Jenny, I do not believe you are. But I had to show
you the danger you might be in if you gave any further
cause for gossip. As long as you continue to work well
and are obedient to me, your master, I will protect you.
But if you give me any cause to doubt you, and gossip
revives, as a man of God I should be obliged to cast you

out, to fend for yourself. And here, on the Marsh, old customs die hard.'

'It won't happen, sir! I am not . . .'

'This has been upsetting for you, no doubt, so you may go to bed now. I trust we will not need to speak of it again.'

It should have been a relief to stumble up to her attic, but her spirit did not lighten. The interview haunted her. She tried to tell herself that as long as she worked well she was safe, that the parsonage would be a sanctuary to her. Yet she still had the uneasy feeling pressing on her that there was more trouble to come.

But the next few days brought Gentian some reassurance. The night-time Bible-readings continued, but Leviticus and Deuteronomy were left unread, and Mr Bolton made no reference to the frightening interview. In fact he seemed to go out of his way to be pleasant to her, and more than once complimented her on the way her reading had improved.

Then one evening he said to her, 'Now you are reading with more fluency and expression, Jenny, we will progress to something different, something more poetic. We will turn to the Song of Solomon.'

She found the first chapter.

'In this the love of Christ for his church is likened to human love. Begin with Chapter one.'

She started to read, and found that the words flowed musically from her tongue. She could not see the religious significance; to her it was like an old-fashioned love-song; but if Mr Bolton found it religious, that was possibly just as well, and she stifled her embarrassment at reading verse thirteen. *'A bundle of myrrh is my wellbeloved unto me; he shall lie all night betwixt my breasts.'* She continued to the end of the chapter.

'That is better than ever, Jenny. Now the next chapter.'

And she read on, quite lost in the beauty of the words.

'It occurs to me, Jenny,' he said when she paused, 'that since you are here as my pupil and not my servant, you should remove your cap.'

Rather surprised, she did so, and looking up, saw that his eyes were fixed on her hair. His gaze was strangely intent. Was it just because it was threatening to loose itself from its pins?

'As I thought,' he murmured. 'It is plentiful, and a very pretty colour. You are looking a little tired, Jenny. I am going to give you a glass of negus, for it will be like a medicine, and will do you good.'

It was a long time since she had drunk wine. She did not care for the beer—strong at the bakery, flat and weak for the Boltons' servant—that was all she had been given in the months since her father died. She took the glass gratefully. When she sipped, she fould that the drink, hot with the addition of water, was none the less rich, spicy and delicious, and it gave a most comforting glow, first in the pit of her stomach and then spreading warmth throughout her body right to her fingers and toes.

'Continue reading when you are ready, Jenny.'

When she had drunk most of her negus, he took the glass and replenished it, then paced slowly up and down behind her chair as she read. The chapter heading said it was a further description of the church's graces, but to her it seemed like a man cataloguing his sweetheart's beauty. However, the drink was so comforting that it gave her confidence, and she continued. *'How fair and pleasant art thou, O love, for delights!'*

'You may pause there, Jenny, and drink some more of your negus.'

She did so. Her legs felt strangely weak, and her body almost weightless, but it was a pleasant sensation, and she was quite lighthearted that Mr Bolton was being so kind to her now.

'Go on drinking, and I will read the next verses over your shoulder.'

She vaguely realised that he was leaning over her, because his voice was very close to her ear, and it seemed to have changed. There was a hoarse tone to it; he did not sound like a parson. The words flowed into her consciousness. *'This thy stature is like to a palm tree, and thy breasts to clusters of grapes.'*

She felt his hands upon her shoulders; then, before she had time to register surprise, they slid forward on her bosom, enclosing her breasts. She did not realise how befuddled she was, but was aware of a wave of shock, and oddly she was too shocked to move. The next moment his mouth was on hers, his tongue forcing her lips apart and thrusting over hers, pushing to and fro, while his fingers pressed the soft flesh of her breasts against his palms. Suddenly her head cleared a little and she began to resist, pulling at his hands and trying to move her head back and release her mouth from his full wet lips and revolting, searching tongue, but it was surprisingly difficult to free herself.

Then he shifted his hands and let her struggle to her feet, but he still held one arm about her, the other hand now turning her face up to his. 'Remember, Jenny,' he said, and she saw his eyes, narrowed and lustful. 'Remember your obedience. I require obedience from you —I am favouring you as my handmaiden.' He moved his hand down to the bodice of her gown, fumbling at the buttons fastening it at the throat. Still she resisted. 'Jenny,' he said, 'if you are obedient to my wishes, you will not suffer. If not, I must drive you forth. Think of that.'

Shock and the negus were working on her so that she was almost unable to stand, but it made little difference, for he was holding her so tightly against him. He stopped trying to unbutton her bodice and pushed his hand downwards, passing it over her body. His hoarse voice was speaking slowly, bringing out the words with a crude relish. *'Thy two breasts are like two young roes that are twins . . .'* His hand explored her bosom again. 'Thy two breasts! I must see the beauty of them. You will come to my bed and show me your nakedness. You will pleasure me, like a good handmaiden.'

His eyes looked down at her as if they had already stripped her of her clothes. His fingers went to her bodice again, and she knew he was about to open her dress. She was paralysed with horror—why was she so helpless?

'You will be a sensible girl, Jenny. I am giving you the choice, but think, it will be more agreeable to be my concubine than to be hunted as a witch.'

Choice! What choice was it, between two equally horrible alternatives?

She looked up at him, her flesh crawling with revulsion. His face was flushed with liquor, his eyes bloodshot, but he was not drunk. She knew he had taken plenty of wine and brandy during the evening, and then the negus, but he was used to drink, and was capable of doing anything he chose with her. Now the buttons of her bodice began to release themselves under his fingers. His look spoke lust, and he smiled triumphantly.

'Thy breasts shall be as clusters of the vine,' he murmured, and thrust his hand inside her gown as his full soft mouth covered hers again.

CHAPTER SIX

ALL THE TIME she was helpless under the parson's kiss, Gentian's mind was working desperately. Her body was weak with the drink, but her mind was clearing under the shock, and her brain sought frantically for some way of escape.

The parson raised his head, but his hand still fondled her. 'Well, Jenny, are you going to be obedient?'

A man's cynical voice came into her mind. 'Promise a little, but give nothing . . .'

'Yes, Mr Bolton,' she whispered.

'Good. What do you know of the carnal delights, Jenny?'

'Of . . . what . . . sir?'

'Of the pleasures of the flesh, when a woman surrenders to a man—when they are united . . .' He rolled the words out with relish.

'Nothing, sir.'

His hands were stilled. He spoke eagerly. 'Is that true? Do not lie to me! Has no man enjoyed you—not even William Bartlett, or his father?'

'No, sir. No one.' She felt physically sick, and fought for control.

'You swear that? I shall know if you have lied to me.'

'I swear it, sir.'

A satisfied sigh drifted from between his lips. 'So you are still a virgin. I am well rewarded for choosing you. And that explains your shyness.'

'Yes, sir.' She must try to delay him. 'So, please . . . It will all be strange to me—will you not wait a little?'

'Wait? I must test the obedience you promised me. You must learn your lesson: to be swift and complete in your submission. You must be more than willing—eager —to learn what I require of you, and how you can best please me.'

She felt like a bird trapped in a cage, beating the bars from which there was no escape. He had pulled down the neck of her dress, and now he thrust his face against the base of her throat, nuzzling her and muttering.

'Such a round little shoulder! Such delicate skin for a poor girl! Perhaps you are a witch—you have captivated me with your innocence, your pretty face and bright hair, and your shapely body, which I long to see and enjoy. You little witch! But as long as you please me, I'll say nothing.'

She did not even dare to struggle. This dreadful man was going to force her to submit to his lust in a way she was beginning fearfully, almost incredulously, to guess. She would prefer William Bartlett's beating to what lay ahead. If she screamed and woke Mrs Bolton, it would do her no good. He would tell some tale his mother would believe, and would still make sure she did not escape his desires. The room was silent except for the fall of a cinder in the grate, the sound of the parson's breathing as he pawed and kissed the soft swell of her breast—and a faint scratching at the curtained window.

'What was that?' she gasped.

'Nothing . . .'

The sound was repeated, louder this time—too loud, too deliberate to be a branch brushing against the window-pane. The parson raised his head, and abruptly released her.

'Is it someone outside, sir?'

'Yes. A prowler, I think—perhaps a thief. I must look.'

He went to the window, jerked the curtain aside and then let it fall again—too quickly to see anything, she thought.

'Yes. Go up to bed, Jenny.' His face showed the annoyance of thwarted lust. 'It may take time to make sure—and then . . .' She held her breath. 'Then it will be late, and my mood will be broken. We will postpone our delights until tomorrow. So you have a day to prepare yourself. Now go to bed.'

'Yes, sir.'

She snatched up her cap, and clutching the bodice of her gown together, fled from the room. As she stumbled up the stairs her heart was thumping so hard that she felt half-suffocated. She collapsed on her bed and put her head in her hands. Hardly could she believe her good fortune, that the parson had put off his conquest for that night. Suppose he changed his mind? It would not take him long to scare off a prowler with the gun he kept in the hall.

Everything was quiet. She went to the window and looked out. There was little moon and the sky was cloudy, but she thought she could see movement, and more than one figure going to and fro. Realisation came to her. Bolton's twitching of the curtain had not been so that he could see outside. He had recognised the furtive noise, and had made an answering signal. The man outside was not a prowler or a thief. Adam had told her that the parson had dealings with the smugglers. The parson had responded to the signal at the window, and he knew it would be some time before the smuggler—or smugglers—left. He might be engaged with them for hours. Time for his lust to cool—perhaps, time enough for her to escape. She knew that flight from the house was her only safeguard, no matter what it might entail. She remembered her attempt at the bakery, and must be more careful this time. She drew the curtain over her window, lit her candle and pulled out the basket from beneath her bed.

Hours later, under the wan light of a half-moon, she was trudging out of the village, exhausted with all the tension and fear that had racked her. She had been terrified that she would not be able to make her escape. She had packed her few possessions, leaving on her bed the caps and aprons and the Sunday gown that Mrs Bolton had provided, and listened to hear Mr Bolton go to his room. All was quiet and still outside. She waited —interminably—to make sure he would be sound asleep before she crept downstairs. Every creak of a floorboard, each dull rasp of a bolt, each grating of a hinge renewed the terror within her. But no sound came from the darkened house, and she stole down the path, on to the road, and hurried on. She had no plan but escape.

She had not a penny piece in her pocket, for she was to be paid her miserable wage at the end of the quarter, and all that stood between her and starvation was a hunk of bread and a piece of cheese she had filched from the larder: nothing else. She could imagine the vindictiveness that would burn in the parson's mind when he discovered he had been tricked, and could guess what he would do. He would accuse her of theft, for a start, while he hatched up some accusation of witchcraft. People were hanged for theft. But surely if it came to a trial, any judge would consider that the bread and cheese were hers in lieu of wages? But how strong would be her truth against the parson's lies? She had taken the bread and cheese in order to have strength to travel; she could not work for food, or beg, yet awhile, for she dared not show herself in this neighbourhood. She guessed that as soon as he discovered her absence, the parson would mount a search. He would not risk the tale that she might tell.

She clutched her clothes-basket under one arm.

Nothing, she thought, would induce her to part with it. Even when she had been close to dying in the snow she had not cast away her father's books, and the herbal was now more precious to her than ever, while her few scraps of clothes seemed to her the last remnants of her dignity. Abandon them and she would feel no better than an unwanted animal, a dog beaten and kicked from every door.

Thoughts continued to flow through her head. Now she knew what the 'load of scandal' was that the previous servant-girl had tried to tell Jane Tozer. She had wanted her to know that she had been seduced by Mr Bolton, that it was the parson's child she was carrying. Did Mrs Bolton know? If so, it put her 'kindness' to the girl in another light; if not, the parson would certainly have wanted the girl out of the village as soon as possible. Was the parson's lust, and his need for secrecy, one reason for the lack of living-in servants? Adam had driven the last girl away in his cart—had she perhaps confided in him? That would explain his air of anxiety when he had called, and his relief on hearing Gentian say she was being well treated. Oh, Adam, she thought, I need you now—but there is no way you can help me. Even if she could go to the bakery, she would not dare to do so. As for Charles Claverton . . . No, she must think about that later.

She walked through the rest of the night and the early morning, with only a few brief rests. There was but one road through Losely village, and she had taken the direction that was new to her, for that must lead away from the Marsh. She must try for the coast, for was Charles Claverton not sometimes at Hythe?

Dawn crept up, with a faint lightening of the sky and a swirl of mist over the fields. In the darkness after moon-set, before dawn broke, it had been almost impossible to see the way; now at least it was light enough to choose one's path amid the stones and mud-filled ruts of the narrow road. She was very tired, and she longed for sleep. Before the labourers were up and about she must find a place to hide—but *sleep*? She could not risk discovery by anyone; everyone around would be anxious to keep in the parson's good books, and would tell him if they had seen her. Sleep, and someone might come upon her unawares.

At last she had to rest. She found a place in the damp hedge-bottom, and crouching there as unobtrusively as she could, she ate some bread and cheese. The bread was dry, the cheese hard, and she needed a drink, but could not face the brackish water of the ditch. Perhaps, later, she would find a spring.

She began to walk again. Soon, some way ahead of her, she saw a cluster of cottages, the outskirts of a village. She could not go through it, for by now people would be stirring, labourers leaving for their work. A narrow lane appeared; this was better, for somehow she must skirt the village and try to pick up the road on the other side. The lane twisted and turned, until soon she had only a vague idea of where the village lay. She had not been born a country girl, and her sense of direction was poor. I mustn't go back on my tracks, she told herself. If I try to keep the sun on my right hand, that should lead me the way I want to go.

It was strange how in such flat countryside landmarks could disappear; she had found a road, but lost the village. There were a few clumps of trees—the village must be hidden by one of them—but they all looked much the same, and the countryside still consisted of open fields, some tilled, some harbouring sheep, and a road which ran, ditch-bordered, between low hedge-rows. It became a mechanical exercise of pushing one foot in front of the other, and her head nodded forward, her eyes half-closed as she went on. Suddenly she was jerked out of her trance of exhaustion by a new sound. Somewhere there were horses—and the voice of a man. She could not distinguish any words, but the tone of the voice was chillingly familiar.

Frantically she looked around. As bad luck would have it, the hedgerows here were particularly low and sparse, so that the only possible source of cover was a clump of willows beside the ditch. The sounds were coming from behind, and growing louder; she was at that moment hidden from the riders by a bend in the road, but at any moment they would round it, and then . . .

She dived for the willows, plunging through the ditch in water above her knees to reach the further side. Thrusting her basket low down among the spreading branches, she forced her way in and crouched over it, pulling her dark shawl over her head and face and praying that the sounds made by the horses would mask the light clashing of the branches. They were as yet not in full leaf, and might not be thick enough to hide her. She had an awful certainty of the riders' identities.

Hooves thudded on the road; voices and words were now intelligible. As they spoke to each other, she knew the men to be Mr Bolton and his groom.

'You don't think she might have gone the other way out of Losely, sir?'

'No. She has no liking for the Marsh.'

'The crossroads are ahead. Which of the ways shall we take?'

'I think she will avoid the coast. She is known there. Since all these silly girls head for London, I will take the Ashford and London road. You may take the inland road, but if you have found no trace of her after another half-hour, turn back. She cannot possibly have got much further—there would be no passing carts to take her up until daylight.'

The voices were now very close. The groom, a middle-aged countryman, went on. 'And if I find her, sir?'

The parson's voice was cold and clear. 'You bring her back, of course. If she makes a fuss, and there is anyone by, tell the truth—that she is a little servant-girl, half out of her wits, and you are taking her back to the parson who has charge of her.'

'I'll do that, sir.'

Gentian dared not move—she hardly dared to breathe—while the horses thudded past. The sound of their hooves grew fainter, and still she crouched, with water swilling round her legs, the lower part of her skirts sodden and soaking up more of it every minute. I must give them time to reach the crossroads they spoke of, she thought, I must let them get well on their way, but I must not wait too long, or they will have turned back. But how can I judge that?

She was just about to drag herself out from the willows when more voices approached. She cowered back again, straining to hear what was being said. They were rough country voices, accompanied by plodding footsteps.

'. . . and the pigs, then?'

'Middling.'

There was a pause. Then, 'What be you thinking of doing if we find the maid parson's after?'

'Take her back, of course. There'll be a coin for anyone who does.'

'He be right bothered, riding out so early!'

'Ay, but she be half-crazed and in his care. And pretty, by all accounts—"well-favoured" he said—much could happen to her afore he finds her. The witless ones are often more than willing to let a man give 'em a tumble!'

They both laughed.

'What be you thinking of, Thomas? Showing her your

manhood afore taking her back?'

'I'll tell 'ee when I find her.'

Gentian felt sick with fear. The morning wore on, and each time she thought to leave her hiding-place, something prevented her. It might only be the figure of a man two fields away, but if she could see him, he could see her if she came out of hiding, and would probably recognise a stranger. Occasionally people came along the road in ones or twos, mostly on foot. She expected every moment to hear Mr Bolton retracing his steps, but he did not come. At last she concluded that he had gone home another way.

When she could leave, she would take the coast road. There was always the risk that having drawn a blank elsewhere, the parson might search in that direction, but it was the area he considered least likely, and as time went on, he might not be so thorough. And, peeping through the willows, she saw that it had another advantage; in the distance along that road the fields turned to woodland, so that after the first few miles she might find more cover.

It was growing dark before she felt it was safe to drag herself and her basket out of the willows. Her limbs were so cold and stiff, so utterly benumbed, that they would not hold her, and she fell full length into the underbrush of the hedge. She ached all over, and she lay there for some minutes, sobbing, before she could struggle to her feet. Somehow she managed to lift her basket and plunge through the ditch to the roadside. Her skirts, full of water, hung about her like bags filled with lead, for the moisture had crept up to her waist. With a quick look about, she pulled off her petticoat and wrung out the skirt of her gown, then her petticoat, and scrambled into that again. She had a dry gown and petticoat in her basket, but now was not the time or place to change her clothes. Besides, if she had to hide, she might get wet again; she would keep her dry clothes for a better moment.

She forced her chilled, cramped limbs to walk, and this time had better luck. At the crossroads she took the turn to the right, where a fingerpost said 'Dymchurch'. Along this road she encountered no one before darkness fell, by which time she had reached the woods. Now, when she heard anyone about, it was easy to slip into the woods and lie down among the trees. Fear of capture still drove her on until exhaustion overcame her suddenly and completely, and she stumbled blindly into the trees and lay down—or rather fell down—behind a clump of bushes. Her head fell back upon her basket, and she lapsed into unconsciousness.

The sun was up when she awoke, a pale sun that gleamed like silver between the branches above her. A bird was chirruping near by; another answered; around her there were faint rustlings of indistinguishable life. She moved, and groaned. Her body seemed one great ache, and her stomach was so empty that she felt sick again. But although she had been lying on damp ground, her clothes were much less wet and would finish drying as she walked. Those in her basket she would keep for later on, when she would want to look more respectable. She must somehow reach Dymchurch and look for work.

It was strange that her body did not seem to want to obey her, and she could not think very clearly either, for her mind would hold only three ideas—to keep away from Mr Bolton, to get to a town, and to find work. Work meant food and shelter. But not with Mr Bolton. There was no need for her to tremble so, and why were her teeth chattering, when surely the worst of her danger was past? Or was it? Wasn't he behind her, chasing after her, coming to seize her and take her and do unspeakable things . . . No, it was her imagination . . . No, it was not, she could hear wheels bumping on the rough road.

She was about to turn and run into the woods when she remembered—he would be on a horse. Flight would be suspicious, so she must walk on, like a travelling woman, with her shawl over her head . . . walk on, while the wheels rumbled and rattled nearer. They were coming up abreast of her . . . They were passing . . . Oh, God, they were stopping . . .

A woman's voice, a country voice, but not rough or unkindly, was saying, 'Sister, you look tired. Can we help you on your way?'

Gentian saw a round rosy face, with lined cheeks and pale grey eyes that held an anxious look. The woman was sitting beside the driver of a little trap, stout and middle aged, decently dressed in dark clothes, with a kind of shapeless bonnet tied under her chin. Gentian took this in, and also that the driver was a man somewhat older, wearing a thick dark coat and breeches, and a flat wide-brimmed hat over a broad weatherbeaten face fringed with sparse grey hair, yet she found herself incapable of speech.

Then the man said, 'Why, she's only a maid!'

The woman clambered down from the trap. To Gentian the world seemed to be rocking to and fro; then she felt an arm about her.

'Are you ill, child? What is the matter?' Then, 'Enoch, help me to get her into the trap.'

She was beyond protesting. If they were taking her back to Mr Bolton, she could not resist, not while her body was shaking and shivering like this. She found herself half sitting, half lying in the back of the trap.

'I think she has a fever.'

'The marsh ague, perhaps.'

'Perhaps. Look at her clothes—they have been wet, and dried on her. Why, they are still damp, and her shoes are in ribbons—poor child!'

'See if she will drink from the flask.'

He passed something to the woman, and Gentian felt a cold rim against her lips. She swallowed a trickle of liquid, not knowing what it was, but feeling a blessed glow in her stomach. She managed to smile.

'I can see you're tired out, child. Are you hungry, too?'

She nodded.

Like a miracle, bread and cold meat appeared, and she found the strength to eat a little.

'Where are you going, my dear?'

Gentian could not think. Where was it? Did it matter? She must get away from Mr Bolton . . .

'Away . . .' she whispered. 'Away from that man —don't tell him you found me!' Renewed fear gave her another moment's strength. 'They're all looking for me—He told them I was crazy—He wants me back—He made me promise, but I could not . . . so I had to run away—Hide me, please hide me!'

'Hush, my dear, hush. You're safe with us. We will look after you. Enoch—we'll hear the full story later, but she needs rest and care, and, besides, the poor child is terrified. Shall we . . .'

'Of course, my dear, and the sooner the better. I'll pick up her basket and we'll get home as fast as we can.'

The trap rocked and swayed; the woman's face, and then the pale sky, swung above her, and Gentian slipped into unconsciousness.

The door closed behind the servant, and Mr Bolton and Captain Claverton savoured their glasses of brandy.

'You've changed your maid, I see,' said Claverton. 'What became of the last one?'

'Ah—Jenny—yes. I intended to speak to you of her.'

'You did? Why?' he asked with casual amusement.

'Simply because I entertain some suspicions of her, which I think may concern you.'

'Really?' If the officer was at all interested, he did not show it by so much as the flicker of an eyelid.

'Yes. And the fact that the girl has run away seems to confirm them.'

'And in what way could the flight of your maid concern me?'

The parson leaned back in his chair. 'I will tell you what I know, and you shall judge for yourself. You will probably not have noticed, but the girl seemed rather superior to the general run of servant-girls about here—she was better spoken, and I considered her to be above the average intelligence.'

Claverton nodded.

'It surprised me,' the parson continued, 'for she left a very poor position to come to me, and I knew nothing of her antecedents.'

'But you do now?'

'You know how gossip travels in the country. But let me not anticipate. Thinking she was an intelligent girl, I believed it my duty to give her a little help, a modicum of education, if she could profit by it. I asked her if she could read, and to my surprise she said she could, a little—and write a little, too. However slight her attainment, that would be unusual, you would agree?'

'Certainly.'

'When I tested her, I found she could indeed read, though slowly and haltingly at first. I now regret very much that I did not test her writing. But I concentrated on her reading, and decided to give her practice. I then found that when she lost herself in what was before her she read, not stumblingly, but fluently and well.'

'Surprising indeed, but how does it concern me?'

'I am coming to that. In the meantime, I had been

informed by someone who thought I should know, of some gossip—and some facts. It seems the girl had not been long at Markinge—a mere month or two—and before that she had been living in New Romney with her father. There they were suspected of being witch and warlock before he died—of natural causes, I am convinced.'

Claverton's mouth twisted contemptuously. 'So? Do you share that suspicion?'

'Of course not—it is all ignorant superstition. But it points to her father being a man of learning. The ignorant always confuse learning with witchcraft, except in men of the cloth.'

'Which is fortunate for you,' the officer murmured.

The parson ignored the remark, and went on. 'I then found out that the two of them had arrived in New Romney only last summer—and that they had come by sea. They were carried there by a fishing-boat, *from France*!' He paused, as if expecting to have made a great impression.

'Is that all?'

'My good sir, do you not understand? Think of the situation—a man of learning and intelligence, coming from France, and remaining on the coast—living unobtrusively, not following any profession—it's plain the man was a spy! And, what is more, on his death his daughter decided to carry on her father's infamous trade.'

'That girl? A *spy*? You cannot believe it.'

'Indeed I do. And I blame myself for what has happened. I was troubled, knowing you had been here since she has been in my employ and that you are supervising this great defensive canal. Who knows what she might have discovered? Foolishly I hinted at my suspicions to her—and that very night the girl decamped, which looks to me like proof of guilt. What is more, though I arranged a search, I could find no trace of her—she might have disappeared like the witch some believe her to be—which to me argues that she has gone to ground, and is being hidden by an accomplice.'

Claverton stretched lazily. 'An interesting tale. But I think you are exaggerating both my capacity for secrets and the girl's ability to profit by them. You cannot hide a canal, and I dare say Napoleon knows as much about it as I do. And the girl—when all's said and done, even though she can read and write, she is only a little serving-wench. Now if she were a society beauty, or even a governess in some house where she might contact serving officers or politicians, or be in the company of their servants, I might consider her a possible danger.'

'You think that I am making too much of this?'

'I think your patriotism and your conscience are making you unduly sensitive. I suspect nothing more serious than a girl running away with a sweetheart —some handsome gypsy or a pedlar with a persuasive tongue.'

Mr Bolton nodded thoughtfully. 'You reassure me somewhat. You could be right; I sincerely hope you are. But you would be doing me a service—if not our country—if you would stay aware of the possibility of finding her. If you should come across her, please let me know. Such girls, when they run away, have to find some excuse for their conduct. All too often they invent some tale and lay the blame on their employer. If I am to be accused of starving the girl or beating her, I should prefer to know about it.'

'Naturally. I will keep my eyes and ears open, and if I come across the girl I will make discreet enquiries. And I will remember your theory: sometimes a little suspicion can save a lot of trouble.'

On the whole, Mr Bolton was well satisfied with the conversation. The effect on Captain Claverton was rather different.

CHAPTER SEVEN

'WELL, MY DEAR, I see you are better today.'

The gentle voice stirred memories in Gentian's brain, and so did the kindly, rosy face, but she was at first confused and could not think what had happened to her. She was in a soft, comfortable bed between fresh-smelling sheets, her body, though weak, was no longer racked with violent aches, and she was clean. That in itself was bliss.

'How did I get here?' she whispered.

'We brought you—me and my husband Enoch. You've had a bout of fever.'

'And you have been looking after me?'

The woman smiled in the most cheerful manner. 'It was certain you could not look after yourself, my dear.'

'But you don't know me, and I . . .'

'You are one of God's creatures in need of help, and we came by when you needed us. Now you're still very weak, so don't start fretting. Just lie there while I get you a bowl of broth. Time enough to talk when you feel stronger.'

She bustled out of the room, and Gentian lay thinking it was a miracle. The world which had been utterly hostile had shown mercy, had thrown her in the way of two good people. And they were caring for her. It was heaven merely to be clean and comfortable; to feel protected was paradise.

The women reappeared carrying a steaming bowl and a napkin. Setting the bowl down, she tucked the napkin into the neck of Gentian's nightgown.

'Now let us see if you can drink this.'

Gentian slowly sipped the brew. 'It's delicious,' she said gratefully. 'And—And you have even dressed me in one of your nightgowns.'

The voluminous, high-necked, long-sleeved garment of substantial creamy linen was certainly not her own. As memory returned, she recalled dragging herself along a country road, remembered the horse and trap stopping, and then . . .

'My basket!' she gasped. 'What happened to my basket?'

'Don't fret, my dear, it's here. I thought you might have a nightgown in it, but I didn't look. I didn't want you to feel your things had been disturbed, that I might have been prying. So I put you in one of mine.'

Gentian sighed with relief. 'I was so afraid I had lost it. I have some precious things—oh, not valuable, but precious to me. The books my father loved . . .' Tears of sorrow and weakness came to her eyes.

'Now, now, dear, don't grieve. You're weak, poor soul—but you'll feel better soon. Finish your broth, then go to sleep. We'll talk later.'

When she was stronger, she was given answers to the questions that had formed in her mind. The good couple were named Sarah and Enoch Homewood; he was by trade a saddler and harness-maker, by vocation a Methodist lay preacher. They had been returning from a preaching visit when they had come across Gentian and had taken her back with them to Hythe. She now lay in their little spare bedroom above the workshop, from which the sociable stirrings of his labour filtered up. To her the house seemed surrounded by sounds of activity: the creaking of a pump, a woman's voice calling, a boy whistling, a huckster crying his wares, the rumbling of horses and carts—she loved each one of them.

'I must tell you about myself,' she said to Sarah.

'There's no hurry, my dear. Just tell me your name so that I know what to call you.'

'My name is Gentian Summerlee.'

'Why, that's pretty! Gentian—that's a rare flower, I'm thinking. The wild gentians are few. So your parents thought you were a rare flower. They must have loved you dearly.'

'My mother died. My father—he was a herbalist—he told me that in a country over the sea there were gentians the colour of my eyes . . .'

'And he is dead, too?'

'Yes, last winter. Since then, I have been on my own.'

'And you've had a hard struggle, I don't doubt.'

'When you found me, I was running away.' Now painful, frightening memories were pressing on her. 'If he comes after me, please—please don't send me back?'

'You're safe here! But there are a few things I ought to know—for instance, did you break contract with your master?'

'Contract? I don't think I had one. I was to be given sixpence a week, but I never had any money while I was there—and I won't go back!'

'Do you want to tell me about it?'

'I think so, but I fear you will not believe me.'

'Why should I not? I think you are an honest girl.'

Gentian told her.

Soon she was strong enough to get up and do light tasks, and she tried in every way to help the good Homewoods, for besides feeling immeasurably in their debt, she had also developed a great affection for them. Her mind often turned to Charles Claverton, and she told herself that before long she would be able to make discreet enquiries. She would find him and explain; her happiness with him was only deferred.

Sarah Homewood watched as Gentian worked,

noting her abilities, and discovering in her unusual accomplishments such as the knowledge of reading and writing and the fact that she could even cast accounts. In the privacy of their bedroom she discussed with her husband what they could best do for her. They both agreed that she was no ordinary girl to be put out to service, and between them they thought of a possible opening.

When she was beginning to regain her strength, she had unpacked her basket in front of Sarah, and from the folds of her few garments she had brought out her books.

'These are the things that are so precious to me—my father's books: a book of meditations, a book of essays and a herbal.'

'How beautiful they are. He was a great scholar, then?'

'Yes. For years he lived—and taught—in Oxford. I can just remember that. There he was respected, but here, because he had knowledge, they called him a warlock.'

She could not keep the bitterness out of her voice, and Sarah nodded gravely.

'Ignorant people always distrust what they cannot understand. We must see that you do not suffer any more because of it.'

Some days later Gentian said, 'You have been so good to me, and I have no words or ways to thank you.'

'Stuff and nonsense! You show me all the time, with your willingness to help. You must not feel beholden to us—we are doing God's work.'

'All the same, I must look for a position as soon as I can. But I do not know how to start, and I am so afraid of Mr Bolton finding me and taking me back.'

'Master Bolton! We are a long way from Losely—and if he did find you he could do nothing! Enoch and I have been talking about you between ourselves, and we agree it would be wrong for you to go back into service. You need something better.'

Gentian smiled. 'I should like something better. But I have no idea what I could do, and that seems the only thing . . .' Somehow she knew she could not mention Charles Claverton and his suggestion.

'But Enoch and I have an idea! I can make no promises, of course, but we have a plan. Tell me what you think of this.' Her hands paused for a moment from preparing pot-herbs for a stew, and she looked at Gentian intently. 'So far, you have not been beyond the end of the street, so you have no knowledge of Hythe. I can tell you it is a nice, bustling little town, with good tradesmen, quite a few of the military, and a sprinkling of gentry in the neighbourhood. In the High Street there is an apothecary's shop, owned by a Master Clark. He is an old bachelor, a good man, not one to take advantage of a young maid. He needs help in the house and shop, but he is most particular whom he employs, partly, he says, because of the substances he has there, which must be carefully treated. He has a woman who cooks and cleans for him, and a young man who helps in the shop, but as he—Tom, that is—is often out delivering medicines, Master Clark would be glad of someone else to help him there. Enoch and I think it might be just the place for you.'

Gentian gazed at her in happy surprise. 'If only I could do that! It would be so much better . . .'

'As I say, I can promise nothing. But this afternoon we will go there and see him.'

When they walked down the High Street, the excitement of the outing brought a delicate flush of colour to Gentian's cheeks and made her eyes look an even deeper blue. She's so pretty, Sarah said to herself, and she has such fine features; with that fair skin, blue eyes and golden hair almost too pretty for her own good. She is a maid to be cherished. If the Lord wills it, Master Clark will have her and take care of her.

Gentian was thinking: It is so kind of Sarah to help, to find me a decent pair of shoes and stockings, and a bonnet, so that I look fit for the place she hopes to get for me. And if I can get the place, I shall be able to look for the Captain. She sped along the cobbles beside the stout Sarah, looking at the houses and well-stocked shops, noticing the carriages that passed, the loaded carts, the men on horseback—some soldiers, some gentlemen, some solid farmers—and the folk on foot that hurried to and fro. Everywhere there was an air of cheerful prosperity and a busy purpose. But scan the faces of the military as she might, she could not see Charles Claverton.

They reached a shop with a bow-fronted window in which were displayed apothecary jars and decorated pots, and flasks of coloured liquids which glowed like great jewels. They went inside. At the back were shelves of bottles, behind a counter were rows of labelled drawers. A young man stood at the counter; behind him, in a corner at a long bench which held scales, bowls, a pestle and mortar and other utensils, a small stooped man was working.

Mrs Homewood spoke to the man at the counter. 'We should like a word with Master Clark, when he is free.'

At her voice the older man looked up, peered over his spectacles and came towards them. 'Mistress Homewood! What can I do for you? Your husband is not ailing, I trust?'

'No, he is well, I thank you, Master Clark. I have come to see you on a matter of business, if we could have a private word?'

'Business?' His eyebrows shot up, his high bald forehead wrinkling in surprise. 'Then you had better come into the parlour.'

He raised the counter-flap and ushered them through a door into a narrow passage and then through another door into a room plainly furnished yet snug, with rugs on the floor, clay pipes on the mantelpiece and a shelf of books on the wall. He motioned them to sit down.

'Master Clark, this is Gentian Summerlee,' said Sarah. 'She is the reason for my visit.'

'Mistress Summerlee, you are welcome.' He gave her a grave inclination of the head, and turned back to Sarah. 'If you would explain?'

'Master Clark, I will be brief. Later I will tell you any details you wish, but the core of the matter is this. Gentian finds herself alone in the world, and penniless. She needs work. She is a clever, educated girl, such as are rarely found, I think. I believe she could be of great use to you in the shop, and in return, a small wage would be of value to her.'

'A *young woman* in my shop?'

If Sarah had suggested a hippopotamus, he could hardly have been more surprised.

'It would be unusual, I know,' Sarah replied swiftly. 'But consider the possibility, I beg you. You may test her knowledge, and I think you will be astonished.'

'A young woman! It would never have occurred to me. But I can find no young man to my liking, that is certain. But a woman . . . I should not expect to meet one with any suitable accomplishments.'

'Please, sir, will you not try me?' Gentian pleaded.

He looked at her critically. 'Educated, you say? But in what way? Well, Mistress Summerlee, what do you know that might be of use to me?'

'I can read and write, and do accounts. I have some knowledge of the uses of herbs.'

'I am an apothecary, not a herbalist!'

'Yes, of course. I also have a fair knowledge of Latin.'

(She thought it politic not to mention her ability with French.)

'Latin, indeed!' He looked at Sarah. 'Your protégée interests me. But we must see how her capabilities match her promise.'

The next quarter of an hour was a period as taxing and yet as stimulating as any Gentian could remember. First, he had her read from a book—a medical treatise with long words and strange terms which were unknown to her. Then he gave her quill and paper and set her, first to write, then to cast up a lengthy money sum.

'I'll own you have been well taught,' was Mr Clark's verdict, 'but let us have one more practical test.' He wrote a few words on a piece of paper. 'Come with me into the shop.' She followed him obediently. He gave her the paper, and indicated the ranks of labelled drawers behind the counter. 'Find them for me.'

The names were curiously abbreviated and totally unknown to her, and the drawers did not seem to be arranged in any kind of order (she was instructed later as to the system), but she scanned them methodically, and found the corresponding words without too much delay.

'Let us rejoin Mistress Homewood,' the chemist said.

Once more in the parlour, Gentian waited anxiously for his verdict.

'Well, Mistress Homewood, you have brought me a curiosity,' he began. 'A young lady of such attainments is an unusual creature; but for such a one to work in an apothecary's shop is rare indeed. May I ask why you have not considered seeking a post as a governess?'

'There are a number of reasons, Master Clark,' Sarah said quickly. 'She would need references, and she has none—only my word that I believe her to be a good and honest girl, which would mean something to you but nothing to such gentry who would want a governess. Then again, such a position might put her at the mercy of unscrupulous men—you understand me—and she has been in that danger before. What she needs is a position where she would be protected.'

'I see.'

'And also,' Gentian interposed quietly, 'I would much rather work here than as a governess.'

'In that case it is worth giving the matter a trial. We will see how we suit each other.'

And so Gentian started on a completely different phase of her life, one of interest, tranquillity and serenity. Her heart ached for Charles Claverton, but since fate had come between them, she must make the best of the turn her life had taken. She continued to live with the Homewoods, and on Sundays, her free day, she would go with them to the Methodist Chapel, although she had been brought up an Anglican. We are all Christians, she thought, and she found much in their simple direct ways that recommended their beliefs to her. After chapel and Sunday dinner she would go with Sarah on visits which were usually errands of mercy, or join her in some homely activity.

One Sunday they had all driven out of Hythe; Enoch had left them to pay a friendly call, Sarah had taken some food and clothing to a poor sick woman, and then, as they had time to spare before rejoining Enoch, Sarah suggested a walk in the fields.

'That would be lovely!' Gentian answered enthusiastically. 'Perhaps I might find some herbs to make tisanes or salves . . .'

Sarah smiled. 'I believe you miss your old occupation. Yes, see what you can find, and though it is early in the year for it, I may do some wool-gathering.'

Since Gentian looked puzzled, she explained. 'The sheep rub themselves against the posts and hedges, and sometimes leave tufts of wool. It is not as good as fleece shorn from the sheep, but it can be spun, and is worth the collecting. There will not be much, for at this time of the year the fleeces are not heavy.'

They made their way slowly along the country road, each with a basket emptied of Sarah's gifts, seeking a harvest. Gentian knew what sort of plants to expect in the hedges and beside the water-filled ditches, where should be something of use. Her searching was rewarded; then as they slowly moved on she saw they were approaching a little copse.

'I should like to go into the trees,' she told Sarah. 'The plants will be different there. I shall not be long.'

There was a plank across the ditch near by; she used it and followed a narrow path into the copse. As she had thought, in the shaded undergrowth grew different plants, and she searched about carefully. There were faint rustling sounds in the wood, which she disregarded until she heard a jingling and looked through the tree-trunks to see a horse cropping the sparse grass. It was not a farm horse, but a fine riding-horse, and saddled. She moved nearer, and then could discern, lying motionless on the ground, the figure of a man.

Her first reaction was that he must have been thrown, and was injured, unconscious. She hurried forward, and as she did so she recognised Charles Claverton. She reached him and knelt swiftly at his side. At that moment his eyes flew open, his hand shot out and grasped her wrist. Then he gave a mocking laugh, and let her go.

'Why, it's no pickpocket! It's the little witch!'

She drew back. 'Please do not call me that,' she said stiffly.

'Why not? You behave like one—casting spells and then disappearing.'

His look was hard and critical. Would it be any use trying to explain? He looked as if he did not care.

'I thought you had been thrown and were injured. I

was wrong—so I will bid you good day, Captain Claverton.'

Before she could stand up, he had caught her wrist again.

'Not so fast! You owe me an explanation. You ran away from the parson's house. Did you have a better offer? Has some country oaf married you?'

'No! It wasn't that . . .' How could she tell him the shameful story?'

'What, then?'

'I had to leave the parson. I couldn't wait . . .'

'No?' One eyebrow lifted as he gazed at her cynically. 'Who helped you? There was a fine hue and cry, but you weren't found.'

'No one helped me. Not when I ran away. I had to go because the parson . . . He was going to accuse me of witchcraft.' That was the easier explanation. Claverton looked incredulous. 'I was found by the road by some good people,' she hurried on. 'I was starving and ill with fever. They took me home and cared for me.'

'How fortunate for you.'

She ignored his sarcasm. She could not help it if he did not believe her. It was plain he did not want her now.

'Yes. And they have found me a good post in Hythe. At last I am doing something which would not disgrace my father.'

'Then I congratulate you on avoiding the disgrace of following the drum with me.'

She flushed, and did not answer. If only he would soften and smile, coax her to tell him more. But he did not. Yet he still held her wrist. Then with cold casualness he threw a remark at her.

'In his ramblings, Bolton told me he had heard your father had been a herbalist and a scholar.'

'How did he know?' A pang of fear shot through her. Bolton knew too much.

'No doubt he has his sources. So it is true?'

'Yes.'

'Then why pretend to be a servant?'

'*Pretend?* I was desperate—there was nothing else to do. I had no one to turn to.'

'But now you have. You have protectors and a position. Perhaps you had found them before you left. In any case, you do not need me. And I do not need a little chit who breaks her word. Being my woman is plainly below your ambition now. So I will bid you goodbye.'

He let go of her wrist. With the breaking of the contact of his fingers on her flesh, she felt as if her heart's desire was being snatched away, and she could do nothing to prevent it. If there had been any softening of his expression she would have spoken, if his eyes had told her he still desired her she could have confessed her love, she would have said she was prepared to throw away her post with the apothecary, leave the good Homewoods, forfeit their respect, humble her good name, anything to be with him—but he no longer wanted her.

She got to her feet. 'Goodbye, Captain Claverton.'

She turned and hurried away through the trees before he could glimpse the tears that were welling in her eyes. Now she knew that her dream of life with Charles Claverton had been nothing but a foolish girl's illusion.

For several minutes Charles Claverton did not move.

The meeting had been a strange coincidence. He had ridden out in a black mood, hoping to shake off his dark thoughts with hard riding but he had failed, and while resting his horse he had lain back and let himself sink into despair and self-pity. Why did he ever marry Charity? *Charity*—never was a woman so inappropriately named. And her extravagance denied him the means of buying promotion and thus serving abroad

—the only way to personal satisfaction left to him. These thoughts had been eating into his brain when he heard someone moving close by. There was the rustle of skirts, and expecting some gypsy girl to be trying to pick the pocket of a sleeping man, he had grabbed her—and opened his eyes to see Gentian's face bending over his.

Gentian—the girl became more interesting every time he came across her. How different she was looking now. Better dressed, no longer downtrodden, with most of the time a new air of assurance—and a greater beauty. She had been running away from him when she left Bolton—perhaps with a better offer—was that air of innocence false? She had regretted giving him her word, and had broken it in the only definite way she knew. She was as false as all other women, but she was still desirable. He cursed the ridiculous attraction she held for him, and thought that it would serve her right if he made an opportunity to take what had once been promised.

CHAPTER EIGHT

GENTIAN'S WORK was not easy at first, and she had to use great tact in order not to antagonise Mr Clark's two other workers. Mrs Potter, who lived in and acted as cook and housekeeper, was at first much on her dignity and ready to take offence, but she soon lost her hostility when she found that Gentian treated her as the one in authority and was willing to help with household tasks. Tom Treadwell, a serious young man nearing the end of his apprenticeship, began by dogging Gentian's every movement in case she made some mistake, but when he discovered that she was both capable and careful, he became aware of her as a girl rather than as a potential inadvertent poisoner. Although he never presumed by a single word or act to show her his feelings, his looks and the tone of his voice spoke his admiration. As long as it stops at that, thought Gentian, all will be well.

At first she did only the simplest and most menial tasks in the shop—sweeping and cleaning, washing utensils with the scrupulous care upon which Mr Clark insisted, and labelling packages of medicines for delivery. But after a while, when the shop was busy, he began to allow her to help Tom behind the counter, thus freeing himself to continue his dispensing. Mr Clark was elderly, but shrewd, and the result of this revolutionary decision soon came to his notice. Trade had improved.

At first he had thought the increase in customers must be temporary, due to the weather, an infectious ailment or some such occurrence, but careful observation acquainted him of the true reason. It was nothing more nor less than the presence of Gentian Summerlee. More women were coming to the shop, and they would wait for her to deal with them. He realised that delicacy, prudery or mere embarrassment, call it what you would, made them reluctant to divulge their ailments to a man, but when Gentian was their intermediary they were at ease, and he could prescribe and get business which otherwise he might have gone without.

But the extra customers were not only of the female sex. The men were quick to notice such a pretty face and neat figure behind the counter. Previously Mr Clark had not been much patronised by the military, for medical matters were dealt with by the army surgeon at the barracks, and the chemist had kept his shop strictly as an apothecary's, dealing not at all with toilet articles such as the officers might require. Gentian had not been there more than a few weeks before there was an influx of army officers enquiring for pomades and toilet-water. The fact that they went away empty-handed did not seem to deter others from coming. Mr Clark began to see a possible source of profit which he had previously disdained. For a small and doubtful turnover it had not been worth the trouble of stocking such articles, but conditions had changed.

Because of the great canal project and the possibility of a French invasion of the Kent coast, the army strength at Hythe had been increased, and now the officers had found a reason for coming to the shop. As long as they gave no offence to Gentian, the chemist saw no reason to object, for their trivial enquiries could be turned to sales. He bought a trial consignment of pomatum and toilet-water, and both were added to the display in the window, while inside appeared shaving-brushes and razor-strops. He was satisfied to find that trade in these items was brisk—for naturally Gentian handled such sales, since they did not need dispensing. So after the first few weeks, the chemist's shop developed a new atmosphere of tranquillity and good fellowship, coupled with steady industry.

At first Gentian's wardrobe had been hopelessly inadequate, but here Sarah Homewood came to the rescue once more. She was known in Hythe for her good works, and there were ladies in the district who used to send her second-hand clothes to pass on to the needy. Generally these were much-worn servants' gowns, but sometimes were of much better quality and condition. Little by little, with Sarah's gifts, her own small wages and their combined ingenuity and needlecraft, Gentian was equipped with enough good refitted gowns and everything necessary for decency, comfort and a proper appearance in the shop.

One day as she was dusting the shelves, a lady she had not seen before came in. She entered with a great rustling of skirts and thrust like a battering-ram between two small children who fell back quite intimidated at the sight of her. She was large, with an imposing bosom covered in pinchbeck chains over which loomed an out-thrust chin, a beaky nose and steely eyes. Ignoring everyone else, she passed behind the counter and confronted Mr Clark.

'Jonas! I am here!'

'Why, Harriet! I was not expecting you.'

'Then you should have been. You know I visit you two or three times a year, and always about this time.'

A man came in carrying a large trunk.

'Put it there,' the formidable lady continued.

He did so, and waited as if hoping for a tip, but seeing that none was forthcoming, he hunched his shoulders and went out with a surly backward glance.

'Did you see that? He expected a tip, when I have already settled with him and he has done nothing to deserve it! Carters nowadays are bold as brass!'

'Come inside, my dear.'

She turned to leave, first sweeping Gentian and Tom Treadwell with one long glance.

Tom went at once to the trunk and with it followed them through the door; it was plain that he had encountered this lady many times before and found it politic to do what was expected of him. A few minutes later when he rejoined Gentian—somewhat out of breath from carrying the heavy trunk up a narrow flight of steep stairs—he remarked in none too pleased a voice, 'I should have known she'd turn up! Never leaves him alone for long.'

'Who is she?' Gentian asked.

'Mistress Sumner—his sister. She lives the other side of Ashford. The way she keeps her eye on him, you'd think she had a half-share in the business.'

In the parlour, Harriet Sumner was making her presence felt. 'So you still have Ada Potter with you. I hope she airs my bed properly. Sometimes I think she is getting too old for her work.'

'I find her very capable.'

'And what, may I ask, was that little hussy doing behind the counter?'

'If you mean Gentian Summerlee, I should have thought that was obvious. She is serving the customers.'

'*Serving the customers?* A girl—a little flibbertigibbet! Are you out of your mind, Jonas?'

'No, I am not. She is a very capable girl.'

'A girl in the shop! It's unheard-of!'

'It makes sense to me. She has had an excellent education. I could not find a young man with her abilities—why, she even knows Latin.'

'*Latin!* I cannot believe it! She has gulled you! You simply cannot keep her.'

'But I intend to. She is more than satisfactory.'

'You *must* be out of your mind! It's madness! You will have a nice packet of trouble on your hands!'

'I cannot think why I should.'

'With that *girl*! You must be senile, Jonas, not to see that she will be after the men for one reason or another, and they will be after her, for their own ends.'

'Harriet, I cannot control your imagination, but I must ask you to curb your tongue. Miss Summerlee is a most respectable young woman, and I will not allow her to be insulted.'

Mrs Sumner was too surprised to do more than snort at the rebuke.

The visit lasted for a fortnight, during which time Mrs Sumner totally upset the atmosphere and routine of the household. Whenever they worked together, Ada Potter regaled Gentian with a recital of Mrs Sumner's sayings and doings, her arrogance and her lack of consideration.

'It's always the same,' she said. 'Poor Master Clark—I don't know how he bears it. If only he had a wife, it would be easier for him. That Mistress Sumner! I'll wager her husband is glad to see the back of her for a while. The sight of her is enough to sour cream. She looks as if she sups vinegar from a red-hot spoon.'

Thinking of the pursed-up mouth and bitter expression, Gentian could only laugh. She did not expect to come into conflict with Harriet Sumner. Time was to prove otherwise.

One afternoon, the moment came which Gentian had both been hoping for and fearing: Charles Claverton came into the shop. She had not seen him since their chance meeting in the woods. He was with two other officers, and stood back to let them be served. Behind their backs he smiled at her with a slightly cynical amusement. Her heart was pounding, she could feel the blood mounting in her cheeks as she attended to the other men, but she had regained her self-control by the time she had to turn to him.

'In what way can I serve you, sir?'

'Some soap, if you please.'

She asked him what sort he preferred, she showed their stock, and all the time they behaved as if they had never met, as if she had never confided in him, never accepted the wonder of his kiss, never agreed to go to him. He made his purchases and left, with not a word or a sign. Only his eyes had indicated that he knew her. His indifference seemed complete. Two more officers passed him on the threshold; she left Tom Treadwell to deal with them, and went to a substantial countrywoman who was waiting to be served.

The woman confided her ailment to Gentian, who relayed it to Mr Clark. Then she had to wait while he dispensed a remedy. Unable to face a conversation on the weather and the laying idiosyncrasies of hens, Gentian turned to the drawers behind the counter and pretended to tidy them, her mind still in a turmoil. The sound of a name brought her back to the present, and she found herself listening to the conversation of the two officers.

'I see Claverton's back from his marsh patrol.'

'And not in too black a mood. His wife must be keeping away from him.'

His wife! Gentian felt as if her legs had turned to jelly, and clutched the edge of the counter for support. Why had it never occurred to her that he might be married? At his age, it would be strange if he were not.

She realised that Mr Clark was calling her.

I must be mad, Charles Claverton told himself. He was letting his curiosity take hold of him, he was allowing it to reinforce a simple physical attraction and become far too absorbing of his time and thought. A little slip of a girl with golden hair and dark blue eyes—she was nothing more than that. Of course, as a healthy male, he had the normal sexual reaction; if he could bed her a few times he would probably get her out of his system. The idea he had of her was something that had generated in his own mind, totally unfounded on fact. Why should he think of her as someone whose natural simplicity hid an intelligent mind, whose innocence masked a depth of passion? It was contradictory, it was ridiculous. The girl had made him a promise, had had second thoughts or had got cold feet, and had broken it. He owed her nothing. But she still attracted him.

Very well; all he wanted of her was some gratification, so that he could free himself from the thought of her. Taking her, proving to himself that she was just another body, however beautiful—he would not admit that there was anything about her to enslave him as he had once thought himself obsessed by a woman who had turned out to be shallow, fickle, greedy and selfish, as they all were—that was becoming more and more necessary if he were to regain his peace of mind. He had put himself to the test of seeing her, not once, but several times, in her own surroundings, and had found that his desire, his need had only increased. So it was foolish to go on like this. He was behaving like a lunatic, but something had to be done.

It had not been difficult to find out Gentian's habits. She went out very little; at irregular times she left the shop to make household purchases, that was all. Then, some time after the shop closed, she walked through the town, back to the Homewoods' cottage. If he wanted to engineer a meeting, there would be no difficulty.

Gentian had left the shop after clearing up, and was walking briskly down the street, tucking her shawl round her against the cool autumn breeze. There were still plenty of people about in the late afternoon, as Hythe was always busy. She had no reason to notice footsteps behind her, and paid no attention when someone came alongside until she heard her name.

'Gentian . . .'

The voice was unmistakable; before she had time to turn her head she felt that lurch of the heart, that thudding in her bosom. Charles Claverton was walking beside her, his figure less striking than usual since he was bareheaded, his hair as was the custom among the officers clubbed into a neat pigtail, and he was wearing a long dark cloak—a campaign cloak, she thought abstractedly, reluctant to raise her eyes to the face whose look could cause such havoc to her feelings. But whatever he wore, he would stand out among men with his bearing, his looks, his eyes . . .

'Oh—good afternoon, Captain Claverton.'

'I see you have not forgotten me. May I walk with you a little way?'

'Oh, no, please do not—do not inconvenience yourself.'

'It is no inconvenience; I am going this way.'

He was already slowing his long stride beside her swift little steps.

'No, please do not. It would not be right.'

'Not right? For me to escort you when I find you alone? You cannot mean that.'

'Indeed I do! There is no danger in my being alone here, and—and . . .'

'And the gossips will have some amusement, is that it? Well, let them. Our consciences are clear, are they not?'

He did not intend to leave her. To insist would cause a fuss, which would be more gossiped about than if she simply let him accompany her to the Homewoods' door. So they walked on, side by side.

'I believe you sometimes choose the shore path,' he said casually. 'Let us go that way today.'

How did he know? Perhaps she should not agree, for it

was less frequented than the main streets. Did it matter? There would still be people along the way, and it was only a little further. She liked to go that way unless she was short of time, as she loved the open sky and the sound and sight of the sea. With a light hand on her elbow, he was steadying her across the littered cobbles of the street.

Soon they were on the path above the strand. The breeze was stronger there, whipping her skirts about her, snatching at the escaping tendrils of golden hair and whisking them across her face, but she lifted her head to it and took into her lungs deep draughts of cool air laden with salty scents of tide and seaweed. Not far below them the sea splashed and sucked at the pebbles along the shore, a soft grey-green expanse stretching to the horizon, where its colour melted imperceptibly into the misty skyline. Somewhere over there, lost in the soft obscurity, was France.

His voice recalled her to the present.

'This place seems to suit you, Gentian. For once you look as if life held some pleasure for you.'

'For once?' She turned to him in swift surprise. 'There is much pleasure in my life. But, of course, you have seen me before only when I was unhappy.'

'I am glad conditions are better for you. And here I find you are using your real name—not Jenny, but Gentian Summerlee. Is that your real name?'

'Of course! I told you it was not suitable for a servant. I am proud of it—too proud to let it be degraded, as I myself was.'

'And now you are satisfied to be a chemist's maid-of-all-work?'

'I am not a maid-of-all-work! I am his assistant. I am treated with respect, and beholden to no one!'

Mercifully the nearest person was only a fisherman on the beach below, cleaning out his boat. This was not the sort of conversation she cared to have overheard.

'And is that all you want from life?'

She looked at him, and her breath caught in her throat. Oh, no, it was not. She wanted more, much more, but she could never admit it to him. Another gust of wind caught her, and she shivered and pulled her shawl closer, but it was not only the wind which sent a shiver down her spine and made her draw a quick gasp of breath between parted lips.

'You're cold!'

In one swift movement he twisted his cloak from his shoulders and swung it about her, wrapping her in its folds, and enclosing her in his arms. She felt the thickness of it warm from his body, felt the strength of his arms holding her close to him. She could not move, her arms were pinned under the cloak, and if she tried to take a step it would only bring her nearer still to him. He was no longer smiling, but looking at her with a sudden intentness. The next moment his mouth was on hers.

As if in a dream she gave herself up to his kiss, her body relaxing in his embrace, her mouth soft under the pressure of his. At first that was all it was—a gentle contact—then his hands tightened, his mouth pressed harder, opening her lips. This is what the parson did, she thought, and it was loathsome, but now—the searching tongue seemed to be drawing her very soul to him, sending tremors of exquisite delight through her body, so that her stomach turned over and even the points of her breasts tingled. It's true, she thought, it's loving that makes all the difference, and I love him. I think I have always loved him. She let him take the sweetness of her mouth, she held both mouth and body against him with no thought of resistance, for this was a rapture outside her experience, beyond even her imaginings.

At last he raised his head. 'Gentian, why do you run away from me?'

'Because . . . I must.'

'No! You know I want you, and now I know you want me.'

'No!'

'Don't deny it. You are ready for love—you would still like to come to me.'

He kissed her again, quick teasing kisses.

'And I say you *are* a little witch!' He smiled. 'Haven't I seen you transform yourself? First you're disguised as a downtrodden slavey, next you're a prim serving-maid—now you're a capable bourgeoise, but one glowing with passion—what next?'

'Please don't mock me! There was a time when I was nobody's servant, and it is good to hold up my head again.'

'Then hold it up and look at me! Every time I see you, you are more desirable.'

She was fighting the emotion that rose within her. She did not know how to answer him.

'Look at me!'

Against her will she did so, and saw his eyes lit with a dark fire. She drew in her breath between her lips as her heart beat more madly.

'So we feel the same. We were meant for each other, and you know it. Admit it . . . Tell me you will come to me, and this time you won't fail me.' When she still did not answer, he spoke even more urgently. 'Admit it! Tell me you love me!'

The words were forced from her. 'Yes—I love you.'

Now his eyes were no longer sardonically hooded, but wide and sparkling, his look open and eager, his mouth smiling with pleasure.

'Then let's have no more shilly-shallying! We want each other—we've a right to our happiness.'

He kissed her again, this time with even greater passion than before, and she was swept away on a tide of emotion that drowned all thought, that left her nothing but the love she felt for him, so that she surrendered and responded as she sank into the strength of his arms. At last he raised his head.

'When will you come to me, sweet? Tomorrow? Today?'

At his words, the flood-tide of passion ebbed enough for thought and reason to surface a little, for memory to come rushing back.

'You know it's impossible!'

'Impossible? There's nothing to stop us.'

'But there is! You are . . . I know . . .' Her voice tailed off. She could not bear to say it.

'Know what? There's nothing . . .'

'There is! I—I know you have a wife.'

He threw back his head and gave a short derisive laugh. 'A wife! Yes, what a wife! The greatest mistake of my life. Put your mind at rest. Forget her. There's no love lost in that quarter, on either side.'

'But you *are* married.'

All these weeks she had hoped against hope that the men had been wrong, that somehow they had misunderstood, that Charles Claverton was a free man, that she could love him with a clear conscience, though more than that she could not do . . .

'Yes, I'm married. But I've told you, it does not signify. We do not live as man and wife. You can leave the old apothecary and come to live with me. I shall see that you want for nothing.'

'You don't understand!'

'No, I don't. Explain to me—and for God's sake, call me Charles.'

'If—If I did that, I know what it would mean. I couldn't live like that—not now, when I've just got back some respectability.'

'*Respectability!* We're talking about *love*!'

'But it's not just that. You're married, and anything could happen. You might have to leave me, and I've been adrift before, without protection . . .'

All her old fears were rushing back. She had been defenceless, a prey for the sadistic bakers, the lecherous parson . . . If Charles Claverton stopped loving her she would be nothing but his discarded mistress, a prey once more for the lascivious and the rapacious to fasten on. She loved him, but how could she risk it, now that she had at last reached a respectable and sheltered position.

'Protection! *I* am offering your protection!'

'But it wouldn't be real protection. At best I'd be your mistress—at worst, anything could happen.'

'So you don't trust me, when I say I'll provide for you? That's a fine sort of love.'

The bitter lines had returned to his face, the eyes were hooded, the mouth hard.

'I do trust you! I believe you would do your best—but I would still be nothing.'

'So it's status you want, is it? Was it that all the time—marriage or nothing?'

'It's not like that! But don't you see, I need to be secure, for I have no one.'

'*You would have me!*'

She gazed into his eyes and thought: If only I had the strength. If only I could take the risk. But I might snatch at happiness only to find it didn't last, and I should be alone again, in far worse case than before.

'It's no use. I can't do it.'

For a long moment he did not speak. Then he nodded. 'I see. I'm always too abrupt for you, I try to take things too fast. Very well, I'll learn to bide my time long enough to court you, but this isn't the time and place. Later I'll explain, I'll make you see that you won't be badly off, that there is a future for us together. Believe me, I shall do it.'

She believed him. That was the worst of it. She knew that a few more meetings, some urgent words, some passionate kisses would be enough. She would give in. She loved him enough for that. But what would happen to that love? Once she went to him, she would be a mistress, without status, living in the shadows, a creature who could be dispensed with when passion faded. She was not clever enough to know how to keep his love once the first delights were over. She loved him too much to endure all it might entail. Better to kill her love now, than let it live to suffer.

'No, you can't do that. I cannot be your woman.'

'You mean you will not?'

'I will not.'

'I shall not take that for an answer.'

'You must.'

She slid out of his encircling arm, took off his cloak and handed it back to him. 'I'm going on alone. Don't follow me.'

She began to hurry along the path. He took a step towards her, checked and turned away, thought better of it and turned back, to stand and call her name.

'Gentian!'

Still the slim figure fled from him.

'Gentian! Come back!'

She had nearly reached the houses, where she would be out of his sight. She heard her name blown past on the wind; it would lose itself over the waste of sea, taking her love with it.

Charles Claverton stood for a few seconds longer looking after her hurrying figure, then flung his cloak about his shoulders and turned back along the shore path.

CHAPTER NINE

AUTUMN DREW ON, and there was more work than usual for Gentian. Mrs Potter was feeling her age, and Mr Clark, who up till then had been a wiry little man, surprisingly fit for his middle sixties, began to suffer from a succession of ailments. There were times when both she and Mrs Potter had to take it in turns to nurse him, and though he rarely stayed abed and never quitted the shop for more than a day or so, everything took longer to do and Ada Potter had not the strength to catch up on all of the tasks. But Gentian was not afraid of work, and between them they managed, for a time.

Then one evening Ada Potter had a talk with Mr Clark in the parlour, and on returning to the kitchen where Gentian was preparing vegetables for the next day's dinner, she said flatly, 'I've told him.'

'Told him what?' asked Gentian, somewhat mystified.

'I've told him I must leave.'

'Leave?'

'Yes. My daughter needs me, and it will be best for me to go soon, while I can look after her youngsters for her and perhaps make a few coppers working at home. I don't want to leave Master Clark in the lurch, and I'll stay until he comes to some arrangement—but I must think of my daughter and my future, and I can't go on here for ever, particularly now Master Clark isn't so well.'

'I'm sure he'll be better in the spring, and I'll do all I can.'

'Bless you, I know you will. I don't want to be selfish, but I think it's best. I've told him to get a good day woman if he won't have a stranger to live in. You'll manage.'

Gentian was not so sure; she knew how particular Mr Clark was over the sort of person he employed. When he spoke to her about it, he made his objections very obvious.

'I simply cannot find anyone I am prepared to have living in this house, with all my stock of drugs about.'

The drugs are partly an excuse, he just doesn't like strangers who might be curious or interfering, Gentian thought.

'I think Mistress Potter's suggestion is the best,' he went on. 'I have tried to get a daily woman, but even there it is impossible to find one to suit. I think I shall have to ask Tom to live in. It's time he took more responsibility. Well, we shall see.'

Gentian talked it over with Sarah Homewood. They were sitting in the little downstairs room behind the shop where Enoch was still working. Gentian, wearing an apron to protect her dark dress, was helping Sarah as they chatted by teasing out the sheep's wool that she had gathered. Gentian loosened the oily wool, picking out the burrs and seeds and little knotted lumps and laying the fibres all one way in fluffy piles, while Sarah, using a drop spindle, laboriously spun them into a thread. When Gentian had asked her why she did not use a spinning-wheel, Sarah had answered, 'Wheels cost a lot of money, my dear. This way is much slower, but it works.'

'I can see it's going to be difficult,' Sarah was saying. 'Jonas Clark will not take just anybody. From what you tell me, there's not a daily woman to suit him. Though he might get a young girl, it would hardly be fair to ask you to train her and be responsible for her—you have enough to do already.'

'We certainly have plenty of work in the shop.'

'Another apprentice might help.'

'He cannot find one.'

'And if he did, it would turn you into a housekeeper.'

For once Sarah had no suggestions, and Gentian had to agree that the matter must be left to Providence. It did not occur to her that her own feelings and actions might be the deciding factor.

Try as she might to tell herself that she must not, could not, love Charles Claverton, that everything between them—and it had been little enough—was in the past, Gentian still felt grief for a happiness denied. Sometimes she thought she had been foolish not to throw overboard her principles with her present way of life and go to him, to snatch what joy she could; at other times she knew that her conscience could not so easily be stifled, that it would constantly gnaw at her delight, and that if—as was only too possible—Charles Claverton should tire of her, she would end up with a broken heart and a life in ruins. But her emotions were constantly under siege.

Claverton quite often came into the shop, and one look from him was enough to set her feelings in turmoil. Then there were chance meetings in the street—or were they by chance?—when a polite word from him would be accompanied by a clear gaze that set her heart thudding and turned her limbs into green sticks. He did not press his attentions on her, but she knew her own vulnerability, and she guessed he was only biding his time. She knew also that there was only one way in which she could armour herself against him. But so far the right sort of protection had not presented itself. Or had it? It could be closer to hand than she had dreamed.

'I can see no possibility of doing any better,' Mr Clark was saying, 'and yet it is not satisfactory.'

In his quest for a woman servant, none had come up to his exigent standard; all he had found was a young girl who could come in daily as a junior maid.

'If I engage her and let Mistress Potter go,' he went on, 'it will mean extra work for you, Gentian, which is hardly fair—and if I insist on Tom Treadwell living in, that will not help you. Besides, that was never in his contract.'

'No, please do not do that. Could you not find a reliable boy to help with the outside work and do the less important deliveries?'

'That is a possibility. But it would not help you—and, on the other hand, it is another extra wage.'

Gentian had long since discovered that Mr Clark, though he could not be called miserly, was at times parsimonious. He wanted value for money.

'But Mistress Potter will be leaving. Surely the wages for a daily girl and an errand-boy would not come to more than you pay her?'

'Well . . . that could be so. Would you be prepared to manage with such an arrangement? I will not have the daily girl working upstairs or in the shop, that is definite. She must confine her activities to the kitchen and the parlour.'

It was flattering how Mr Clark had of late taken her into his confidence and treated her as an equal. She supposed it was because she was able to discuss his books and even his treatments of ailments with intelligence.

'I do not mind the extra work, Master Clark, but there will be difficulties,' Gentian said tentatively.

'Difficulties? What sorts of difficulties?' The chemist peered at her sharply over his spectacles; he had thought Gentian's acceptance of a daily girl would solve everything.

'First of all, I should have no authority over a daily servant.'

'Stuff and nonsense! I should tell her you are in charge of the household.'

'Telling her might not be enough. If I were older it would be easier, but as it is, I doubt if she would accept orders from me very willingly. And I shall be reluctant to give them.'

'You must try. I see no other way out of this confounded business.'

Gentian nerved herself. This was her opportunity, if she had the courage to take it. 'There is only one thing that would settle the matter; but I think for you it would be out of the question.' Could she go through with it? It was a gamble that might lose her everything.

'What is that? I will consider any reasonable suggestion.'

Now she must say it, come what may.

'There would be no problem—if you would marry me.'

'*Marry* you?'

'Do not misunderstand me—there would be no alteration in our relationship. I would wish us to be exactly as we are now. But if—if I were your wife . . .' she checked the tremor in her voice, 'I should then have authority over the maid and the boy, and would work the same as before, while living here to look after you. I would not ask for anything more.'

He looked at her for a long moment without speaking. She could not tell what he was thinking. Oh, it had been too presumptuous, he would turn her out . . .

'You know I have never found for myself the necessity of marriage. Such an arrangement never occurred to me. But now you mention it, I can see its advantages. Yet—there will be gossip.'

Of course, people would say he had married her for a housekeeper, and she him for his money.

'That would not bother me.'

Mr Clark clapped his hands on his knees. 'Nor would I care! I think it is an excellent idea! We will sort out the details and go ahead as soon as possible.'

I shall be safe, Gentian thought. Charles Claverton will have lost all power to tempt me; he cannot make advances to a respectable married woman. And I shall have forestalled my own desire.

She admitted it to herself, she wanted to go to him. When she had been in his arms, surrendering to his kiss, her whole body had cried out for fulfilment. But they could never marry; he had a wife, and she knew instinctively what misery becoming his mistress would bring to her. He wanted her. He wanted her to supply a physical need—and that was all she would be to him, an object for his satisfaction. He did not know her as a person, he did not want to know her in that way. She, who had never given her body to any man, realised that if only she did not love him, they would meet on equal terms. And when desire was satisfied, and sated, they could part the same way. But to belong to him, loving him as she did, would be torture, whatever the physical delights, and parting from him when he tired of her would be one long never-ending agony. It would be a suffering far worse than never knowing fulfilment. But it was an avoidable agony—avoidable if she did now what was sensible and right. She could not imagine ever wanting to belong to another man, but a form of marriage with Mr Clark would solve his problems and cut her off from Charles Claverton for ever.

Sarah Homewood was surprised, and treated the news with modified pleasure. 'Master Clark is a good man,' she said, 'but he is somewhat old for you. Are you sure this is what you want to do? I imagined you taking someone like Tom Treadwell, and I must say I never thought Master Clark would marry.'

'I am quite sure,' Gentian told her. She had not revealed the details of the marriage arrangement, since that was between Master Jonas, as she now called him, and herself. 'As you say, he is good and kind, and I shall be happy.'

'Well, you are a sensible girl, not a flibbertigibbet. He will give you security, and that is important to a woman.'

They were married as soon as possible, very quietly. Master Jonas was in his Sunday best with a large buttonhole, Gentian in a refurbished gown and be-ribboned bonnet, with a little nosegay of flowers. The Homewoods and Ada Potter attended, but no one else, for Master Clark had not sent word to his sister, and Tom Treadwell was simultaneously nursing a wounded heart and minding the shop.

When the ring was on her finger, Gentian and Master Jonas left the church, got into a hired chaise, drove to Folkestone where they had dinner, walked along the promenade, decided the wind was too cold to linger, strolled about the town and took the chaise back to Hythe in time for supper. The honeymoon was over.

Ada Potter had bidden them a tearful farewell after the service, for she was going at once to her daughter's house in Dymchurch, so on the day after the wedding Gentian set about changing the rooms. It had been agreed that she should take over the best spare-room used by Mrs Sumner on her visits, and she, when she next appeared, would have what used to be Ada's room. She won't like that, Gentian thought, but I must make some show of being mistress of this house. I shall smarten it up as best I can.

The transition worked completely smoothly and with-out fuss; the new girl accepted Gentian as mistress of the house and was willing to learn, while in the shop everything was as before, with one exception—Tom Treadwell was most punctilious in calling her 'Mistress Clark'. Jonas Clark's wedding was a nine-day's-wonder among the tradespeople, who at first speculated about how on earth Gentian had managed to catch him; but when they found she gave herself no airs and did not flaunt her new status, most of them decided that Master Clark had made a clever move and wished Gentian well.

Sooner or later, Gentian thought, Charles Claverton will find out. However he reacts, I must not let it disturb me. Unknowingly, it was Tom Treadwell who told him.

A young lieutenant who had recently come to the shop with a noticeable frequency had taken to eyeing Gentian in a lovelorn fashion and becoming daily bolder; he was now attempting to grasp her hand as she was showing him some new shaving-brushes. Tom, who made an excellent watchdog while Mr Clark was stooped over his bench, moved along the counter towards her. The shop-bell jingled for another customer, but Gentian was only concerned with extricating her hand.

'Excuse me, *Mistress Clark*,' said Tom—and that was enough.

The lieutenant looked up sharply, dropped her hand as if it had turned into a hot potato, and mumbled, 'I'll take this one.'

One moment he had been playing the cavalier, the next he was a shamefaced boy, and Gentian was almost sorry for him. He was transparently relieved to move up the counter and let Tom wrap his purchase.

Gentian found herself confronted by Charles Claverton. It was he who had come in, and Tom's words had been spoken loudly and clearly. He knew. There was no doubt that he knew, and that it had taken him unawares; his face was pale, his eyes bright with incredulity, and then with pain. Pain—his pride is hurt, she thought, because he wanted me, and I have now gone to someone else.

She could almost feel his emotion coming at her like a wave lifting itself to crash on the shore. Her heartbeats had quickened, her stomach felt uneasy, she clasped the edge of the counter; and his eyes left her face and travelled down to her hand—her left hand, with its plain gold band.

He leaned towards her, and at last he spoke, in a whisper so quiet that no one else in the shop could hear, yet so intense that his words seemed to burn their way into her brain. 'There was no need for that. I'd not have persuaded you against your will.' And so they stood, facing each other across the counter, aware only of the other's presence. His mouth twisted. 'So you defended your honour and bought respectability. I trust it will be worth the price! As far as I am concerned, you may go to hell!'

She felt as if he had stabbed her through the heart. So that's what he thinks. Well, the result will be what I intended, she told herself, trying to ignore her misery. He will not trouble me again. I have seen him for the last time.

She flung herself into the business of house and shop. When the shop was closed and young Meggie had left, she spent companionable hours with Master Jonas in the parlour. When the time came to retire, she would take her candle and go to her own room, leaving Jonas to check that all locks and bolts were secure before going to his. It was as if each appreciated that the other made no demands.

One evening Gentian ventured to ask, 'Master Jonas, have you informed your sister that we are married?'

He gave a mock groan. 'Ah! Not yet. I suppose I should, but to tell the truth, I do not relish it, particularly since I know full well she will not settle for writing me a letter full of recriminations. Even if she had complete command of the written word she would still, I know, have to deliver her opinions in person.'

'Then that is all the more reason why you should

write, so that she may get used to the idea before she pays you a visit.'

'Bah! She will never get used to the idea! And when she comes, you will suffer too, for she will of course assume that you have married me simply to inherit the business.'

'Oh, how dreadful! Then you must tell her that indeed I had no such intention. In fact, I beg that you will ensure that your Will leaves everything as it would have been before.'

'I know, Gentian, that it was never in your mind. Now, I am not discussing my Will with anybody, but though ours is not an ordinary marriage, I must consider you . . . Any arrangements I make will be governed so that my sister does not suffer . . . On the other hand, I shall remember your loyalty.'

'Master Jonas, I do not want anything like that from you. I hope you will live a long time to give me your protection—that, and the friendship we have, is all I want.'

'You are a good girl, Gentian, and I hope my sister will appreciate it.'

That was all he said—but he wrote a letter.

Mrs Sumner must have packed her trunk and set off as soon as she received it. She arrived in a fine state, her temper barely under control, giving Gentian one venomous glance and then sweeping her brother before her into the parlour. Gentian waited while Tom took her trunk up to Ada's old room, and then, when he had returned to the shop, she went to the kitchen where she prepared a tray. She carried it to the parlour, breaking into what was apparently an endless monologue being delivered by Mrs Sumner to her luckless brother. Setting the kettle on the hob, she took the tea-caddy from its place on the shelf.

Harriet Sumner turned on her. 'You have done very

well for yourself, *Mistress Clark*! But there is no need for you to play the fine lady with your tea-caddy. I am used to making my own tea, here!'

'I wish to save you the trouble,' was the calm reply.

'Now, Harriet, you have said enough,' interposed Mr Clark. 'If you are going to stay, let us be agreeable.'

'*If* I am going to stay? Do you intend to turn me out into the street after that exhausting journey?'

'Of course not. The choice is yours, but I cannot have you quarrelling with Gentian. She has done me a great kindness.'

'*She* has done *you* . . . ! Great heaven! She knows which side her bread is buttered, I'll say that! You must be in your dotage, Jonas, to marry a little serving-wench.'

'*Harriet! That is enough!*'

Mr Clark's voice was so sharp that for once she subsided into silence, drinking her tea and biting into her sponge cake as if she had a grudge against it.

Gentian met the force of her resentment alone when she showed Harriet Sumner to her room.

'And why, may I ask, have I been given a servant's room?' she demanded.

'I am sorry, Mistress Sumner. I have made it as comfortable as possible. You see, I have moved into the second best bedroom.'

'I see. As mistress of the house you move into *that* room, when as a wife you should join your husband. I begin to understand. You are taking everything from Jonas, and giving him nothing—not even his married rights, after bewitching him with your blue eyes and yellow hair! It is scandalous! Don't think I shan't see Lawyer Thornhill about this!'

Gentian had tried to be conciliatory, but this was too much. 'It is not Lawyer Thornhill's business—neither is it yours! Master Jonas chose to marry me, and we are both happy with the arrangement. Please keep your speculations and your comments to yourself.' With that, she went into her room and shut the door.

She should have foreseen that Harriet Sumner would assume she had married Master Jonas in order to inherit his property, and had made herself indispensable in business and attractive in person to that end. It was what the woman herself would have done, given the opportunity. Jonas must tell his sister that she was not going to suffer financially by his marriage, and it was to be hoped that she would believe him. Gentian had the uncomfortable feeling that even such assurances would not greatly soften Mrs Sumner's vindictive nature, and that Harriet was now firmly her enemy, and likely to remain so.

Charles Claverton did not understand why he felt such bitterness and rage. Gentian had only confirmed his belief that women were shallow, greedy and self-seeking. It was plain he had not offered her enough. Presumably his promise to see her well settled had not been sufficiently definite; she considered the old chemist a better investment. In the very nature of things he would die before Gentian was middle-aged, and she would be left a young widow owning his business and in possession of such money as he had saved. And for that, he told himself, she was prepared to give her body to an old lecher. Oh, the chemist had made a good bargain: with that beauty he no doubt expected to renew his lost youth. It was obscene. And Gentian—by God, how she had altered!

He had hoped she was a pure innocent; he had found her in his arms to be aware of desire and ready, he believed, to seek satisfaction with him; he could ignore the possibility that she was now sexually experienced —but not that she had been playing with him. It must have amused her to see how quickly he had been aroused. She must have known then that she intended to marry Clark the chemist.

He cursed her. He hoped that every night she would be revolted by an old man's fumbling intimacy, that she would bitterly regret the bargain she had made. He owned to himself that he had expected her to come to him for something more than physical passion—that he thought she had a girlish affection for him. He would have respected that. He now admitted that he felt more than the instinctive desire to possess her, that something in her mind or spirit attracted him as he had never been drawn before to any woman. Was that too an illusion? But desire was still there, and strong; she was young and beautiful, he was in the prime of masculine vigour, they would have been well suited. For Gentian instead voluntarily to go to the bed of a bent and bloodless old man, to offer herself to his groping fingers and shrivelled shanks—it was foul, sordid, lewd, a degradation!

He took himself off early on his next canal duty. His darkened looks and curt commands warned his men that his temper was at flash-point, they had seen it before, but normally a few hours' riding worked off the black mood. This time a few hours—a few days—made no difference.

The party reached Losely, and as a matter of politeness Claverton called upon Parson Bolton. The parson was most kind, but no, he would not stay the night—he did, however, when pressed, accept the invitation to dine. They had not met for a few months, and there was a certain amount of social chit-chat and news to be exchanged—passed on, would be more accurate, for most of the information came from Claverton, since Mr Bolton lived in such a quiet retreat.

Charles Claverton had not informed Mr Bolton when he discovered Gentian working in the shop in Hythe; it was no longer the parson's business where Gentian had found employment, he had thought. But now, just as illogically, he felt impelled to mention her, to see if Bolton showed any interest. And so, over the brandy, he said casually, 'I saw your one-time maid—Jenny, that is—the other day.'

There was a sudden gleam in Parson Bolton's eyes as the lids flashed up in surprise, than lowered again. He was in no hurry to answer, and his voice was slow, almost indifferent, but Claverton was not deceived.

'Indeed? Where was she?'

'In Hythe. She has gone up in the world. She was working behind the counter in the apothecary's.'

'So? I am glad for her sake. I always thought she was an intelligent girl. She knew you, of course?'

'Oh, yes, she knew me. But we had no conversation over the counter, you understand.'

'Of course not. Did she seem well?'

'In the pink of health, I would say.'

Mr Bolton nodded. His nostrils were a little compressed, the corners of his mouth tightened. He is not pleased, thought Claverton, and withheld the information that Gentian was married. That he could try out another time if he chose, for Parson Bolton was already changing the subject.

The villages on the Romney Marsh were small and widely scattered, the ways between them narrow, rough, ill-kept; in winter the tiny communities were frequently cut off from each other by drifts of snow or deep impassable mire. And yet news spread, not always swiftly, and sometimes becoming garbled, inaccurate and altered in the process, yet by word of mouth people somehow kept in touch. Since almost every family relied on the 'owling' to keep them above starvation level, contact was necessary; smuggling was by its nature a combined operation. When Harry Smart visited the parsonage, under cover of night and with a couple of ankers of brandy slung on his pony, he expected to be informed of any movement of the military or the Excise in the district of which Mr Bolton had become aware. The parson was useful, and generally earned his fee of brandy, tobacco and tea.

The maid had earlier been sent to bed, and parson and owler sat together in the kitchen, with one flickering candle and two pewter pots between them. They had by now exchanged all their important information.

Harry took a long swig at his pot. 'By God, you brewed some good ale this time, parson.'

'Well, Harry, this is my best. I thought you deserved it.'

Harry drank again and wiped his mouth with the back of his hand. 'No more news, then?'

Mr Bolton considered for a moment. He remembered that Harry had once said Joseph Bartlett held a grudge since he, the parson, had taken Jenny Sumners into his employ, and had thus been in his turn amused by Jenny's flight. So he might as well give Bartlett something to think about.

'Nothing of importance. But—you remember the servant-girl I had from Bartlett the baker of Markinge?'

'The one what skipped?' said Harry briefly.

'Yes. Well, I have found her again. She is working for an apothecary in Hythe. I really think I may renew her acquaintance.'

He knew Harry would not be able to resist passing on the information. He overlooked the near certainty that what Bartlett was told, Adam Brenzett would also learn.

CHAPTER TEN

MR CLARK WAS changing his way of life—by almost imperceptible degrees, it was true, but the change was there. For one thing, he was becoming a little more sociable. He had one or two cronies who at infrequent intervals would call after the shop was shut and smoke a pipe of tobacco with him; now he suggested that their wives might like to join them and bear Gentian company. The wives accepted perhaps as much from curiosity as kindness, but once they had arrived they found Gentian so agreeable that they were ready to come again. It was on one such occasion that the matter of the ball was mentioned.

The Pumphreys owned the best grocer's shop in Hythe, and Mrs Pumphrey, a stout jolly woman, knew everything that happened in the town and enjoyed all the social functions.

'Have you heard, my dear,' she said to Gentian, 'that there is to be a ball?'

'No, indeed. Pray tell me about it.'

'Well, the mayor is holding an assembly in honour of Mr William Pitt's regiment of Cinque Ports Volunteers —you know that Number Eleven Company is stationed here.'

The names meant little to Gentian, but she was aware of the presence of the Volunteers in Hythe, and she nodded agreement.

'It is to be held in the Town Hall, and will be a fine affair! The military will be there in strength, so there will be no shortage of partners, and all the best townsfolk will go. You should persuade Master Clark to take you—I am insisting that Pumphrey obtains tickets for us.'

'What am I to be persuaded to do?' asked Jonas, who had caught the tail-end of the conversation.

'It's the ball at the Town Hall, Master Clark. It will be a splendid business, Pumphrey and I shall attend, and I was hoping that you might take Mistress Clark.'

'I am not one for balls and routs, Mistress Pumphrey.'

'Then you do not realise the advantages of them, Master Clark!' she rejoined, wagging a finger at him. 'Much good business has been done over a glass of claret at a social occasion, and there will be officers' wives at the ball, who might if they saw Mistress Clark be encouraged to set foot in your shop for the first time.'

'Well, Pumphrey, I can see why your business prospers! Mistress Pumphrey has a shrewd head on her shoulders. But, Mistress, I do not dance, and too many glasses of claret might lose me business and give me gout—have you thought of that?'

'Ah, you will have your jest! But I can answer it. There will be cards for those who do not dance, and I happen to know that you play a fair hand of whist.'

'In that case, I promise you I will think about it.'

Gentian expected that to be the end of the subject, but to her surprise Jonas broached the matter the very next day.

'Well, Gentian, would you like to go to the assembly?'

'I had not thought seriously of it. I hardly know . . .'

'Is there anything against it?'

'No . . . Yes, for I should not do you justice.'

'My dear, you would always do me justice, anywhere,' he replied, with a warmth that brought a flush of pleasure to her cheeks.

'That is kind of you, Master Jonas, but indeed I should make a poor showing, even in my best gown.'

'Is that the trouble? I should have thought of it. Then

you shall have some furbelows for the occasion. Ask the mantua-maker to call.'

Mr Clark was careful with his money, but he recognised a good investment. It would do him no harm, quite the contrary, to be seen with a pretty, well-dressed wife.

From different corners of the Marsh two men were making their way to Hythe to see the same person—but with very different motives. They arrived on the same day, Parson Bolton being ahead of Adam Brenzett by an hour or two.

Mr Bolton, as was his nature, acted deviously. First he found out there was only one apothecary's shop in Hythe, in a good position at one end of the High Street. He did not enter, but strolled along the opposite side of the street, making observations. The second time he passed he was nearly abreast of the shop when the door opened and a customer was shown out. This was a well-dressed woman, and bidding the lady good morning was a slim figure, a girl with golden hair showing from beneath a cap trimmed with lace. He could not be mistaken—it was Jenny.

The first stage of his curiosity being satisfied, he retraced his steps as far as the White Hart—a good coaching inn standing next to the Town Hall—deciding that he would dine there. An inn was a good place for gathering gossip, and he would like to know what was being said in Hythe of Miss Jenny Summers.

Adam Brenzett was not devious. He found the apothecary's shop, and with very little hesitation pushed open the door and went inside. There was no sign of Jenny, which was disconcerting. A young man behind the counter moved towards him.

'How can I help you, sir?' he asked politely, in spite of the fact that Adam in his rough country clothes looked no better than a carter.

'I thought—I was told—that a Miss Jenny Summers worked here. I have a message,' he stammered.

The young man smiled with faint encouragement. 'I think you have the name a little awry. She *was* Miss Gentian Summerlee—she is now Mistress Clark. Can I . . .'

He was interrupted by Gentian herself, who came through a door behind him.

'Adam!' she cried. 'Adam Brenzett!' The tone of her voice and her smile showed how glad she was to see him. 'Just wait a moment.'

She went to a corner bench where an old man was pounding with pestle and mortar, and said a few soft words. The man looked up, listened, and replied. Jenny—or what was it the young man had called her?—came back.

'Come through here, Adam.'

Still bewildered, he followed her behind the counter, through a door and into a cosy parlour.

'Pray sit down, Adam. You must be hungry. You could take something while we talk?'

'I don't want to be no trouble,' he mumbled.

'You are not any trouble!' She disappeared, like a will-o'-the-wisp, he thought, and was back again before he had collected his wits. 'The maid is getting some bread and meat and ale. Now tell me, Adam, how is everything with you?'

'Middling,' he said. 'But you, Jenny—I be fair mazed —what has been going on? First you be not Jenny Summers, but something else, and then you be Mistress Clark. I can't make head nor tail of it.'

'It's simple enough, Adam. My real name is Gentian Summerlee, but when you knew me I thought something simpler would better suit a servant's life. When I came here, I felt I could use my own name. And now—now I am married to Master Clark.'

'*Married!* Why, Jenny . . .'

He was at a loss for words. He had always known it was hopeless to dream of her; he could not marry her, and it was inevitable that someone so lovely should be courted. Still, it was unexpected, and a bad blow, but he pulled himself together. He was, after all, no worse off than before.

'Well, he looks a good sort of young man. As long as you be happy . . .'

'Young man?' She looked at him questioningly, then understood. 'Oh, that was Tom Treadwell. Master Clark was at the bench, dispensing medicines.'

'*Him!* But he be *old*, Jenny!'

'Older than I am, yes, but he is kind.'

She said no more, for the door opened and a maid came in with a tray, and set out food and ale on the table.

'Will that be all, mistress?'

'Yes, thank you, Meggie.'

When the door had closed behind her, Adam, his face flushed with embarrassment, tried to smooth over his remark. 'I be that sorry, Jenny, for speaking thus.'

'You don't have to apologise, Adam. You were surprised, I know. Now take some food, for you have come a long way.'

'I shouldn't be here. I be dressed so rough—the kitchen would be good enough.'

'The kitchen is *not* good enough for my friends. Besides, Meggie is there and we could not talk privately. Oh, Adam, it's so long since I saw you!'

'A couple of years, I reckon.' He remembered his mission, and went on, 'I came to warn you, but reckon you don't need the warning after all.'

'Warning? What about?'

Adam munched on a hunk of bread and meat and tried to think how best to put his ideas. 'You ran away from Parson Bolton,' he said finally.

'Yes. I had to.'

'I can guess why. The maid who was there before you—she told me things when I was driving her in my cart. But when I saw you after, you said you was all right, being treated well.' Adam put down his mug. 'What happened? Did he . . . ?'

'He wanted to. He tried to. I—I knew he would not be refused, so the only thing I could do was run away.'

'And he came after you, I know that. He be a sly one, but I have his measure. He be a lecher, but more than that, he be covetous and unforgiving. I know he tried to find you, and since you escaped him, I reckon he still wants you. And now he knows where you be.'

It was a long speech for him; he had been driven on by emotion and conviction. Now he stopped and waited for Gentian's reply.

'It's not possible he could try . . .' Her words tailed off.

'I reckon it be. But now I see there be no need to worry. You be married—and though your husband bain't a young man, it'll do. Trying to get back a servant be one thing, but even a parson can't claim another man's wife.'

'Oh, Adam, it is so good of you to trouble about me,' Gentian said impulsively. 'And if I were not married, I should be frightened, I know, for I think he is a man who would not forget a grudge.'

'Ay. And is that why you married Master Clark, Jenny—because you were frightened?'

'I suppose—in a way—it was.'

He leaned towards her, his voice low and his eyes kind. 'Frightened of what, Jenny?'

'Of many things.'

He looked at her, considering the expressive features, the soft sensitive mouth. 'I know you feared William, and the parson. You be very attractive to men, Jenny. But fearing men be the last reason for marrying.'

She flashed him a sudden surprised look, and all at once he knew, or thought he did. Unsteadily he took her face in his two hands.

'Look at me, Jenny. You be still a maid, I be thinking?'

She clasped his big brown wrists.

'Adam! You must not ask such a question.'

'I be not asking. I be saying it. You be still a maid. Well, that do beat all.' He allowed the little hands to draw his away. 'Well, Jenny, safe be safe, no matter how. But if you need help, you know where to find me.'

'Thank you, Adam. But, come now, you have not told me how you are getting on.'

'Oh, it be a funny old life at the bakery now. My father be ailing—had some queer turns in the last few months, he has, and can't work so hard. We've had to find another worker, and I be afraid . . .' He stopped, and shook his head.

'*You* afraid? Of what, Adam?'

He looked at her with his straight, honest gaze. 'I be afraid my father will die. There be no love lost between us, but I would not wish that on any man before his time. And if he does, then William . . .'

'What about William?'

'I fear he'll not keep the bakery. With all this talk of Boney coming, and the canal being cut just below the bakery, he fears there'll be no one to buy our bread. We rely on the little cottages on the Marsh. When the bakery becomes his, I reckon he'll try to sell.'

'And it means a lot to you. Can you not prevent it?'

He laughed bitterly. 'How? I shall have no rights. Once I hoped my father might give me a share. I be his son, though a bastard—and there was no need for *that*. He were a widower then. Now I reckon he'll defy his conscience, for I know he'll leave me nothing. And I have no money. If I had, William'd not sell me a share. No, he'll sell elsewhere, for spite.'

'There must be some way. You could borrow, perhaps, and buy through another man?'

'Borrow? I'd never make enough to pay the interest. Oh, I be trying to save—I make more by the owling now my father can't do so much—but it be hopeless. It'd take me a lifetime.'

'Don't give up hope, Adam. You never know . . .'

He stood up. 'Ah, Jenny, if only I could think hope might be some use. But you do me good—you've given me some cheer. And thank you for the food. Now I'd best be getting back.'

They went through into the shop.

'Master Jonas—this is Adam Brenzett. As I told you, he is an old friend, and helped me in the past.'

'I am glad to meet you, Master Brenzett.'

'And I to know you, Master Clark. And now I'll bid you good day.'

'Good day, Adam. Let it not be so long before we have news of you again.'

Adam went back to where he had left his horse and cart, and took the marsh road back to Markinge. He had no reason to call at the White Hart, so he and Parson Bolton, though within a score of yards of each other, did not cross paths.

The glimpse Parson Bolton had had of Gentian in the shop doorway had reawakened his desire, and the sight of her, no longer dressed as an insignificant servant-girl but as a tradeswoman of some substance, made the luring of her back to Losely a challenge he had not expected, and he began to relish it. Now she had greater value and he wanted her all the more.

At the White Hart he skilfully drew information from

a talkative pot-boy under the pretence of enquiring about a one-time parishioner he thought he had recognised.

'Oh, *that* young lady! She *was* Miss Summerby—something like that—until a short while ago. Now she's Mistress Clark. Master Clark the apothecary—an old bachelor, everyone thought—has done well for himself. It's December marrying May, as they say, but she be a nice, well-thought-of young lady.'

'I see. I am mistaken, it cannot be the same person.'

Married to the old apothecary! That altered everything. He could hardly bring pressure to bear at this stage to get her back. Nevertheless, if he could, he would have some revenge for the way she had slipped from between his fingers. The best plan would be to find out what he could regarding her circumstances.

'December and May, you say? And what did Master Clark's family think of the match?'

'Oh, there be no family to speak of, only one sister, and she don't live hereabouts. It's said she were furious, for she thought to inherit the business. Still, she be married to a farmer over Ashford way, and he don't see much of her.'

'Then it is to be hoped that time will heal their differences.'

'Time!' The pot-boy laughed. 'It'll need more than that! That Mistress Sumner cherishes a grudge as dear as gold!'

He could hardly believe his luck, to be handed her name like that! It would be easy to trace a Farmer Sumner in the Ashford area, and he resolved to do so. He and Mistress Sumner had something in common —they each had a score marked against Mistress Jenny's account.

The White Hart was a good inn, so he decided to dine there. The pot-boy who brought the tankard of ale he had ordered with his meal was the same one, and as talkative as ever.

'Be you here for the ball, sir?' he asked.

'Ball? What ball? I did not know there was one.'

''Tis to be held tonight, in the Town Hall, next door. A grand affair, in honour of the Cinque Ports Volunteers. I made sure a gentleman like yourself would be going.'

'I should indeed like to attend, but there will be no tickets left—and, I dare say, no bed for me here.'

'Oh, don't 'ee worry about that! I can get 'ee a ticket—and there's a bed free here tonight, since most of the folk attending be local, you see.'

'Then I should be glad if you would arrange it.'

Parson Bolton liked a social occasion. He was not expected back at Losely until the following day, and there was no knowing what gossip he might pick up about the chemist and his young wife.

Gentian dressed herself with more than usual care. This was the first public occasion she had attended in Hythe, and she wanted to look her best. She was pleased with her gown. The mantua-maker has told her that in London flimsy materials in white and pale colours were all the rage, the cut very décolleté and the style figure-clinging, but they agreed that would not be suitable for Hythe. They had settled on a silk, striped in sapphire blue and burgundy, cut with the fashionable high-waisted fitting bodice and full skirt, with a neckline low but not too revealing, and little puff sleeves. The gown was trimmed with burgundy red ruffles, and she had a ribbon of the same dark red with which to knot up her golden curls. She had no jewellery, since everything had been sold during her father's last illness, but to reduce the bareness of her throat and bosom she tied another piece of the ribbon round her neck. It emphasised the whiteness of her skin, and was becoming. When she went downstairs, Master Clark gazed at her with approval.

'You look very pretty, my dear. To complete the picture, would you care to wear these? They belonged to my mother.'

He held out a pair of drop earrings. They were of gold set with garnets, old-fashioned but delightful, and a perfect match with her burgundy ribbons.

'How kind of you, Master Jonas! They are beautiful.'

She set them in her ears and smiled back at him.

'Perfect! Keep them, my dear. You had no present when we married. Call them a wedding gift.'

'I cannot thank you enough. I regret I have nothing for you.'

'Your presence is gift enough, Gentian. Now, shall we go?'

Well, we have Napoleon to thank for this, thought Parson Bolton as he looked about him at the prosperous and lively gathering. It was the threat of Bonaparte that had greatly increased the military presence on the Kent coast. In 1801 the handsome new barracks had been built for the Royal Staff Corps—the specialists in the construction of fortifications—and Hythe was now their permanent station. With them came their wives, and so the need for suitable entertainment. Left to themselves, the citizens of Hythe would still have had assemblies, but they would have been on a provincial, almost rural scale. Here, tonight, there was a cultivated air, with richness, elegance, uniforms and stylish toilettes, well-bred accents intermingling with and diluting the provincial and bucolic flavours and the broad Kentish speech.

He saw one or two people with whom he had a nodding acquaintance, but he did not wish to attach himself to anybody, preferring to move slowly in the background of the activity, listening, observing, waiting. He could dance or play cards later if he wished, and had in mind the possibility that the apothecary and his wife might attend the ball. If so, he was not going to miss the opportunity of a little amusement.

Gentian felt a surge of excitement as she entered the ballroom. It reminded her of gatherings she had witnessed years ago with her father, when, little more than a child, she had been so proud to accompany him and try out her carefully-practised steps. She had not danced since that time.

The rooms were aswirl with colour and the flash of gold under the many candles, and chatter and laughter competed with the music of the fiddles. At present the air was tolerably fresh; later the smell and heat from the burning tapers would combine with the odours of perfume and sweat to make the atmosphere oppressive. That was usual at any function, and people were accustomed to it.

Mistress Pumphrey, with her husband in tow, soon bore down upon them. The four of them talked together, and Gentian did not notice the dark figure of the parson until he was a mere yard or two away. Then she thanked heaven for Adam's warning, for had Mr Bolton not been brought to her mind earlier in the day, she might have betrayed herself. As it was, she was able to suppress the start of surprise and the exclamation that sprang to her lips, and quell the unreasoning fear which rose within her.

Now he had approached them, and was making his bow. 'Miss Jenny, I am overjoyed to see you again.'

'Master Bolton . . .' she acknowledged him, and could say no more.

'Will you not present me to your delightful company?'

'Why, yes.'

She recovered herself and made the introductions, naming 'Master Clark, my husband,' last.

'Your husband? Sir, I must congratulate you. Miss Jenny—forgive me, Mistress Clark—I wish you well.'

He took her hand and raised it to his lips in a gallant gesture, but the too-tight pressure of his fingers and the cold look he gave her before he bent his head invested it with menace. Gentian felt a shiver down her back, felt her throat contract.

'It is a long time since we met, is it not?' he went on. 'I had such hopes from our Bible readings, and regretted that you had to leave so suddenly.'

What is he going to say? Gentian wondered. Does he intend to disgrace me by making it public here that I was his servant? It would be such a blow to Master Jonas's prestige—my position at apothecary's was very different from being a general servant.

Mrs Pumphrey was speaking. 'Bible readings? You hold Bible classes, then, Master Bolton?'

'Yes. But these were special classes, since Mistress Clark is such a talented reader. We were thus able to study . . . in depth. But Mistress Clark disappointed me.'

'Indeed? How as that?'

'She left Losely before we had pursued our studies to the full consummation of knowledge.'

His lips smiled as he measured every word, and Gentian understood his foul meaning. She knew he was baiting her. How far would he go? She forced herself to look at him with a calm unconcern.

'It is too much to hope that we can return to that footing now,' he went on smoothly. 'For that disappointment I must seek some other compensation, in time. Life is full of trials, is it not?'

Mrs Pumphrey turned to her, curiosity sparkling in her eyes. 'Why, Mistress Gentian, you never told me you had lived in Losely! What were you doing there?'

'I was there—such a short time,' Gentian stammered.

The parson smiled again. 'She was my most valued . . .' he paused, and Gentian held her breath. 'My most valued parishioner,' he finished.

'Do you play cards, parson?' Master Jonas suddenly interposed in a cheerful voice. 'I am desirous of taking a hand at whist, and leaving the ladies to their dancing. They will have plenty of partners. Will you join me?'

'Thank you, Master Clark. I trust we shall meet again, ladies.'

His departure made Gentian only a little easier. She was saved for the moment from personal and public disgrace, but who could tell what the parson might say to Jonas on the way to the card-room? His presence was a constant menace to her, and she could not breathe freely until he was gone—and even then, what had he meant by seeking some other compensation for his disappointment? Adam was right: Mr Bolton was cherishing a grudge because she had once outplayed him.

She did not dare to think about it, and to distract herself she threw herself into the diversions of the ball. She noticed that the military and gently-born civilians were mingling only with each other, while the trades-people were keeping to themselves. Will barriers be lowered later in the evening? she wondered.

Mrs Pumphrey soon found a dancing partner for Gentian—the tailor's son, who had plainly been too shy to ask her for himself, but led her on to the floor with more alacrity than grace, his face covered with blushes and smiles. Together they got through the dance reasonably well, and the ice having been broken, she found she was then not short of partners. If it had not been for the nagging fear of what Mr Bolton's intentions might be, she would have enjoyed herself hugely, for she found that she remembered all the steps and was, in fact, a better dancer than any of her partners.

After an hour or so, a dance having finished, Gentian was sitting with Mrs Pumphrey when a stir at the end of the ballroom indicated that more people were arriving. She glanced up, and saw a group of officers with their ladies, and there among them was Charles Claverton. On his arm was a handsome woman, fashionably dressed in a high-waisted gauzy gown trimmed with gold. Her hair was stylishly arranged, smoothed back into a mass of dark brown ringlets. Her features were too large and bold for beauty, but she would have looked well had it not been for a proud and supercilious expression that hooded her eyes under drooping lids and gave her mouth a downward twist. She was staring about her with undisguised distaste. So that is his wife, Gentian thought. Although her hand was resting on his arm, there seemed to be no real contact between them. They did not speak or even exchange glances; she continued to look proud and disdainful, while Claverton's face could have been a mask, it was so devoid of expression. Gentian remembered his words: 'There's no love lost in that quarter'. She felt a wave of sympathy for him, then she told herself not to be so foolish. He had chosen to marry, so perhaps the situation was his fault. If he had shown his wife more understanding, more affection, they might have grown to love each other. Plenty of people managed to turn marriages that were less than perfect matches into tolerably happy unions. And if, as it seemed, Claverton had a taste for liaisons with other women, that could have been enough to sour his wife and cause a permanent rift between them. She realised that Mrs Pumphrey was talking to her.

'. . . really quite unsuitable!'

'I beg your pardon?' Gentian had no idea what had been said.

'Captain Claverton's wife—I suppose it is she—*her gown*! *Most* unsuitable for this gathering.'

'Oh, I see—I suppose so. But it is very pretty.'

Mrs Pumphrey eyed the flimsy white gown, with nothing over the arms and but two narrow gold straps over the shoulders, low-cut, the bosom cross-banded with gold ribbon which also trimmed the hem of the diaphanous skirt—and snorted.

'It might do for London, but here it is most immodest!'

Gentian supposed it was, but secretly wished she could have worn it. It was like something out of a dream.

Claverton led his wife into the next dance, though it seemed to afford neither of them any pleasure, for their expressions did not alter, and she could not see that they exchanged a single word. Though she tried not to watch, she could not help her eyes straying back to the couple, outwardly so handsome and privileged, who yet seemed to take no delight, or even interest, in each other's company.

A little while later, when she was sitting alone, she looked up to see him approaching. His eyes were on her. The last thing she wanted was to have any conversation with him in public or private, but short of sudden and conspicuous flight, she had no means of avoiding him. So she sat, hypnotised by his gaze, feeling tension growing within her and praying that the conversation would be brief.

He reached her and gave her a small bow. 'Mistress Clark. I trust I find you well?'

'Very well, I thank you.'

'I regret I cannot present you to my wife,' he went on. 'If I did, she would undoubtedly be extremely rude to you, and that offence would be greater than my apparent incivility.'

Did he expect her to believe that? Of course he was reluctant to introduce a shopkeeper's wife to his superior circle. Perhaps his wife would think that any woman outside that circle might be his current mistress?

'There is no reason why I should be presented,' she answered stiffly. 'And I do not wish it.'

She did not know what else to say. She wished he would leave her, because she already felt the flutter of excitement his presence always provoked.

'I have come to apologise,' he went on. 'When I last saw you, I made some unforgivable remarks. I realised afterwards that what you had done was your affair—and that your action no different from that of thousands of women, many of whom have less reason . . .'

'I trust it will be worth the price . . . you may go to hell!' The words were branded on her mind, and she flushed to remember them. So he still thought she had given herself to Jonas for money and security, but was now excusing it as common practice.

'I accept your apology,' she said coldly, 'but I find your condescending justification as offensive as your original remarks.'

His first reaction was of total surprise, then he laughed. 'Why, Gentian, how you have grown up! That was a fighting retort. You have put me in my place. I apologise again, unreservedly. So will you dance with me?'

'I think not.'

'Please do. It is time that someone from the town stood up with one of the military to show that, unlike oil and water, they can occasionally mix.'

It was weakness to do so, she knew, but she danced with him. His hand clasped hers, and her fingers tingled at the warm pressure; his eyes kept returning to her face, bringing a glow to her cheeks and making her heart beat faster. When they moved closer together in the dance, he murmured, 'Gentian, you are no toy to me now.'

They swung apart, came together again. 'I have learnt to love you,' he whispered.

How can I believe him? she thought. His dark saturnine looks were lightened by the fire in his eyes, the slight smile, neither cynical nor condescending, that curved his well-shaped mouth. The mouth that has kissed me, she thought, but must never do so again, for there is no knowing what madness it might tempt me into.

'Don't tell me that means nothing?' he murmured.

She had to say something, and could think of nothing but the truth. 'It means a lot, but it alters nothing.'

'I can't believe that.'

As the dance ended, he bent his head to hers and said softly, 'Gentian, will you reconsider?'

'*No!*'

However much she loved him she could not leave Jonas . . .

'This time I would be very discreet. Surely something . . . ?'

'No!' she repeated. 'You must never speak of it again.'

'I see. Well, if you choose to be an old man's plaything and martyr both of us, it seems there is nothing I can do.' He took her back to a chair, bowed, gave her a long unsmiling look, and said, before he left her, 'Thank you, Mistress Clark.'

CHAPTER ELEVEN

'WELL, MISTRESS GENTIAN, you certainly had a success last night!' It was the day after the ball, and Mrs Pumphrey had not been able to resist calling to talk it over. 'After Captain Claverton asked you to dance, there was no holding the military back!' she continued.

'They are all customers,' Gentian murmured in explanation.

Mrs Pumphrey's ample frame shook with laughter. 'Some of them are customers of mine, but they did not ask me to stand up with them! It is a strange thing, I have noticed—some women try to attract men and fail completely, while others who do nothing to draw men's attention are like honey to wasps, the men come buzzing from all directions! It's a good thing you are a sensible girl, not likely to have your head turned—and so mindful of Master Clark into the bargain—or else I might fear trouble. Some men are so unscrupulous that they'll lure a girl, steal her affections, have their pleasure of her, and then abandon her without a second's thought.'

Gentian had a spasm of fear—did she know or suspect anything about Charles Claverton? But Mrs Pumphrey's face was honest and open, her manner conversational, she meant nothing.

Even if it had been a warning, it was not necessary. Gentian had no intention of trusting Charles Claverton even though her heart was breaking. She must make herself forget him, and in time, please God, the hurt would heal. If she had gone to him, her life would have been spent on the constant rack of desire for the love which, in spite of last night's words, she felt he could not

135

give her. Here with Master Jonas, life was uncompli-
cated, safe, secure. And Jonas was a cleverer, kinder
man that she had suspected.

'Don't worry about that Parson Bolton,' he had said to
her that morning. 'Mistress Homewood told me about
him before you came here. He's a most un-Christian
man, but he'll keep his mouth shut for his own good.'

She knew then that he had deliberately taken the
parson to the card-room to spare her torment. She swore
to herself that she would be a better wife than ever to
him, that he would never have cause for the least
complaint.

There was much to interest her in the shop. Not only
was she absorbing some of the apothecary's craft, but
Jonas was also, in a small way, letting her use her own
knowledge. He had given her a space at the end of the
counter where she placed little baskets full of articles she
had made—lavender bags, pot-pourri, packets of herbal
tea and other herbs for the kitchen, all things that would
appeal to women. They sold well, and when she packed
them in attractive ways and tied them with ribbon, even
the officers bought them as little presents for their
wives.

'What a clever little business-woman you are,' Jonas
said, although he could not agree to her selling the
herbal salves and curative preparations she still made.
But he had no objection to her passing them on to Sarah
Homewood for the treatment of poor and ailing folk, so
Gentian kept in practice and felt her herbal lore was not
wasted.

The morning after the ball, when Gentian was behind
the counter, the shop door was pushed open and a lady
in a riding-habit strode in. In a glance Gentian took in
the smart blue outfit with red facings, the tall blue hat
with a red cockade—and the bold imperious face of
Charity Claverton.

With her habit skirt looped over one arm, a riding-whip in the other hand, the lady marched up to the counter and impatiently tapping a boot with her whip, demanded, 'Where are the bags of herbs that are supposed to be so useful?'

Gentian moved forward. 'For what purpose do you require them, ma'am?' she asked, touching the little baskets with their various contents.

With the end of her crop, Mrs Claverton began to push the sachets to and fro, having given Gentian hardly a glance. Then some recognition stirred, for she looked up and gazed at Gentian's calm and enquiring face. Her lips curved in a sneer, and she gave a brief laugh.

'Why, you're the girl my husband condescended to dance with last night!' When Gentian made no answer, she went on, 'I hope you will not let it go to your head. I cannot think why he should do such a thing.'

'No doubt it was a courtesy,' Gentian responded.

The shop door opened again, and Charles Claverton came in.

'Charity . . .' he began, but his wife ignored him. With an added glint in her eye, she continued to address herself to Gentian.

'A courtesy, yes. Do not mistake it for interest, if like so many you have pretensions to become an officer's mistress. My husband will not be fascinated by some chemist's little servant.'

Claverton gripped his wife's arm. 'That is more than enough!' he said, with the quiet steeliness of suppressed fury.

Gentian's heart was pounding with mingled embarrassment and anger, and she felt herself trembling, but she answered calmly, 'I have no such wish. And allow me to correct you—I am the chemist's wife.'

The answer was first a peal of contemptuous laughter as the elegantly gloved hand pulled out several sachets from the baskets, then the remark, 'And proud of it, it seems! How delightfully bourgeoise!' She had ignored Claverton's hand on her arm, but now she picked it off, and without looking at him, said coldly, 'Pay for these, Charles,' and strode to the door.

Tom Treadwell, who had been watching and listening in horrified silence, moved up to package the sachets and take the coin Claverton mechanically offered. Gentian, determined not to show the shame and distress she felt, stood erect behind the counter. Charles Claverton gave her a long look.

'My deepest apologies, Mistress Clark.'

He took the packet from Tom's hand and followed his wife out of the shop.

After that incident, Gentian saw nothing of Charles Claverton. Whether it was to save further embarrassment, or to avoid gossip, she did not know. She found herself eavesdropping on the conversations in the shop, listening for news of him, but she heard his name only once or twice. The talk was not so trivial now, for there seemed to be more of an urgency in everyone's mind over foreign affairs. Wellesley—some important military commander back from India—was now the member of parliament for Rye, they said, and a young lieutenant remarked,

'That should please Claverton! It seems he got into disgrace by repeatedly championing Wellesley's views against his own commanding officer's, when he was in India.'

'Claverton was always short on tact when he was long on tactics!' was the reply, which caused a burst of appreciative laughter and made Gentian clench her fists under the counter.

It was plain the military believed Napoleon's strength was still growing; a year ago he had defeated the Austrians at a place called Ulm. The grave mood had been lightened, yet mingled with deep sorrow, when it became known that the very day after the battle of Ulm the French fleet had suffered a crushing defeat near the Spanish coast off Cape Trafalgar, but that the great and beloved Admiral Lord Nelson had died during the conflict. There were many signs of mourning, official and otherwise, the ordinary folk responding spontaneously with drawn blinds and black ribbons, but after the grief was spent, there was a comforting feeling of confidence that at least England was supreme at sea. She needed to be; December had brought news that the French had defeated the combined forces of Austria and Russia at Austerlitz. Napoleon was striding victoriously throughout Europe.

The winter of 1807–8 was a difficult time for Gentian. It was not a season that suited Mr Clark; during the previous winter he had frequently suffered illness, and this time the attacks were worse. When he was out of action and needed nursing, it disrupted the business and put a considerable load on her shoulders, so that without the improved status of both Tom Treadwell and Meggie she did not know how she would have managed. Tom was now out of his apprenticeship, and was a responsible chemist capable of dispensing and needing to refer to Mr Clark only over serious matters. Meggie had been orphaned by her mother's death that autumn, and Gentian had persuaded Mr Clark to let her live in; he was accepting her presence above stairs, and she was a good and willing worker. With all the fetching and carrying up and down stairs of food, coal, washing water and slops she was an invaluable help. What was more, under Gentian's tuition, she was turning into a good cook and maidservant. She believed, quite rightly, that Gentian was helping her to 'better herself'; being of an affectionate disposition and now bereft of family, she lavished on Gentian all the loyalty and fondness she would have given them. For Mrs Sumner she cherished an implacable aversion.

Gentian could not blame her. Mrs Sumner's manner to Meggie was brusque in the extreme, and she complained and found fault unceasingly. Gentian she treated at best with a cold hauteur, and often with an only thinly disguised enmity. Once or twice Gentian wondered whether this extreme dislike had prompted the woman to try to investigate Gentian's life before she came to Hythe, but could not decide whether her pointed remarks were based on knowledge or simple spite. Once, when Gentian was serving a particularly dainty tea to tempt Jonas's appetite, she remarked,

'I don't know how you can put on such airs and graces! You were nothing before you came here!'

This Gentian ignored, but on another occasion they came near to open warfare.

Mr Clark had been so ill and feverish that Gentian had asked Dr Derwent to call. When he had seen Jonas, Gentian asked him whether he prescribed 'the bark' for such cases.

'Indeed I do, and find it beneficial, but this obstinate old friend of mine has so far refused it.'

Gentian knew well how the bark of the foreign tree was used for fevers with good effect, and persuaded Jonas to give it a trial. To her delight and his surprise it brought down the fever, and when Mrs Sumner visited them shortly afterwards, he remarked on it to her.

'You see how Gentian looks after me!' he said. 'Without her pleading, I would never have taken it.'

'Then you had best be careful, Jonas Clark! It seems to me that Mistress Gentian meddles with doubtful matters.'

'How can you say that?' Gentian asked. 'There are many good plants, and as for the foreign bark, why, the bark of our own willow relieves pain and headaches.'

'You see what I mean?' Harriet Sumner turned on her brother. 'She pretends to knowledge she has no right to possess—but she doesn't mention the dangers of yew and toadstools and the deadly nightshade! She's too clever by half, and I shouldn't wonder if she got some of her knowledge from the devil! She certainly seems to have bewitched you!'

'Harriet! If you were not so offensive I would find this positively amusing! It is ludicrous to be suspicious of Gentian's knowledge of herbs. Let me have no more of such remarks.'

'I only speak out of concern for you, Jonas, you know that. I cannot be blamed if Mistress Gentian takes it ill.'

'*I* take it ill.'

They said no more, but the look Harriet Sumner threw Gentian—a knowing, calculating, almost triumphant look—disturbed her for some time.

Gentian saw Adam Brenzett twice during the winter. Each time, though he denied it, she suspected he had gone far out of his way to call, merely to see that all was well with her. The second time he told her that what he feared had happened; his father had died of some sort of seizure, and his half-brother William was in control of the bakery.

'It be what I expected,' Adam said. 'The old man allus used people and gave nothing. He were greedy and selfish. The only person he ever cared about were William—because he be so like him, I reckon.'

'What will you do, Adam?'

'Stay as long as I can. What else? Now, how be Master Clark?'

'He has been ill, but he is recovering. I wish he would eat more, but he has no appetite, and he insists on working in the shop.'

'Ay, I saw him. He didn't look too brave to me. Jenny, if at any time you be in need of help, you send for me.'

'It's a long way, Adam, and I don't foresee . . .'

'You never know. And it bain't that far. It be no use writing to me, for I don't read too well.' He gave her a crooked grin. 'But if you send word you'd like to see me next time I be in Hythe, I shall know it be urgent and you need help. I'll come as quick as I can.'

'It is so good of you, Adam. You are a true friend. I shall remember.'

She did not expect to have need of him.

The winter had been long and bitter, and to Gentian's distress she could see that Jonas was growing older and feebler week by week. Now it will soon be spring, she thought, and he will improve. He will breathe easier in the warm days, and there will be fresh food, more nourishing things to give him. Meanwhile she continued to burn coltsfoot leaves to help his chestiness, and always since she had found that he choked for breath on going from the warm parlour to his cold bedroom, she had a fire lit there, becoming prodigal with fuel in order to save him this terrible discomfort. She warmed his bed with a warming-pan, and when he was really ill she slept lightly, her bedroom door open, listening for sounds of distress, and often got up from her warm bed into the freezing cold, huddled herself into a cloak and crept into his room to replenish his dying fire with wood and sea-coal. Then, if he was awake, she would go downstairs, stir up the kitchen fire and get two bowls of gruel, and they would sup them together before she settled him down and bade him good night again.

He seemed to be responding to her care, and she thought the worst of the winter was over. But February turned bitter, and Jonas grew weaker again. One day, to Gentian's concern, he asked her to send for Lawyer Thornhill.

'There are matters I should have settled with him long ago,' Jonas said. 'I think I must do it now, in case I become ill again and my mind is less clear.'

Gentian tried not to look worried, but to her it seemed very like a man putting his affairs in order because he feared death.

'Surely there is no urgency, Master Jonas? Whatever it is, it has waited long enough, and can wait a little longer.'

'No. I wish to see him as soon as convenient.'

So the yard-boy was sent with a message, and Lawyer Thornhill came the same afternoon.

He was closeted with Jonas for some time, and when he came downstairs Gentian invited him to take tea with her in the parlour.

'I am afraid you find my husband in poor health,' Gentian said, as she passed him his cup.

'Yes. It grieves me to see him so weak. I am glad he had the good sense to send for me; one must provide for the worst eventuality.'

Gentian looked at him in some surprise, and answered, 'I did not wish him to trouble himself with business, but if to see you will set his mind at rest, that is all to the good.'

It was the lawyer's turn to look surprised. 'Did you not realise, Mistress Clark, that he is concerned to alter his Will?'

'No, I did not. Well, that is his affair.'

'It is yours also. But you have no cause to worry. I shall have the new Will drafted immediately, and will bring it for his signature tomorrow.'

'Then I will expect you.'

The next morning Gentian gave Jonas his breakfast in bed, and having attended to his needs and taken the tray away she left him, to tidy her own room. A few minutes later she heard a thud, and thought Jonas must have dropped something from his bed, though she could not guess what. She went to his room, and to her horror found him lying on the floor. She rushed to him, and kneeling beside him lifted him in her arms. His face was contorted and he was gasping for breath. She tried to lift him into bed, but he was a dead weight. She pulled a pillow from the bed and placed it beneath his head, then hurried to the head of the stairs and called for Meggie. Tom Treadwell must have heard the urgency in her voice because it was he who appeared in the passage below.

'Tom! Come up!' she called, and he bounded up the stairs and into the bedroom.

'Master Jonas—he fell out of bed! Help me!'

With Gentian supporting the old man's head, Tom easily lifted Jonas and laid him between the sheets. Gentian propped him on his pillows and tucked the blankets round him.

'Shall I send for the doctor, Mistress Clark?'

'Yes, please do, Tom.'

Jonas made a feeble gesture of disagreement, but Gentian nodded firmly to Tom, and he left. She took Jonas's withered hand in hers.

'Lie easy now,' she soothed him.

'Gentian, I must . . .'

He was struggling to speak, and she thought it too great an effort for him.

'Don't worry. Wait until you are stronger.'

'Can't wait . . .' he gasped, and somehow pulled himself forward and pointed downwards over the side of the bed. 'Help me, Gentian. I want—I want you to . . .'

Suddenly his words stopped on a sharp indrawn breath, he was caught by a terrible spasm, and clutched at her as she put her arms about him. The next moment he fell back against the pillows.

In anguish twice she called out his name, then bent and tried to listen to his heart. She could hear and feel nothing. She snatched up a glass that was standing on a side table and held it before his face. It stayed unclouded. Jonas was dead.

When the doctor came, all he had to do was to confirm that the old man was no more. He did not seem unduly surprised, but shook his head regretfully and said, 'I had thought, Mistress Clark, that between us we might pull him through the winter. You have my deepest condolences.'

During the ensuing hours, Gentian had no time for thought. The laying-out woman came, and between them they prepared Jonas's body for the grave. The undertaker came to take measurements and to find out Gentian's detailed wishes. It was not until late afternoon that she realised that she must acquaint Mrs Sumner as soon as possible of her brother's death. She wrote a brief letter and arranged for it to be sent; she would expect Mrs Sumner for the funeral.

'Mistress, you must rest now, and take a bite and sup,' Meggie urged. 'You've had nothing all day, and you look like a shadow. I've made up the parlour fire—sit and warm yourself, and I'll bring you something.'

'I couldn't eat, Meggie.'

'You must try. It'll be as light as can be, I promise you.'

She came back with a tray on which was a bowl of rich broth and a dish of syllabub—food that had been intended for Jonas, Gentian thought sadly. But with Meggie standing over her—behaving for all her youth like a mother-hen—Gentian made the effort, took the food and felt better for it.

'Now you've eaten, Master Treadwell says you should take a glass of port or brandy, and I'm to see you do.'

'Then I will take the port, Meggie,' Gentian said with a tremulous smile. She was sipping it when Lawyer Thornhill arrived. She had quite forgotten he would be calling.

'What is this dreadful news, Mistress Clark?' he said, as Meggie showed him in. 'I could not believe it when my clerk came in with the rumour. But your servant says it is true.'

'Yes, Master Thornhill. Master Clark died this morning. A spasm of the heart, I think.'

'My deepest sympathies, ma'am. A sad business—a bad business, too. I was just finishing the draft of his new Will. If only he had called me earlier, it would be signed by now. As it is, we only know his wishes . . .'

'But he made a Will long ago, Master Thornhill, did he not? Then the old one must serve.'

'Yes, that is so, Mistress Clark.' His serious professional mien was troubled; Gentian had never expected to see a lawyer disconcerted, but this one was. 'I hardly think you understand, ma'am. The old Will—it must be executed, of course, but for you—your position . . . Well, I really cannot say more in my professional capacity. As I say, I know his wishes, but—well, I shall do my best.'

'I am sure you will do your duty to Jonas as his lawyer, and I can ask for no more,' Gentian replied.

Master Thornhill looked relieved to go.

After his departure, Gentian realised that she must think about her position. She had been either very innocent or very dense. Only now did she guess that Jonas had intended to alter his Will so that she would benefit; in his old Will she had been left nothing.

Harriet Sumner read Gentian's letter with little grief. She had no capacity for loving anyone but herself. She at once busied herself with preparations for going to Hythe, ostensibly to mourn her brother at his funeral, but in fact to safeguard to the utmost her own interests. Her husband could not leave the farm, so she would travel alone as usual. But this time she would alter her mode of travel: she would take the carter only as far as Ashford, and there she would hire a chaise. Thus she would arrive for the funeral with all the dignity it deserved, and the driver would not think it strange that she should wish to convey the sad news to the curate of Losely.

What will happen to me now? Gentian wondered, as she sat in the parlour thinking over the implications of this tragic turn of events. She could guess from Lawyer Thornhill's veiled remarks that Jonas had intended to provide for her, but that death had prevented him. He had not even been granted enough time to tell her his last wishes. Poor Jonas.

As if in a dream she got up, lit a candle—for it was already dark indoors—went upstairs and entered the room where he lay. Something impelled her to bid him goodbye and say a prayer for him while she was quite alone. She stood for a moment looking down at the waxen, untroubled face, then went on her knees at the bedside and bowed her head over her hands. She prayed, and then found her mind straying back to Jonas's last moments. Kneeling there, she thought that her assumption that Jonas had fallen out of bed was not really credible; sunk deep into the feather-bed and weak as he was, it was most unlikely. Yet the only other possibility would be that he had deliberately got out of bed, and then fallen over. But why should he have done that? He had only to call or ring for her. What had he been trying to tell her, and why had he been pointing downwards over the side of the bed? Did he want something from downstairs? Hardly. And he kept nothing under the bed. But that pointing finger . . .

On an impulse, she got up, pulled aside the rug on which she had been kneeling, and looked carefully at the boards beneath. The house had been well built, and it was a good floor, laid with long close-fitting planks, polished over the years to a waxen mellowness. But when she looked closely she could see from the joins that under the rug were two short lengths of boarding side by side. She glanced about her. On the dressing-chest lay the contents of Jonas's pockets, and among the items was a strong penknife. She opened the larger blade and went on her knees again.

The blade slid easily between the planks, and after a moment or two of gentle prising she found that the board was not nailed in place, and she could raise one end of it. It lifted out without trouble, and so did its fellow. With some curiosity, yet no excitement, she brought the candle over so that she could look into the gap. When the candle-flame steadied, she could see, resting on the joists below, a wooden box. She put both hands inside, but to her surprise found that she could not lift it. She could not lift the lid, for it was locked, but the keyhole was accessible without raising the box. By now more curious, she returned to the dressing-chest and took Jonas's bunch of keys. None fitted. Then she saw his watch, and on the end of the fob-chain two keys which must normally have been tucked into Jonas's waistcoat pocket. One was the watch-key; the other fitted the box. With the box still in the hole, there was room to raise the lid, and when she did so, she saw that the box was almost full of small wash-leather bags.

She lifted one out, and loosened the drawstring. A thin stream of golden sovereigns poured into her lap. When she looked into a few more bags, each one contained gold. She sat back on her heels, and tried to think.

It had never occurred to her to wonder what Jonas did with his money. She knew he would often take some from the shop to the parlour and use it for their running expenses, but obviously he plied the business at a profit, so there must have been a surplus. This hoard must be his life savings, changed piece by piece into sovereigns for easy storage.

If only he had had time to tell her his intentions! Had this been mentioned in his new Will? But it would make no difference now. If, as Gentian expected, Harriet Sumner was the main beneficiary, none of it would leave her grasping fingers. She would not voluntarily give anyone anything, and Gentian had no doubt she would take a certain pleasure in turning her penniless out of doors at the first opportunity. But Jonas would never have wanted that. Then everything fell into place in her mind, and she knew what she was going to do.

She had worked for Jonas willingly, and after their marriage she had toiled even harder and without a shilling to call her own. She had never expected a wife's portion, but Jonas had intended her to have something. In the years since she had been hounded, starving, across the marsh, she had learnt something about self-preservation. Now she was not an innocent girl but a woman, and never again, if she could prevent it, would she endure the privations and the utter vulnerability of being penniless. Now that there was something she could do about it, it would be foolish to delay.

But for the moment she replaced everything and went downstairs. She and Meggie supped together, and went to bed early. With Meggie fast asleep in her attic room, Gentian spent several hours over achieving the main part of her plan. By the time she got into bed, she had lined her stays and the hems of her petticoats with a multitude of little pockets of soft cotton, and in each pocket was sewn a golden sovereign.

CHAPTER TWELVE

PARSON BOLTON LISTENED attentively to what Harriet Sumner had to say, hiding his satisfaction under an air of sympathetic gravity.

'You have my deepest sympathy,' he told her, 'and I understand your concern. There is no knowing what you will find in Hythe. Naturally you must safeguard your interests against that scheming young girl, and I suggest you go there as quickly as may be. I will travel to Hythe on the day of the funeral and take a room at the White Hart. If you come there and acquaint me of your situation, you can rely on me to use my best endeavours to get you what is due to you—and I am sure you in turn will assist me to persuade the girl to re-enter my service.'

'Certainly, Master Bolton, that will suit me very well. Between us, with what we know, we should do very nicely.'

It was another long day for Gentian. Normally the shop would have been closed until after the funeral, but the nature of the trade being what it was, she felt she must keep it open for urgent requirements such as medicines and nursing needs. Most of the time Tom had to manage by himself, for she had the funeral arrangements to settle. Then she had to order her mourning. Besides her own gown she ordered one for Meggie, who was overwhelmed at such generosity, never having possessed a good mourning gown before. Tom Treadwell would be attending the funeral; she ordered the traditional pair of gloves and hatband for him, as well as for those of Jonas's friends who had said they would be present. Then she had to plan the burial meal and do what preparations she could for that. It was ironical to do so much when she had been able to do nothing for her father, but Jonas had become almost like a second father to her, she realised. The preparations left her little time for grief, and she went to bed tired out.

Mrs Sumner arrived, clad in deepest mourning with all the accessories, even down to the black-bordered hand-kerchief. Gentian found time to wonder if she kept everything in constant readiness. There was much shedding of crocodile tears—but the small shrewd eyes were darting everywhere. She then made a great show of pulling herself together and enquired what arrange-ments had been made. These, of course, she wished to turn upside down, but Gentian was in no mood for her autocratic interference. Her time will come, she thought, but until then,

'Mistress Sumner, those are my arrangements, and I am still mistress of this house.'

Harriet was momentarily disconcerted, and contented herself by saying, 'Very well. But we shall see.'

Gentian knew that Harriet could hardly wait for the Will to be read.

The funeral was well attended, a harrowing business which depressed Gentian considerably, in spite of her telling herself that Jonas was better off at rest than suffering constant ill-health. Family and friends re-turned to the house for the mourning meal, and Gentian felt her physical and mental strength ebbing away from her with grief and exhaustion. But I must keep my wits about me, she thought, for Harriet is my enemy and will injure me if I give her the chance. She did not anticipate the depths to which Harriet would stoop.

At last the meal was over, the formal goodbyes said, and Gentian was left alone with Harriet and Lawyer Thornhill. He said, 'And now, ladies, I will read the

Will. There are some small bequests, but I did not think it necessary for these beneficiaries to attend.'

They were seated at the table which Meggie had cleared of food and vessels. The lawyer looked at Gentian over his spectacles. 'Might I suggest a glass of brandy, Mistress Clark? You look very tired.'

Gentian poured out three glasses—to give us courage, or for celebration? she wondered. Harriet made a show of protest, but took hers nevertheless.

'To Jonas's memory,' said Lawyer Thornhill, so Gentian had to drink. Perhaps he thinks I will need it, but I am already prepared, she said to herself.

He brought out a document from a leather case and sat resting his hand on it for a few moments. Harriet tapped her fingers on the table-top.

'This Will was made by Master Clark some years ago,' he said in a dry, solemn manner, 'and it is unaltered, save for the addition of a codicil. However, I am impelled to say that Master Clark was in the process of making a new Will, which was to have been signed the very day he died. Since death supervened, the new Will is not valid. Nevertheless, after reading the valid Will I shall acquaint you of the contents of the new one, so that you will have the opportunity to carry out Master Clark's last wishes should you so desire.'

He avoided looking at either of them as he said this. Gentian was steeling herself for the inevitable. Harriet Sumner could hardly hold back her impatience; Gentian could hear her foot tapping under the table, could see the nervous twitch of her fingers.

'Then let us hear what they are, Master Thornhill,' Harriet demanded.

The lawyer pushed his spectacles up his nose, cleared his throat, broke the seal, and began to read.

There was the usual long preamble. Gentian began to feel a little faint. It is only tiredness, she told herself, and took a sip of brandy. She had been working hard and eating little through the past trying days.

First came the minor bequests. There were generous sums of money for the old servant Ada Potter and for Tom Treadwell; even Meggie benefited under the clause 'any other house servant'. Gentian was glad of that. There were token gifts to his old friends; his parlour clock—Harriet's mouth tightened in annoyance—his watch, a silver tobacco-jar and his pipes, and so on. Then, at last, all his residual property and money '. . . to my sister, Harriet Sumner, since I have no other living relative.' There was a slightly regretful, almost grudging, note about that, Gentian thought, but Harriet did not even notice. Her thin lips were smiling and her small eyes gleaming with triumph. She let out a sigh of satisfaction as Master Thornhill went on.

'The codicil reads as follows: "to Gentian Summerlee I leave the sum of fifty pounds and all my books, in recognition of her faithful service."'

Fifty pounds—it was a great deal of money, when she had expected nothing; more than five years' wages for a first maidservant. Harriet gave a snort of disgust and was about to speak, but Master Thornhill prevented her.

'As I remarked, the Will was made some years ago, and the codicil added a month before Master Clark's marriage. I do not know why he put off the revision of his Will, but in fact he sent for me the day before his death and instructed me to draw up a new one, the minor bequests being the same, but leaving his estate to Mistress Clark, and to you, Mistress Sumner, the sum of two hundred pounds. May I venture to hope that you will see fit to give Mistress Clark something nearer a wife's portion?'

Harriet gave a short, unpleasant laugh. 'Indeed you may not! *Mistress Clark* has done well enough by her influence over my brother—*fifty pounds*, no less! I may as well tell you, Master Thornhill, it is my opinion that she has been a little too clever for her own good.'

'I do not understand you, Mistress Sumner.'

She gave Gentian a cold glare, and then leaned towards him. 'Mistress Jenny has been nursing my brother, *in her own way*. Before they married, he would have nothing to do with herbal medicines. It was Mistress Jenny who prevailed upon him to try them —and it was only since then that my brother's health went downhill so badly. I should think it was obvious to you, as a lawyer. She thought she would be better off with a dead husband, once she had a favourable Will.'

Gentian felt herself growing cold as she gazed at Harriet, speechless with horror. The lawyer was also staring, silent, astounded.

'She was just too clever.' Harriet's voice dripped hatred. 'He was weaker than she thought—he died before he signed in her favour. And you think I should give her a wife's portion? She will be lucky if I do not accuse her of murder!'

At last the lawyer found speech. 'Mistress Sumner! You must be careful what you say! To make such accusations, quite unwarranted, I am sure—I can only think you are a trifle unhinged with grief. Mistress Gentian has been a most attentive, solicitous nurse.'

'Of course she was! That would be part of it! Don't you understand? She could not give him anything harmful from the shop, with Tom Treadwell there—but the plants she could gather from the countryside were another matter! I have seen her giving him herb tea—tisanes, she calls them—but no one could tell what was in them. Deadly nightshade or laburnum, I shouldn't wonder!'

'How dare you!' Gentian cried. 'I would not have harmed him for the world! I did my best to make him well.'

Harriet threw back her head and smiled. 'Next you will tell us you married him for love—you, a chit of a girl with golden curls that all the young officers flocked into the shop to see! Oh, yes, mistress, you were very cunning! Too cunning to run off with a soldier—much better to marry an old man, for a rich young widow can then have her pick of fancy followers!'

Master Thornhill's voice crashed out like thunder. 'Mistress Sumner! Let us have no more of this! I advise you to put an end to these accusations, which are totally unfounded and do no credit to yourself!'

Harriet met his gaze resentfully. 'I'll say no more now, except that for once Providence has taken a merciful hand. Mistress Gentian, I should be glad if you would pack your traps and leave my house as soon as possible—shall we say in two days' time?'

'Certainly, Mistress Sumner.'

'I must protest!' said the lawyer. 'The Will cannot be executed in that time, therefore . . .'

'Therefore nothing! Pay her, and send her on her way!'

'Ah—that reminds me of a detail, Mistress Sumner. In the drafted Will, your brother said that the two hundred pounds he intended for you could be paid from the box in his bedroom. Would you kindly produce that for me? It should be in my care until the bequests are paid.'

'Box? In his bedroom? I've seen none.'

'Mistress Gentian?'

'If there is a box of money, I should hardly think my husband would have left it in an obvious place. I suggest, Master Thornhill, that you go at once and look for it.'

'And I will join you!' Harriet Sumner cried. Then another thought struck her. 'No, Mistress Gentian may have stolen a march on us. I will stay with her.'

'By all means!' Gentian retorted. 'But I assure you I am not going to spirit anything out of the house.'

The lawyer got to his feet and looked at her apologetically. 'Forgive me, Mistress Gentian. Have I your permission?'

'Certainly. And if you do not find it, you may search my room. You will find nothing there except the garnet earrings which used to belong to Jonas's mother, and which he gave me as a wedding present.'

Now the two women were alone together. I must keep silent, no matter what Harriet says, Gentian told herself. It is the only safe way. But Harriet said nothing; she sat and stared at Gentian and gazed about her in open triumph. No doubt she intended her silence to be intimidating, but to Gentian it was a blessed relief. Minutes ticked by. What should she do if Lawyer Thornhill did not find the box? Why was he taking so long? At last they heard his footsteps coming down the stairs, and Harriet looked up expectantly.

'I have found the box,' he told them. 'It was hidden under the floorboards. Mistress Sumner, will you come with me? I wish to count the contents in your presence. I shall then seal the box with both our seals, and take it to my office for safe keeping. Mistress Gentian, could I ask you to bring materials for sealing it?'

'Do you wish for cord to put round it under the seal?'

'Yes, I shall need that for it to be effective.'

'Very well.'

Gentian found cord, wax and a taper, and sent Meggie to get a man with a wheelbarrow, so that when everything was done to the lawyer's satisfaction the box could be taken away under his supervision. But first she insisted that he searched her room in Harriet's presence.

'Mistress Sumner has been over the rest of the house, I know. I do not wish her to have any cause for saying I might have kept anything from her.'

Reluctantly Master Thornhill complied, then told Harriet that she had no cause for complaint, and left—much to her annoyance—with Jonas's strong-box.

Gentian went to sit with Meggie in the kitchen. Harriet could queen it in the parlour in solitary state, while she herself tried to make some plan for her future. She told Meggie of the provisions of the Will—she knew by now of her own windfall—for Gentian liked Meggie, and saw no reason to hide her situation from her.

'Oh, mistress, that be dreadful!' Meggie exclaimed. 'You mean you will have to leave here? That be no sort of justice, when you was such a good wife to him!'

She seemed to have forgotten her own bequest, which to her, since she had always been without a penny, was a great deal of money.

'It's the law, Meggie, since the old Will is the valid one. So I must think where I shall go. First, I am sure, I can go to the Homewoods. Then I must make plans.'

'Wherever it be, I be going too. You be the mistress I want—I'll not work for Mistress Sumner.'

'You must not decide anything in a hurry, Meggie. I may not be able to afford to employ you for long, so you should look for a better situation if you do not want to stay here.'

'I *won't* stay here, and that's flat! I shall go with you, Mistress Gentian, and now I've got some money, if you can't afford wages, you don't have to pay me.'

'Oh, Meggie, what a good creature you are! I should love to keep you with me, and of course I shall pay you. But you should think very carefully.'

'No need, mistress. I've decided. Where you go, I go.'

At that moment they heard the door to the shop being opened and then closed. After that, the outer shop door banged. Harriet Sumner had gone out, and they were both too relieved to be free of her for a while even to wonder where she could be going in her ostentatious mourning.

The next day Gentian was packing Jonas's books in a box when there was a knock on the door communicating with the shop. Mrs Sumner came out from the parlour, and returned to say, 'You have a visitor, Mistress Jenny.'

Gentian looked up, and saw, standing in the doorway, the figure of Parson Bolton. She got to her feet, smoothing down her skirt, and gazed at him, saying nothing.

'I have come to offer my condolences, Mistress Jenny.'

Still she was silent, filled with astonishment and anger that he should presume to come to the house after the way he had behaved to her.

'Your husband was a worthy gentleman, and his loss will be deeply felt,' he went on smoothly.

To Gentian, his presence was so insufferable that she could not stay in the same room with him.

'I have nothing to say to you, Master Bolton, and I am busy. Pray excuse me.'

'So, Mistress Jenny!' Harriet interposed. 'You are rude to a gentleman who comes here with nothing but kindness in his heart!'

Gentian ignored her. The parson made no move to leave, nor did he stand aside to let her pass.

'Pray excuse me,' she repeated.

His look of sympathetic gravity relaxed into a small smile. 'One moment, Mistress Jenny,' he went on. 'I am here with the best of intentions, for I believe you have been left—shall we say?—insufficiently provided for?'

'Then you believe wrong. I have adequate for my needs.'

'But not, I fear, enough money to keep you indefinitely, from what Mistress Sumner has just told me.'

'Mistress Sumner is very free with other people's private matters.'

'Ah, but she knows I wish to be a friend to you. May I sit down?'

Harriet broke in with unctuous hospitality, 'Oh, parson, take this chair, do—I'm sure we beg your pardon.'

'Thank you, Mistress Sumner.' He sat down and folded his hands over his portly middle. 'No, please do not go, Mistress Jenny, but hear me out.'

She paused at the door. If she left now, he would think she was afraid of him. The smooth confident voice continued.

'Let me put the position to you, for it is within my power to be of assistance. My own situation is this. My mother is now ailing, and frequently confined to her bed. I have one maidservant who is capable enough, but cannot singlehanded run the house as I would wish. I am prepared to offer you the place of housekeeper. You would be fully in charge of the house, with the maid to assist you. As a respectable widow and my housekeeper, you would have a good status, and I would allow you ten pounds a year wages—all found, of course. You would not be considered or treated as a servant. You would share my table, and have certain privileges which we can discuss at our leisure. You must agree this is an offer worth your consideration.'

The little smile was fixed upon his lips, the small eyes gazed at her gloatingly. Gentian felt sick. It was quite plain to her what he meant. It was a cover for his lust, nothing more. As a wretched little maidservant she would have been forced into his bed; but now that she knew his intentions and was a widow of good position, she must be treated with some caution. So he was offering her permanency and a show of respectability. Disgust and indignation rose up within her.

'I shall consider no such thing!' she burst out.

'Hoity-toity!' Harriet Sumner exclaimed. 'And who, pray, are you to refuse parson's good offer in such a fashion? Do you think you can do better for yourself?'

Gentian wanted to say, I could hardly do worse, but she had no intention of arguing with either of them. 'I bid you good day, Parson Bolton,' she said, and left the room.

Several minutes elapsed before she heard the parson saying his farewells to Harriet, but very shortly afterwards Harriet sought her out and returned to the attack.

'I advise you, Mistress Jenny, to reconsider the parson's offer. You will need employment sooner or later.'

'That is my business.'

'He asked me to tell you he will be at the White Hart until four of the afternoon. If you change your mind, you can send him a message.'

'I shall not change my mind.'

Harriet gave her a quick, evil glance. 'Then don't expect to stay in this town, Mistress Jenny! You will find people less well disposed as time goes on. They'll not take kindly to a woman suspected of hastening her husband's death.'

'You have a wicked mind, but I warn you, Mistress Sumner, that Lawyer Thornhill will protect me against your slanders.'

'*My* slanders! If I should hear such rumours I should contradict them! But it is strange how gossip starts,' she said with a sly malevolence. 'I believe you were once suspected of dabbling in witchcraft—you were called the warlock's wench, I think? It would be unfortunate for you if those stories started up again.'

Gentian felt a touch of panic tightening in her throat.

Dear God, she thought, Harriet is in league with the parson—they are threatening me. I have the choice of enduring their foul insidious rumours or of becoming the parson's mistress.

Well, I'll not give in to them. I must make better plans.

CHAPTER THIRTEEN

GENTIAN MOVED BACK to the Homewoods' cottage, taking Meggie with her.

'Of course I can find room for her,' Sarah said, 'she's a faithful little soul. It will be good for both of you if she stays as your maid, whatever you may decide to do in the Lord's good time.'

Gentian considered she should not stay in Hythe, where she risked too much enmity from Mrs Sumner and Mr Bolton, and evil tales seemed to be spreading. Besides which, sad memories were always intruding into her thoughts, memories of Jonas, of her contented life with him—and of Charles Claverton. He would care nothing for her now, so better not to risk another meeting.

Sarah urged her not to rush into a decision, and Gentian did her best to carry on a normal life, helping Sarah as she used to before her marriage, sometimes going shopping for her, taking Meggie as companion. She began to feel conspicuous by herself, for Mrs Sumner had done her work well. Some of Gentian's acquaintances greeted her coldly, and did not stop to do more than pass the time of day, while others, who gave her any conversation, did so deliberately with an air of defying the attitude of doubt and suspicion.

She tried to ignore the atmosphere, greeting everyone civilly and pleasantly. On this particular day, she knew she would be glad to return to the cottage. Her purchases were completed when she left Pumphrey's grocery and came face to face with Mrs Sumner. To her surprise, the sour-faced woman smiled at her.

162

'Good day, Mistress Clark,' she said.

'Good day, Mistress Sumner,' Gentian replied. 'I trust you are well?'

The woman produced her black-edged handkerchief and dabbed at her eyes. 'As well as one could expect, after my—after our sad loss,' she whined.

Gentian was aware that among the passers-by some were lingering, intrigued by the exchange of civilities between the two women who had little cause to like each other.

'It is a difficult time for us both,' Gentian agreed, and would have passed on, had not Mrs Sumner laid a hand on her sleeve. She was plainly nerving herself to say something more than a formality.

'Mistress Clark, I must—I wish—to make you an apology.'

Gentian looked at her in silent surprise.

'I was overwrought—by Jonas's death. I am a hasty-tempered woman, and I said things to you—and about you—which I now regret.' The woman's eyes were lowered, and her mouth twisted a little; the words were coming out with difficulty.

'Do not trouble yourself, Mistress Sumner.'

'It was my fault we parted with unpleasantness between us. I am going home soon, and I do not wish to leave ill-feeling between us.'

'Now you have explained to me, there is none on my side,' said Gentian generously.

'That is good of you.' An idea seemed to occur to Mrs Sumner. 'We are not far from the shop, so will you not return with me and take a dish of tea? And . . . I believe I can find you a keepsake of Jonas.'

Gentian had not the slightest desire to take tea with Mrs Sumner, but to refuse the olive-branch she was so publicly offering would be churlish. 'Thank you, Mistress Sumner.'

'Is that the maid you have with you?' the older woman asked. Meggie had been hovering behind Gentian during the conversation.

'Yes.' Gentian turned to her. 'Meggie, would you please take the shopping back to Mistress Homewood, and tell her that I am stopping a little while to take tea with Mistress Sumner.'

Meggie bobbed a curtsy and went in one direction while Gentian and Mrs Sumner walked the other way; the little groups of people around them were suddenly intent on looking in the shop windows or talking among themselves.

To Gentian's surprise, the shop was shut.

'I had to give Tom Treadwell time off, since his father is ill,' said Mrs Sumner as she unlocked the shop door. 'I hope he will return tomorrow. But I fear I shall have to sell the shop. I cannot leave everything in the hands of that young man.'

'He is very capable,' said Gentian as they walked through to the parlour.

'No doubt, as an apothecary. Jonas trained him well. But there are the accounts . . . and how do I know the house will be looked after, with just a maid here in my absence? It might go to rack and ruin. Not every servant is trustworthy.'

'It is a difficult situation.'

Mrs Sumner went out to the kitchen to tell the maid to bring the tea-tray.

The parlour looked different without Jonas's knick-knacks—his pipes, his tobacco-jar, his books—barer and less bright. At least I have his books, Gentian thought; the house has already taken on a Sumner-like severity.

After a few minutes Mrs Sumner brought the tea-tray herself, stirred up the fire, went out and brought back the little copper kettle whose spout was already breathing a wisp of steam.

'This won't take a minute to boil,' she said. She did not, it seemed, trust her maid to make a good showing in the parlour. Had she brought a raw country girl with her? Or perhaps the only maid available to her here was an out-of-work slattern. With so many military and prosperous tradespeople in Hythe, good maids were rarely out of a job.

With her back to Gentian, she busied herself making the tea. When Gentian sipped it she found it rather strong, and was glad of the little sponge biscuit she was offered. The woman was still being determinedly friendly. Gentian was surprised at such a show of Christian charity, and began to wonder whether she had some idea of asking her to return and run the house and help to supervise the shop. After all, no one knew it better, and she worked well with Tom Treadwell.

'Have you made any plans for the future, Mistress Clark?'

The query strengthened Gentian in her idea. 'Not yet,' she answered. 'I have not been able to put my mind to any decision.' She went on drinking her tea. It really was rather bitter. She must finish it for politeness' sake, but did not fancy a second cup.

'Well, I suppose there is no hurry. But a young lady of your talents needs to be appreciated.'

Gentian did not quite know how to answer this, for all at once she felt slightly giddy and confused, and the right words would not come.

Mrs Sumner got up quickly from the chair opposite her. 'Are you feeling faint, my dear? Finish up your tea—that will help to revive you.'

She took the cup from Gentian's hand and held it to her lips, tilting it so that she was obliged to swallow the last mouthfuls.

'There now, lean back—it will pass.'

Gentian leaned back in her chair, for the giddiness was getting worse. She had a dreadful feeling that she might fall.'

'I can't think what is wrong . . .'

'It's nothing. Just a touch of the vapours.'

It was getting worse. The room seemed to be swaying up and down, the ornaments on the mantelpiece advancing and retreating, their outlines blurring. She began to be frightened; she had never felt like this before.

'I fear I am ill,' she whispered.

'Come and sit on the couch.'

Mrs Sumner took her arm. She was a strong woman, which was just as well, because Gentian's legs would not carry her. With her arm behind her, she almost fell on to the couch, and laid her head back, closing her eyes and praying that the strange sensation would pass. Sounds seemed to be blurring too; the singing of the kettle, the rustle of Harriet Sumner's gown, the click of the door-latch. Then another voice, a man's . . .

'Is she . . . ?'

And Harriet's.

'Nearly.'

Gentian forced her eyes open; the room was swaying about her in a blur of colour, but something was blocking out the room. A dark figure, then a pale face, monstrously large, swam before her own. Shiny waxen cheeks—small hooded greedy eyes—moist red lips that smiled gloatingly—the misty, distorted face of Parson Bolton was looming over her, advancing, retreating, clearing, blurring, but always there above her . . . She was filled with terror, with blind panic, yet found her body would not obey her, she could not rise, could hardly raise a hand, could not speak above a whisper. 'No . . . No . . .' She could say no more.

'Get her out of here,' said Harriet.

'Not now. Keep her for . . .'

'*Get her out!*'

'But I have a meeting I must attend.'

'Damn your meeting! I've done what you paid me for. I'll not keep her here, for the girl will be back soon, and the Treadwell fellow in the morning.'

'Let me think. Ah, yes, there is somewhere I can leave her . . . She'll be safe there till morning.'

The parson laid his hands upon her, and she tried to scream, but no sound came. He lifted and held her, and she felt a cloak being wrapped round her and the hood being pulled over her head. The parson was on one side of her and Harriet Sumner on the other; between them they were propelling her through the house, her feet trailing, not walking. She heard the back door open, and on they went. It was nearly dark in the back yard . . . How could she know this and still be unable to move or call out? She heard a strange voice.

'Be anything wrong?'

Bolton replied. 'It's the maid—she is ill. I am taking her to a doctor.'

She was being lifted up, then laid down somewhere that smelt of fusty straw. Then there was a rumbling and a rattling, a swaying and a jolting, and like a rag doll she was lying there, being jerked about, to and fro, her senses failing. She did not know how long this went on, but eventually the movement stopped and she was being dragged out into the fresh night air. An arm was about her, hauling her up a flight of steps and then along a path. Then there were more steps down, and an even greater darkness.

A faint light flickered; there was the sound of a door shutting. Gentian loosed her last hold on consciousness and sank into total oblivion.

It was a nightmare, a terrifying nightmare from which she was struggling to awake. It could not be true. She was fighting up from the black pit of fear, she was now just aware that her body was cold and aching, that wherever she was lying was level and hard. If she tried she might be able to force her eyelids to lift, then she would know she was no longer dreaming.

With infinite difficulty she did so—and screamed in terror. She must be dreaming still, it was such a little noise that came out, yet it echoed about her ears, while her eyes still stared in a horrified fixation. A faint gleam of yellow light came from the level where she lay, and showed her, before her and on either side, piles of pale bones and grinning skulls.

She could see nothing else in the small circle of light. They seemed to stretch around her into infinity, it was a vision of hell, the eyeless sockets were glaring at her, the dropped and lipless jaws gibbering at her obscenely. Her flesh was crawling, her heart was thumping dreadfully, yet she could not move, she was incapable of freeing herself from the nightmare. She tried to scream again but her breath was strangled in her throat, her head swam, her eyes dazzled with a million points of light and she was claimed again by a merciful oblivion.

Sarah Homewood could not understand why Gentian was late, so very late; when she made enquiries, the information she was given shook and startled her. Meggie had left Gentian on her way to have tea with Mrs Sumner; that woman said she had left the shop about half an hour later, to return on foot by the shore path. But no one had seen her.

'I fear some mischief has come to her,' said Sarah.

Enoch shared her concern, and went out to search and ask for any trace of Gentian. Midnight came; Enoch returned. It was not possible to do more that night, and there was no sign of where Gentian could be.

*   *   *

Whether she had fainted or whether it was the renewed effect of the drug which had sent her back into unconsciousness Gentian did not know, but eventually awareness began to return and she found she could think a little more clearly. It had not all been a nightmare. She had gone with Harriet Sumner to the shop, and there she had been given some drug. What had happened after that was complete confusion, but she thought she had been driven away in the darkness. Had she really been dragged along, up and down steps, by Parson Bolton? Could that really have happened? The rest must have been a nightmare, that apparent awakening—as one did sometimes dream one's self awake—to being surrounded by white bones and hairless, fleshless skulls. Nevertheless she must be imprisoned somewhere, for the floor beneath her was hard and cold, the air she breathed was dank and chill.

She opened her eyes, and recoiled in horror again. If it was no nightmare, if it was real, she was facing once again that terrifying jumble of skulls and bones. She forced herself to look, quelling her panic and trying to penetrate the general gloom. The glimmer of yellow light that she could see came from a lantern set upon the stone-flagged floor. Somehow the sight of the homely lantern gave her her first feeling of sanity, though it was illuminating a grisly scene. Trying to master her feelings of horror, she put out a hand and touched the nearest object—a thigh-bone—and it was solid to her hand. That means nothing, she thought, things feel solid in dreams. At that moment the lantern guttered, flared, and was extinguished, so that she was left in utter darkness.

I am going mad, she thought—if I am not mad already. No, no, I must not think that. I know the parson is capable of anything. I must make some reason out of this. What had the parson been saying to Harriet

Sumner while the drug was taking hold of her? Something about taking her . . . leaving her . . .

She was imprisoned somewhere, in some dreadful place of the parson's choosing, whence he would secretly take her in his own time. Then she knew, and with the knowledge a wave of relief swept over her. She was not mad. Parson Bolton had been diabolically clever. He had hidden her in the one place he could visit without comment—a church. She was in the parish church of St Leonard's, the church where she had been married to Jonas—but she was in the crypt, which she had never seen, but knew to be a charnel-house of bones from the old churchyard. She was a prisoner in this gruesome place until the parson chose to release her. Thank God, she said to herself, it does not smell of decay, only the earthy odour of a subterranean room. I can stand this, now I know the truth of it.

Is there no way of escape? she wondered, knowing at the same time that such thoughts were futile. Before the lantern had guttered out she had glimpsed the crypt as a long passage, with bones piled behind and around her, everywhere save for a path which must lead to the door. And that, she knew, would be firmly locked. She felt desperately weak and ill, but somehow she got to her hands and knees and began to crawl along this path, shuddering with revulsion as her hands touched the bones on either side. After what seemed an age, she felt the bottom of the door in front of her. She tried to beat on it with her fists, but her arms fell slack and useless. She tried to call out, but could only manage a whimper.

She realised the irony of her situation to the full. If she had been able to cry out, her shrieks would have been useless. Any passer-by hearing such sounds coming from the bowels of the church and knowing, as all Hythe did, what the crypt contained, would think he was listening to the howling of unquiet spirits, would cross himself, and hurry fearfully away. No, there was no release for her until the parson chose to come. Hopeless, ill, exhausted, Gentian fainted once more.

She came slowly back to consciousness, vaguely aware that the silence was not complete. In the pitch blackness, she lay still and strained to hear. There was a momentary rumbling, a few faint sounds she could not identify, and then—were there voices on the other side of the thick wooden door?

She struggled to her knees, beating the wood with her fists and crying, 'Let me out! Let me out!' Would anyone hear her? The door was so thick, she doubted whether the feeble thud of her fists, the faint tones of her voice, would penetrate it. She tried again, 'Let me out!'

Dead silence. Had she imagined the sounds? No, there was the muttering of voices once more.

'Please, I beg you – let me out!'

Silence again. Then a renewed muttering, hurried footsteps—and nothing. Whoever it was had gone away.

In the darkness before dawn Parson Bolton got out of his gig outside the church of St Leonard's and climbed the steps. To his surprise, figures moved in the gloom. 'Who is it?' he asked sharply.

A voice responded, 'Passon Bolton, be that you?'

'Yes. Who is it?'

'Harry. Us bain't expecting you, passon.'

'I'm not here on business—something different. I had not thought to see you.'

The burly figure came up to him. He heard a chuckle as Harry answered.

'We had a few trifles to stow—goodwill offerings, you might say. Then—it were a queer thing—we thought we heard a voice, more like a whimper, from behind the door of the bone-vault, asking to be let out. Some of the men were right scared.'

'Were they? Then send them away, Harry. You can come with me to exorcise the spirit.'

'To *what*? By your leave, passon, I'm not meddling!'

'Don't be a fool, Harry, it's no spirit. Do as I say. It may amuse you.'

'Amuse me?' Muttering to himself, he sent his handful of men back to their ponies that were waiting in the lane, and rejoined the parson.

'Now you shall see what ghost has been asking to be released.'

They went down the stone steps, and the parson brought a key from his pocket and fitted it into the lock of the door.

Gentian heard the key grate in the lock, saw a faint luminosity as the door swung open, and fell forward over the threshold. Two dark figures stood looking down at her.

'I'll be damned! It be the warlock's wench! She don't look too pretty . . .'

'She has had a trying time, Harry. She was crazed. I had to lock her up to restrain her, and this was the only place available to me. Holy ground—it was appropriate.'

The sailor stooped, caught Gentian by the shoulder and pulled her to her knees. Her head fell back and she gazed vacantly at him. She knew that face. It must be another nightmare.

'She do look fair crazed. What's she been doing?'

'Who can tell? She was out of her mind. I am taking her where she will be cared for.'

She could hear what was being said, yet she could not think, and her body was still incredibly weak and unresponsive.

'Be you going in your gig, passon? Best tie her in, or she'll fall out. I'll give 'ee a hand.'

He lifted her and slung her over his shoulder like a

sack of flour. She could smell his sweaty, unwashed odour above that of tar, tobacco and spirits, and her stomach heaved with nausea. She must gather strength to fight. This might be her only chance to escape from the parson's hands and all that such capture meant.

They went up the steps, along the path beside the church, then down towards the road. After the pitch darkness of the windowless crypt it seemed almost light outside, though dawn had not yet broken. As Harry slid her off his shoulder she could see the gig, with the horse patiently waiting. She tried to stand, and then to force her feet to move, but she could only make one stumbling step before Harry caught her arm in a cruelly hard grasp and jerked her towards him. She tried to raise her hands in a feeble attempt to beat him off, and he gripped her wrists.

'Silly maid!' he sneered. 'Can't have you hitting at the parson when he's driving.'

He pulled a piece of cord from his pocket and tied her wrists together. Then he hoisted her into the seat of the gig.

'Yes, that is as well,' said Parson Bolton. 'And here is a strong leather strap. Fasten her to the seat, so that she cannot fall out.'

Harry passed the strap around her and buckled it tightly. 'Can't think why tha' bothers with her, passon.'

The parson mounted the seat beside her and took the reins. 'Thank you, Harry. I'll be on my way.'

Before the pale light of early morning could show the road clearly in front of them, they had left Hythe by back paths and were out in the country, heading for Losely. Gentian, still half-unconscious, knew she was completely in the parson's power.

Adam Brenzett had left Markinge early, done a round of bread deliveries, and had time to spare before picking up goods for his return load. Why should he trouble any longer to work for his half-brother who gave him nothing but curses? He would never have a share in the bakery. Better cut his losses, get out, take any job that offered. The difficulty was, nothing seemed to come his way. What else could he do? He was a good carter, a good poacher, and a smuggler, but he knew nothing else. There were plenty of carters without jobs, and poaching was unprofitable on the Marsh. Even smuggling hardly paid now unless you were a member of a well-organised gang. Without some other experience there was nothing he could do. He drove moodily along, turning such thoughts over in his mind, until he saw a tavern by the roadside. It was time, he thought, to stop for a bite and sup.

Gentian had no idea how long they had been driving, but it was considerably lighter when the parson drew the gig to a halt. They were in the depths of the country, and the road, edged by a dyke on one side and bordered by hedges, ran straight ahead for some distance, narrow and rutted, the night dew not yet drying on its even surface. The flat fields around were damp, the air misty. Why had the parson stopped?

'Let me look at you, Jenny.' His plump hand drew the hood from her head, pushed the cloak off her shoulders. 'Why, even with a dirty face, you are prettier than ever. And your hair . . .' His hand fondled the tresses falling beside her neck. 'You are not at your best at the moment, of course, but you will revive when I get you to Losely. You belong to me now, Jenny.' He stroked her cheek and chin. 'It was silly of you to refuse my offer. It will come to the same thing, you see, and you would have avoided this rather uncomfortable episode. You should not have run away in the first place. I do not like defiance. At Losely I shall be your master—in every way. And if you try to leave me, the rumours of witch-craft will make my protection necessary.'

His hand slid down from her shoulder and began to caress the round softness of her breasts, and she could do nothing, she could hardly lift her bound hands to try to stop him.

'Aaaah . . .' A satisfied sigh drifted from the thick sensual mouth. 'Soon your body will be naked for my pleasure.' He gazed at her with greedy eyes. 'And when I enjoy you, if you resist me, it will increase my delight in mastering you. Time and again . . . Yes, time and again. You will not be able to run away.'

And so saying, he wrapped the cloak round her again, and drove on.

Adam Brenzett was in the tavern, having found himself a seat in a corner against the wall, where he could lean back and rest. He was attacking bread and fat bacon, his fist curled round a pint pot, when he heard the sound of wheels outside. A few moments later there was a stir as two people came in. Adam looked idly up, and was surprised to see that one of them was Parson Bolton. The other, a young woman in a cloak and hood, seemed to be ill, for he was supporting her and leading her to a bench. She collapsed rather than sat upon it, and her hood fell back from her head. To his utter astonishment he saw that it was Gentian.

Gentian! But what a change in her! Her face was dirty and her hair dishevelled, but worse than that, her look was vacant, her mouth slack, her head rolled from side to side, and she seemed to have no control over her limbs. And then he saw the crowning horror—her wrists were tied together in front of her with strong cord. She was plainly the parson's captive.

Involuntarily he half rose to his feet, but then caution checked him. He was one man against the parson, who would have his story ready, and the parson was a clever devil. Better to wait and see how the land lay.

Already Gentian had excited some notice. The parson, who was giving his order to the landlord, was aware of this, and added, in a voice clear and loud enough for all to hear, 'And something for this poor young girl. She is a sad, crazed creature, as you see, and has to be restrained in case she flies into a fury. She may start to talk wildly, and will attack anyone. I am taking her to a place where she will be cared for.'

So that is your story, thought Adam. A damned crafty one, too. If I challenge it, everyone will believe the parson, not the baker. Already there were murmurs of 'Ay, she'll be better off in Bedlam, poor soul.' 'Good of the parson to trouble with her.'

When food and drink arrived, the parson held a mug to Gentian's lips, but most of the beer spilled down her chin on to her cloak. Adam felt pity for her sorry state, and determined to rescue her. But it could not be here. He needed time to think, for no plan likely to succeed presented itself to him. He quickly finished his meal, paid his score and left, going out from behind the parson unrecognised.

Outside he saw the parson's gig. He thought of cutting the harness, but what good would that do? Parson would stay at the inn until it was mended, and it would alert him as well. Adam got his cart, and drove on down the road. He could not rescue Jenny by himself. But where was he to get help? If he could find a local constable, he saw no chance of being believed. He drove some little distance, turning the matter over in his mind.

At a bend in the road he saw ahead a flash of scarlet. An officer on horseback was leading about a dozen foot soldiers in his direction. The army—could there be any hope from them? It was very doubtful. Then, as they

drew nearer, Adam's heart lifted. He thought he recognised the officer—lean-faced, black-browed—yes, he
was the one who patrolled the canal, who had come to
the bakery, who might remember Jenny. He must
gamble on it.

He pulled the cart to a halt, and as the officer
approached, he called out, 'Sir—will ye give me a
moment? It be an urgent matter.'

The officer did not look inclined to stop, but changed
his mind, signalled the men to pass and reined in beside
the cart.

'Do I know you?'

'I be Brenzett, from Markinge bakery. It be about
Mistress Jenny.' He spoke softly so that the men should
not hear. He saw the officer's brows draw together, his
eyes narrow.

'Well?'

'The passon from Losely—he has her in the tavern up
the road. She be his prisoner.'

'*What?*'

'Ay, sir. He says she be crazed, and he taking her to
Bedlam. It can't be, though she be in a fearful state, and
her hands tied . . .'

'Gentian? The parson's prisoner? My God!' He
seemed about to set spurs to his horse, but checked.
'You are her friend?'

'Ay, sir.'

'Then you'll help me to free her—unofficially,
mind. The parson has a smooth tongue; he'll convince
authority.'

'Ah—and it must be quick, for Jenny's sake. What
shall we do, sir?'

'One moment.'

The officer rode on to the file of men, and called,
'Sergeant, I have important news, and must act on it.
Continue the patrol with the men. I'll rejoin you when I

can.' He rode back to Adam. 'How did the parson get to the tavern?'

'He has a gig, sir.'

'And this is the road to Losely. Do you think he's taking her there?'

'I be sure of it. That passon—he be a devil! And he were allus taken with Jenny. That be why she ran away.'

'Pray God we're not too late! Now this is what we'll do . . .'

Charles Claverton's plan was simple. Adam was to block the road with his cart a mile or so farther on. When the parson arrived, Claverton would take over the gig and they would drive off with Gentian, leaving the parson to fend for himself. So they drove up the road, positioned themselves, and waited. It could not have been better; the road was deserted, the parson's gig was the first thing to come along.

Bolton saw the cart across the road and brought the gig to a stop. 'What is it, my man? Can't you get your cart off the road and let me pass?'

Charles Claverton stepped out from behind the cart's tail. 'Get down, Bolton!' he said in a voice hard as steel.

'Why, Captain, whatever . . .'

'*Get down!*' Claverton repeated, and emphasised his words by pulling a pistol from his belt. The parson scrambled down, pale-faced and protesting. Claverton looked at Gentian, and turned back, his eyes blazing.

'*What have you done to her?*'

'Nothing! Nothing—I swear. She is ill.'

'That is plain. *What have you done?*'

'Nothing, I tell you! I have not touched her. Why should you . . .'

Claverton seized him by the coat-collar and flung him to the ground. '*What have you done?*'

'*Nothing!*' His dignity lost, the stout parson was

grovelling in the dust, hands upraised for mercy. 'The woman gave her a dose—to quieten her—nothing more.'

'A dose! *What else?*'

'Nothing else. She did it—I swear I've done nothing!'

'You caused it! If I find you have done more, I shall seek you out and kill you. Depend on that.'

He pocketed his pistol and went over to Adam's cart, taking the whip from its holder. Then he turned back to the parson. Bolton had just scrambled to his feet when he saw Claverton advancing on him.

'Captain! You would not dare . . .' he began blusteringly.

Claverton said nothing, but raised the long whip.

'I am a man of the cloth! You . . .' His speech was cut off by a shrill yelp as the whip slashed across his shoulders.

Adam watched, and thought, The Captain's a fine muscular man, and he's going at it with a will. Reckon the parson'll feel it for a week or two—serves him right! He deserves more. But when Parson Bolton was whimpering on the ground and Claverton showed no sign of slackening his blows, Adam thought it wiser to call to him.

'That's enough, sir, ye don't want to kill him.'

'Do I not?'

'Sir, there's Mistress Jenny. She needs care more than he needs killing!'

Slowly Claverton lowered his arm. 'You're right.' Without another glance at the creature moaning at his feet, he got up into the gig.

Adam had cut the cords at Gentian's wrists and unbuckled the strap, and was still standing beside her. 'She bain't able to support herself, sir.'

'Then we must put her in your cart.'

Adam made a place for her among the sacks, and they

gently lifted her in. As Claverton laid her down, she gave a little moan, opened her eyes and tried to speak.

'You're safe, Gentian,' he told her. 'You're safe.' He turned to Adam. 'Drive on, Brenzett, and I'll follow. When you reach the branch road to Losely, take the other way. There's an inn a mile or two down that road. I'll set the gig on the Losely road, and catch you before the inn.'

'Ay. It'll do passon good to walk back—if he can.'

'May he rot in hell!' said Claverton. 'We'll stop at the inn.'

CHAPTER FOURTEEN

WHEN THEY REACHED the inn Claverton dismounted, gave his reins to the ostler, went to the cart and lifted Gentian out. As he carried her through the doorway, a stout, middle-aged woman with a pleasant face came up to him.

'What's wrong, sir?'

'The lady is ill. Have you a room where she could stay the night?'

'Yes, sir, I've one ready. This way. Oh, the poor lady!' She led him through the tap-room to a passage and up some stairs. 'What happened, sir?'

'She fainted—and fell.'

She opened a door, and they entered. Claverton laid Gentian down on the bed. The woman looked at her, concern in her face. 'She's not—the lady's not . . . with child?'

'No.'

The quick denial leapt to his lips, but at the same moment he thought, it's possible. That would make it worse. The parson had admitted she had been 'dosed' by some woman—at his orders, no doubt—but with what? What harm might have been done?

'She needs rest. I wonder, would you be so kind? If you could put her to bed, I can go and have a word with the carter who helped us.'

'Certainly, sir! The poor lady—you can leave her to me.'

He bent over Gentian. 'Don't worry, you are safe. This lady will get you to bed. I shall not be long.' He hurried downstairs to see Adam Brenzett. 'Come inside, man, and join me over a pint pot. There are things we must settle.'

Somewhat abashed, Adam agreed. The tap-room was nearly empty, and they sat together in a corner where the pot-boy would not overhear them.

'She must stay here until she is fit to travel,' Claverton said. 'Can you get a message to Hythe to tell her husband where she is?'

'Husband? She be a widow, sir—he died a few weeks ago.'

'Died! . . . Ah, that would explain in part how Bolton was able to get his hands on her. He gave her some drug. If I find he has touched her, I swear I'll kill him!'

'He said not. Please God she be still a maid.'

Claverton gave him a dark look. 'Maid? She is—was—a married woman, Brenzett.'

Adam looked at him, sidelong. 'Yes, sir. A married woman, but . . .'

'But what?'

'But never a wife, sir . . .'

'*What?* How can you know?'

'I know Mistress Jenny, sir. And I know Master Jonas didn't want a wife. She let it out to me—she wouldn't have married him if he had wanted that. No, it were a kind of business arrangement. They both knew that if she went as his housekeeper—her being young and pretty—there'd be gossip. So she married him. It suited them both.'

Claverton was staring into his pint pot as if he had forgotten Adam's existence.

'We must tell Mistress Homewood that Jenny be safe,' Adam said.

'What's that? Tell who?'

'Mistress Homewood. Jenny were living with them.'

'Then—of course. Can you do that?' Adam nodded.

'And would it be possible to bring some clothes—some toilet things for her—whatever she may need?'

'Mistress Homewood'll see to that. I'll bring them.'

'We must wait till Gentian is better to decide what to do. She must not go back to Hythe in this condition.'

'No, sir. So I'll be off to Hythe, and tell them she be in good hands. Shall you be here when I get back?'

'I'll not leave her, Brenzett.'

Claverton went upstairs and met the landlord's wife at the bedroom door.

'Your lady's in bed, sir. But she's in a sad way—very weak, and she don't seem to know what goes on.'

'Yes, that is part of her illness. I think she needs some nourishment, if she can take it. Have you any broth?'

'Not made, sir, no—and it takes time. I could get some gruel?'

'Yes, that, or some warm milk.'

'Some brandy with it, sir?'

'No, I think not . . . as yet. Just milk or gruel.'

Claverton knew enough about drugs not to mix them with spirits. He went into the room. Gentian lay in the big double bed, her face frighteningly pale—the good woman had washed off the dirt, he noticed—with her fair hair spread on the pillow. Her eyes, dark-ringed, were shut, and he could barely see that she was breathing. He bent over her, and stroked a lock of hair from her forehead. 'Gentian . . .'

Her eyes opened, but it seemed they would not focus. He could not tell whether she recognised him or not.

When the woman came with a bowl of warm milk, Claverton took it from her, and supporting Gentian with one arm, her head on his shoulder, he fed her sip by sip. Then he let her slip back on to the pillows.

'Now try to sleep,' he said, and stayed watching her.

Mrs Hollis of the Flying Swan Inn took them for man and wife. In good health she'd be a pretty young lady, she thought, and she had a look of refinement; her gown was plain but of good quality, her underclothes simple but fine, and she wore a wedding ring. She was no fly-by-night. The Captain—Captain Claverton, he had said—was a handsome man in a dark and devilish sort of way, and it was plain he cared for his wife, he was so gentle and soft-spoken to her, and hadn't he taken the milk and given it to her himself as carefully as a nurse would do? And he hardly left the room. Where they had been, and what they had been doing when the lady was taken ill, Mrs Hollis could not make out, but it was none of her business, as long as the Captain could pay for the best room and the services he required, and she had already seen the colour of his money. Oh, yes, he was a gentleman, she could tell. He paid well, but not too lavishly, and she liked the cut of his uniform and the quality of his linen.

Gentian stirred and opened her eyes. Panic at once seized her—where was she? There was a flickering light, the rest was shadows—was she still in the crypt at St Leonard's? Something between a cry and a moan escaped her lips. At once someone bent over her, and she cringed back. 'Skulls and bones . . .' she whispered. 'Skulls and bones . . .'

Claverton felt a shudder run down his spine. She was not better; her mind was destroyed!

Gentian's voice rose to a moaning cry. 'Every-where—skulls and bones—all round—skulls grinning at me—eyes with no eyes watching me—bones under my hand . . .'

He lifted her in his arms and held her close. 'Hush, Gentian, they are gone. You are safe, and with me. Don't you know me?'

'All night—the skulls watching me—I knew they were there in the dark . . .'

'They're gone now, dearest.'

What could he do but talk gently, reassuringly? Would she come back to sanity, or was her mind permanently unhinged? If so, the parson would pay, but at present he must only think of Gentian.

She began to toss to and fro, moaning to herself. He kept his arms round her, trying to reassure her. Her eyes were wild, and did not seem to see him. Perhaps if he went on talking to her he might draw her mind back to reality. Well, there were many things he wanted to say, whether she could understand them or not.

'Gentian, my darling, listen to me. I have misjudged you—misjudged you dreadfully, from the very beginning. In the past I was hurt—betrayed—by two women. I lost my trust, I couldn't believe in virtue when I saw it—in you.'

Now she was lying more quietly, but there was still no sign that she understood. He went on talking, his voice a low murmur that would not be intelligible in the passage outside, yet he spoke intensely, trying to pierce the mists that seemed to cloud her brain.

'I understand now. I see that in every action of yours which I interpreted as betrayal, you were in fact being faithful to me. You ran away from the parson, not from me. You married the chemist because you loved me too much to let me soil our love by treating it lightly. Gentian, I understand you now. It mustn't be too late—you must know what I am saying. Oh, listen to me!'

Her eyes were wide open, fixed. Could she see him or not? Could she register his words in her mind?

'I love you, Gentian. I love you for what you are, the person I had lost all hope of finding, the person I did not believe in when our paths crossed, and kept on crossing. I've been a fool; now I know my folly. And now, I promise, I shall treat you honourably, whatever happens. Fight back, dear, fight back to reason, let us see what we can make of our wretched, broken lives, our ill-used love . . .'

He paused, for emotion so long denied had been pouring out from him in a spate of words that had rocked his whole being. Until these last few hours he had not known himself how deeply he felt, how he had longed to find one woman who would live up to his ideals—the ideals he had for years affected to depreciate and scorn. Had he found her too late, when she was trembling on the verge of insanity? No, somehow he must drag her back; he must atone. If he could do no more, he must do that. For more than an hour he talked, repeating over and over again his explanations, his pleading, and above all, his love.

'Gentian, I love you—don't leave me!'

Her eyes at last turned to him, rested upon his face. She smiled.

'Dearest, do you understand? I love you.'

She gave a little nod, then closed her eyes, still smiling.

'Then sleep now, my dear. I shan't leave you.'

Later, when she could take food, he gave it to her himself. Before night came he ordered plenty of candles so that she would not wake in the dark and think herself back in the vault of bones. She was too weak to talk, but he believed her to be sane. He pulled off his boots, half undressed and lay on the bed beside her, to be there in case she roused and needed him.

It seemed the natural thing for him to assume total responsibility. He knew he had to be with her. He rejected the idea of calling a doctor, for he had no very high opinion of them, and considered that without knowledge of which drug Gentian had been given, they could do no more than he was doing for her.

He had sent a message to barracks. For the officers, discipline was lax and they did very much as they pleased. He would stay here while she needed him; he could amplify his excuse with some tale when he returned. He did not question his feelings towards Gentian. Now, when she was so utterly spent, so completely vulnerable, he felt a compelling tenderness for her, overriding the passion which he knew would return and which must be held in check—for how long, it was impossible to tell.

Meanwhile he was able to smile saturninely at the news that the parson from Losely had been thrown from his gig when the horse had bolted, and had been found, in a state of collapse, by a passing farmer. Mrs Hollis heard it too, but had no reason to connect it with her two guests.

Gentian awoke the next morning, weak but sane, and was able to tell Claverton briefly how she came to be Bolton's prisoner. But talking tired her, and he would not let her say much more. He was sitting beside her on the bed; having finished her story, she looked up at him with wondering eyes.

'You and Adam rescued me, and you have stayed with me since then . . . What should I have done without you?'

'The first credit goes to Brenzett—and no doubt he would have cared for you as well. I was in a better position to do so, that is all.'

'But—the army?'

'The army is managing perfectly well without me! I have sent my excuses—discipline for the officers is very slack.' Not as it was in India with Wellesley, he thought.

'But what do they think here?' she asked.

'They know you were ill, and they think we are man and wife. We will let the landlady go on thinking that, for the sake of your reputation, and to avoid a great many unpleasant explanations—that in any case would not be believed.'

'Yesterday, when I was so ill, I think you said a great many things to me.'

'I did, but did you understand them?'

'I think so. I hope so.'

'And do you believe them?'

'Whatever you tell me now, I shall believe. So, please, tell me all of them again.'

He took her hand, and very seriously repeated all he had said the night before. She listened in silence.

'Thank you, Charles. And now you must tell me about yourself. It is so strange, to love you and yet know nothing about you.'

'There's very little to know.'

'But tell me.' Her breath was laboured, she was tiring, but still she looked at him enquiringly, almost eagerly.

'All right. If you'll promise to let me do the talking, and rest. The story of my life should send you to sleep in short order.'

'I only want to listen.'

'Very well.'

He slipped his hand under her head and moved to hold her cradled in the crook of his arm. She sighed, and snuggled her head on to his shoulder. His hand tightened the merest fraction.

'That's better! Then, here goes. I am the middle son of three. My elder brother, Edward, naturally inherits from my father.'

She nodded.

'So, it was the army for me. That suited me very well, as I didn't covet the estates.' He paused. Then, 'You may as well hear all my ridiculous story. It was always understood that Edward would marry Charity—it was a suitable match, since the Wentworth estates march with ours, and I was very taken with a pretty little blonde miss of no fortune but many superficial charms. In fact, I considered myself madly in love, and thought she was as infatuated with me. Preparations were already in hand for Edward's wedding when, without a word of warning, he and my *inamorata* contracted a secret marriage. Charity was furious at being jilted—I did say she was most unsuitably named?—and came to me with a proposition. To put it in a nutshell, she suggested that we should marry. It would then look not so much as if we had both been rejected, but more as if the four of us had decided to change partners. Neither of us cared for the other, but we were both suffering from wounded pride. Pride, I think, was the only thing we had in common. I was to blame for agreeing; so in pride and folly we married, and have been at loggerheads ever since.'

Gentian turned her head to look up at him. 'You must have tried to make the best of it. Was there nothing you could do?'

'To sweeten Charity? You are being kind to me. Yes, I tried, but not persistently. It is true I had little encouragement. I could do nothing right, so I gave up the attempt. She was, of course, a disappointed woman. She had expected to marry the heir, and had to settle for me. She could still live well—she has her own fortune, and I will not touch it—but the social position of a Captain's wife is different from that of the wife of the heir to an earldom.'

'An *earldom*! So you are . . .'

'I am Captain Claverton, a serving officer, in love with you.'

'And your wife? Why won't she stay with you?'

'She prefers her own friends. She lives as she pleases.'

'You must have been very lonely.'

'I found other consolations. Please do not enquire too closely about them—I am not proud of my behaviour. Well, I have had good times in the army, good times and bad, and have learnt to take life as it comes.'

'And now you are looking after a sick girl, a nobody.'

'Nobody! You are everything to me! But I have talked too long, and it is time you slept. Then you may be able to take some solid food.' He drew his arm from under her shoulders, and obediently she settled her face against the pillow.

Although she closed her eyes, it was some time before she slept. The disaster of Charles Claverton's marriage explained so much. He had said he had married out of injured pride, but he had also been desperately hurt. He had covered his wounded feelings with a carapace of cynicism that was now second nature to him, but he was nevertheless still a man capable of tenderness.

Later in the day when she questioned him again, he told her about his campaigns, but said no more about his personal life. 'And now,' he said, 'it is time I learnt about you. You told me how you came to be at Markinge, and that your father's name was Summerlee, and that you once lived in Oxford, but nothing more.'

'Father was for some years a tutor in Oxford.'

'And he educated you?'

'He taught me a great deal. How I wish he had lived to teach me more . . .'

So his instinct had been right. She could meet him on equal terms. Damn his marriage, damn Charity, the only stumbling-block in the way of love and companionship. And most of all, damn himself, for being the young, proud, wounded, weak and thoughtless fool who had placed it there!

That day Gentian felt well enough to get up and dress. Claverton had meals brought up to them in their room. It seemed so natural for them to be together. With every hour their knowledge and understanding of each other grew, every word exchanged strengthened the bond between them.

In the room which had past associations for neither of them they were isolated in a world apart, alone with each other, living a uniquely separate existence which had nothing to do with their real lives. All pretence was dropped; now there were no secrets between them. They sat together, Claverton's arm round her. At intervals he kissed her, softly, gently, and her body was warm and pliant, her lips soft and yielding. She was loving, she was also weak and vulnerable. He did not take any advantage of this; he did not even wish to. He was happy merely to stroke her hair and feel her sweet acquiescence, her growing pleasure.

'Oh, Gentian, what wouldn't I give to keep you with me,' he murmured. 'There was a time when I thought possession of you would settle everything for me, that I would then soon forget you. For I wouldn't admit even to myself that I was in love with you. But now it seems so obvious that I've loved you a long time—and you love me. So what are we going to do?'

'What can we do, Charles? Knowing we love each other alters nothing, once we leave here.'

'It alters everything! Doesn't it give us the right to shape our own lives?'

'We can't alter what is fixed.'

'You mean my marriage. But it's empty, it means nothing. Charity doesn't want me, or my love. She only wants to prevent me from finding love with anyone else. But my need of you is like a fire inside me, I need your love, and I need you with me, not only for the times of passion, but so that we can talk and listen as we do now, so that we can live together free from bickering and bitterness, jealousy and pride and envy—of which I've had more than my fill—to be two human beings happy just to be together.'

The dark eyes that gazed into hers had lost their mockery, and held within the fire of love a light of sincerity, and she felt her heart go out to him. They could never marry, but if they were together it would be more real than the marriage he had so long endured. He seemed to read her thoughts.

'Yes, being together, Gentian, to love each other and find our own happiness, that is what matters. Why should we care what other people think? You have had a hard life these past years, and difficult times, while I think I have paid enough for my folly. Why shouldn't we grasp at happiness?'

'Oh, Charles, if only we could!'

'We can! Come and live with me. I'll have no hole-and-corner affair; you shall be known as my wife. There will be talk, of course, there is always gossip, but it will die down. We can ignore it and go our own way. And in time people will get to know you and find we intend to stay together, and it will be accepted.'

Accepted as what? she wondered, and then realised that she no longer cared. Now she knew that Charles loved her, that he did not intend to pension her off in weeks or months when physical passion had run its course, she could believe that fate had willed them to come together, to stay united.

'You are right, Charles. I will come to you.'

His eyes widened, then filled with an overwhelming happiness. He drew her close and kissed her, and the kiss, passionate yet controlled, was the seal to their bargain.

They began to make their plans. Gentian would go back to the Homewoods for the time being until Charles could arrange somewhere near the barracks for them to live. They were discussing it all with the pleasure of new-found lovers when there was a knock at the door. Mrs Hollis was outside.

'There's a soldier asking for you, sir. He has a message.'

Claverton went downstairs, to return a few minutes later, a note crushed in his hand. Gentian looked at him, and saw that he seemed disgruntled, and yet in a strange way elated.

'Damme, it would happen now!' he exclaimed. 'I don't know whether to be glad or sorry!'

'What is it?' she asked, apprehension striking at her heart. 'It's not bad news?'

'At any other time it would be good news. I must go back to barracks at once. I've had a warning from a brother officer that there's something afoot, and we are all put on the alert. I must be there, or I shall miss the action—and run the risk of a court-martial!'

'Then you must go at once.'

Why now, she thought wretchedly, just as we were in sight of happiness? But she smiled bravely.

'This alters nothing, my sweet,' he was saying. 'It will delay us, that is all. When I find out what is happening, I will write, and as soon as I am settled, I will send for you.'

'We have waited so long that we can wait a little longer.'

'It should not be for long,' he said encouragingly. 'And if you stay with the Homewoods, I shall know you are in good hands.' He took her in his arms and held her close. 'My little sweetheart,' he murmured. 'This is the way of the army. I did not think you would have to learn so soon. It brings together, it separates, it goes its arbitrary way, and we all have to follow and make the best of it. You must trust me to work things out for the two of us.'

She nodded and smiled up at him. He stroked her hair as he kissed her long and lovingly, then snatched up his campaign cloak and was gone.

CHAPTER FIFTEEN

Hythe was in a state of ferment. In all the time she had spent there, Gentian had never known anything like it. The town was full of rumours, and the sober citizens would interrupt their daily business to exchange the latest stories, enlarge on the most recent speculations.

There was a sound enough basis for rumour, since much was plainly afoot at the barracks. A force was being mustered, and detachments from Hythe would be part of it, but what it was for, how large it was to be, where it would be assembled, and whence it was bound—these were matters on which everyone held his own opinion. No one knew, and the theories grew wilder day by day.

Gentian was no wiser than anyone else. She had been with the Homewoods for nearly two months and had had but four brief letters from Charles. He was only able to tell her that he had been transferred to another regiment, and did not know where he would be sent next. They must wait until something was settled, then if possible he would come to her in Hythe, or send for her to join him. And so she waited, trying to quell the disquiet she could not help feeling, wondering how much longer fate would prevent her from taking the happiness she yearned for.

Then another letter came, and she broke it open, excitement and apprehension battling within her. It was longer than usual, and as she read it her heart sank. When she had finished, she folded the sheet and sat staring at nothing, conscious only of a great emptiness within her, a feeling of desolation as she struggled with her tears. Charles had written;

> I cannot send for you, my dearest; the fact is, we are on the move, and it is possible we may be leaving England. So you see, there is no way we can be together until I am settled. Keep up your courage, sweetheart. I feel this as deeply as you, and would give anything to have you with me, but tell myself I must possess my soul in patience and pray that the future will be kind to us. Always remember, my dearest girl, that I love you, wherever I may be and whatever may occur. I shall hope to come through Hythe and see you before I leave, but if I cannot, take care of yourself and wait for me.
>
> Your loving Charles.

She read the letter again. She was not a fool—there were matters unstated, yet plain enough to her. 'We may be leaving England'—that meant the army was going to war. He prayed that the future would be kind, so he knew there was a possibility that he might not return. And in case he did not—'whatever may occur'—he sent her his love.

She might not even have the opportunity to say good-bye to him, and her grief became tinged with anger. She knew that officers' wives frequently went with their husbands; if she had been married to Charles she could have accompanied him. Would Charity go? Of course not. She would not even go to the ship to bid him goodbye. Gentian thought, How can I bear Charles to go and not know what is happening to him? God knows how long it will be before I see him again. She would not let herself add, 'if ever'.

A week later he came. She opened the Homewoods' door to a knock, and there he was on the doorstep. She drew him inside, closed the door and was caught in his arms. His embrace was long and passionate; she gasped for breath and smiled at him with tears of emotion and relief filling her eyes. Reluctantly she dragged her gaze from his face, and shy of expressing her deep feelings, said, 'Charles, what is this? Where is your red coat?'

He was clad from head to foot in dark green, and to her it looked strange; were it not for the frogged pelisse slung over the left shoulder it would hardly be uniform at all. He smiled at her surprise.

'I told you I'd been transferred. I'm now with the 95th—the Rifles. This uniform is a new thing, and we're the only ones to have it. "Rifle green", it's called.'

'It doesn't look very . . . military,' she ventured, feeling it lacked the dash and glamour of scarlet.

'On the contrary! It's much less of a target than those red rags. And I tell you, we're a proud regiment! Don't dare disparage us!'

'I wouldn't dream of it! And now I begin to get used to it, I see it is very smart.' Then her feelings overcame her. 'Oh, Charles, why can't I go with you?'

He drew her down to a seat in the simple little parlour. 'My darling, you must trust me to know what is best. If only we were married it would be different. Then you could sail with me and stay at base, you could live a comfortable pleasant life in my absences. But as it is—oh, there are officers who take women to whom they are not married, and the women get on reasonably well for a time . . .'

'Then why not take me? I don't want to be comfortable. I want to be with you!'

'Because, my sweet, we must be practical. I could care for you up to a point, but if anything happened to me everything would change. One must face the worst possibility, and the fact is that as soon as you were left alone things would alter drastically. No provision would be made for you, you would be entitled to nothing, not even basic rations. You would be in a sorry situation, and you would have extreme difficulty even in getting back to England.'

'I will risk that, and face it if it comes. Please God, it will not. Don't ask me to leave you.'

'Gentian, I'm not asking you. I am telling you that in your own interest you cannot come with me. And in mine also. I don't want to go into battle thinking that if I die, Gentian will be unprotected. I must know you are safe here. You don't think I want this separation? I am praying that, wherever I go, the campaign will be short and then I'll be posted back and able to send for you.'

'*Please*, Charles!'

'No, darling. This is a hard lesson for you, but you must learn it. Trust me to know what is best.'

Gentian felt a desolation near to despair. It was plain to her that wherever Charles was to be sent, he expected fighting. Death on the field of battle was always a possibility, and he would not risk leaving her alone and unprotected in a hostile country. Yet he wanted her; and how could she bear to stay secure in England not knowing to what dangers he might be subjected, ignorant whether he lived or died?

He did not stay long. The troops were assembling in Hythe, he said, and would soon be moving out. He might not see her again before he sailed. He gave her one quick fervent kiss, and left—before I could even say goodbye to him properly, she thought.

Later that day Sarah Homewood suggested a stroll in the town. 'It's buzzing with excitement,' she said. 'Who knows if we'll ever see the like again?'

Largely in the hope she might catch a glimpse of Charles, Gentian agreed.

She had never seen the main street so crowded: soldiers and civilians, gentry and lower orders rubbed shoulders with each other; there was a hubbub of talking and shouting, the bustle of men and horses; everywhere was colour and movement. Since she had been out of doors very little in recent weeks, she saw for the first time a number of dark green uniforms, the same colour as the one Charles now wore. She looked for mounted officers, but only saw private soldiers on foot. There were red coats too, but she looked only for the dark green. She scanned the faces of the riflemen, thinking, Will you soon be fighting side by side with Charles?

She was walking close to Sarah, their arms linked so that they would not be divided in the crowd, when she suddenly stopped, pulling Sarah to a halt. With her free hand she caught the dark green sleeve of a man in a group they had just approached.

'Adam!'

Adam Brenzett swung round and his face broke into a delighted smile. 'Jenny!'

They clasped hands. Gentian was for the moment speechless, and he drew the two women aside into a doorway, away from the main crush of people.

'What luck meeting you, Jenny! I didn't know whether I should call.'

'Of course you should! Come back with us now?'

She did not need to ask Sarah.

'I'll gladly walk you back, and stay a few minutes.'

He offered an arm to each, and they started back along the street. Adam in the army! Gentian was confused by the discovery. It has altered him already, she thought; he'd never before have thought of taking us one on each arm. And he's marching as proud as a peacock.

In the hubbub, conversation was impossible, so it was not until they were inside the cottage that Gentian was able to ask, 'How long have you been in the army, Adam?'

'I 'listed just after you came back here. I'd given up hope of the bakery, and there was nothing else.'

'But you're not sorry?'

'Sorry I joined? No, it's not a bad life, and I'm in a fine regiment. And I'm with Captain Claverton—only he's a major now.' And she had barely congratulated him on his promotion!

'Yes, he was transferred. I have seen him.' She could not keep a tremor from her voice. 'How long do you expect to be here, Adam?'

'No time at all. We are bound to move out soon—in a couple of days, I should think—for tomorrow the wives are drawing lots for who are to go.'

She was totally ignorant of the procedure for the wives of privates. 'Drawing lots? I don't understand.'

'The army regulations allow six wives for every hundred men to go with the regiment, so they draw lots for the places. I've heard it's a pitiful business.'

'I knew some were able to go, but I did not know how it was arranged. Yes, I can see there would be many more who did not wish to be parted.' As she spoke, she saw another life-line, and turned to him in a flash. 'Adam, would you do something for me?'

'If I can, Jenny.'

'Then say I am your wife, and let me take a place in the draw.'

'*Jenny!* You can't mean it!' His face was a study in amazement and incomprehension.

'I do, Adam.'

'Why should you? Not for me! Oh, I love you, Jenny, you know that, but you don't want me for a lover—and as for going campaigning . . .'

'It's because we're such good friends that I can ask you. If you said you were my husband . . . Oh, Adam, I must go, if I can, and this is the only way.'

Slowly his expression altered to understanding.

'You're in love with *him*—with the Major! But if he won't take you with him . . .'

'He won't. And, Adam, I can't bear it. He loves me, and yet . . . to have him go, and not to know where he is, whether he's at peace or war, alive or . . .' Her throat tightened so that she could not say the word. Adam reached out and clumsily patted her hand.

'There, Jenny, don't take on. You must learn to bear it, I reckon, as so many women have to. At least, since he's an officer, you'll have more news.'

'I don't want *news*—I want to be there, near him! Adam, please, it's my last chance—let me draw as your wife?'

'Jenny, I've not seen active service yet, but from what I've heard it's a rough life for the women—it's not for you.'

'I've had a rough life before, at times.'

'Not like this would be. And if we go to America, as they say . . .'

'*America!* So far! Then all the more reason for me to try.'

'No, Jenny. If he doesn't want it, how can I . . .'

'It would be my responsibility.'

'I'd be to blame.'

'He's a just man, Adam. He'll know I persuaded you.'

'Jenny, you must get used to parting. Women have to. Only six out of every hundred can go.'

'Then, as it's so few, I stand little chance—at least let me try. If I should win, I'll stay with you, do everything I should—I won't even let him see me, but I shall find out how he fares.'

Eventually, against his better judgment, and counting on her losing in the draw, Adam agreed.

Sarah was horrified when Gentian told her her plan, and painted a black picture to Gentian of all the horrors she could envisage, but when she found she could not alter the girl's decision, she too contented herself by the thought that the chances were against Gentian in the draw.

The next day Gentian joined the crowd of women outside the barracks. She was already feeling nervous, and this state increased minute by minute. To her, the number of women wanting to take their chance was immense, and they were in the main a rough lot, pushing for places, none giving way, shouting and arguing or exchanging bawdy conversation; but she suspected that some of the high talk was concealing anxious feelings. Although she was wearing her plainest working gown, it was still conspicuous by its quality, and the women around her made no bones about staring at her curiously. She stood in the crowd, waiting for something to happen, not daring to speak to anyone.

Then a plump, red-faced middle-aged woman with a more agreeable face than most, who was standing close to her, looked her up and down, and then said in an unmistakable Irish brogue, 'It's the first time for you, I'm thinking, and you not knowing about it at all?'

'Yes, the first time,' Gentian answered.

'Then you're the brave one, for sure, since you're used to a softer life, by the looks of you. So your husband couldn't bear to leave you behind. But he should have thought . . .'

'No, he tried to stop me, but I must go, if I can.'

'Ah, what we do when we love the creatures! He'll be counting on you drawing a "Not-to-Go", then.'

Gentian tried to smile. 'I expect so.'

'And mine expects the other. I always go. I've the luck of the divil, you see. I've followed the drum for ten years, for each time Paddy has sailed, I've gone too. They say the army can't move without Mary Mulvany!' She gave a roar of laughter. 'I tell you, I've washed clothes in more strange streams than you could shake a stick at!'

Gentian was glad of the Irishwoman's talk, as it distracted her somewhat and made her less aware of the curious looks she attracted. At last a sergeant and some soldiers appeared, and the draw began.

It was, as Adam had been told, a pitiful business. The women were ready to fight for positions, and a few unfortunate privates had the job of marshalling them into some semblance of order. As each card was drawn, there was a burst of shouts and cries. There were ex-clamations, cheers, sometimes tears of joy from the women who drew 'To-Go', and from the rest, the great majority, came cries of despair, sobs of anguish, even shrieks and screams of hysteria. Gentian was sick with nerves, keyed up to desperation-point by her longing to keep some contact with the man she now loved with all her heart and being. At last amid all the shuffling for places, the Irishwoman, with Gentian in tow, came near to the sergeant who was presiding over the lots.

Mary Mulvany looked absolutely confident. Was it just a fine pretence? 'You'll see—I'll go,' she said.

Three more women were unlucky after a long suc-cession of blanks; then Mary Mulvany's hand went into the bag. 'To-Go!' It was a cry of triumph. She turned a smiling face to Gentian, and stretching across two women who had pushed between, she said to her, 'I'll give you a bit of me luck, dearie!' and tapped her on the shoulder before she was moved on.

The two women drew; both 'Not-to-Go'. Another pushed in front, and was also unlucky. Gentian, feeling sick and faint, would have been shouldered aside again had not the sergeant said brusquely, 'Keep in line, and take your turn!' and motioned her to the bag.

She was trembling as she put her hand inside. Six out of a hundred—the odds were high against her. Her fingers fumbled among the cards. With one so recently drawn, what chance had she got? She fastened on one and drew it out. She held it and stared at it, and could hardly believe it.

'To-Go!' She stumbled on, and Mary Mulvany caught her arm.

'Don't faint, dearie, now you've won! Didn't I say I'd give you a bit of me luck!'

The regiments moved out of Hythe the next day, the townsfolk lining the streets to wave and cheer them on their way. They marched with full pack in good order, to cover the thirty miles to Deal; the women who were to go—and many who were not—followed as best they could. Gentian, with Mary Mulvany and a few others, at her suggestion, rode in a carrier's cart. While they had a little money, she considered, there was no point in spending their energy to no purpose.

At Deal, in sight of the fleet, the waiting seemed interminable, and then there were harrowing scenes between husbands and wives who could not bear to be parted, the unfortunate women who were not to go sometimes having to be separated from their men by force. To Gentian it was sad in the extreme. Whatever hardship the women who went would face, to some of those who were left behind life might be as hard, with no means of subsistence and possibly young children to keep. To her amazement she saw some children boarding with their mothers; they were allowed to go, and she could only suppose the women thought it best for the whole family to share the father's fortune.

She expected accommodation to be rough and crowded, and was prepared to share a small space with a number of other women, but the reality was far worse than she had imagined in her most pessimistic moments. Women were herded together with the men below decks; at night they would lie down side by side. The men were issued with one blanket each, and a mattress between two men; the sleeping space allowed was eighteen inches each. There was no chance whatever of privacy; all would live, eat and sleep together. With the shock of the discovery, the noise and the confusion, Gentian was in a daze; she followed Mary Mulvany, who was using her experience to get a relatively good position.

'The sooner we can find our men and all stake our places, the better,' she said. 'You didn't expect this, I'm thinking.'

She was pushing her way through the crowd, her bundle held before her, and Gentian kept close, clutching her own; she had been warned by Adam and the Irishwoman that she would be allowed to take only one bundle that she could carry herself.

'There's my Pat—he's seen us. Bless you, don't be taking on! Tonight, when we settle, you sleep beside your man and I'll take the other side of you. It's a tight squeeze, but you'll get used to it.'

Never, thought Gentian, numb with misery. Nevertheless she forced a smile when Adam came up to her, his face full of worry and concern.

'Jenny—I didn't know! No one said it would be like this. You must go back, it's not too late.'

'No, Adam, I'm staying. It's only for the voyage. Mary says it's not like this once we leave the ship.'

But her heart almost failed her. How long would it take to reach America? At every moment the reality of the conditions proved to be worse than she could have envisaged. But no matter how long it lasted, she would endure everything to be near Charles.

It was a splendid sight in the Downs, with all the ships of the great fleet spreading sails to the wind as they put to sea with twenty thousand men aboard. God knows what lies ahead, Gentian thought, and endured the conditions with a numb acquiescence until the ships dropped anchor in the harbour at Cork.

At once conditions were temporarily better. The women were allowed to go ashore as they pleased, but not the men. The four companies of rifles were taken each day to drill in the countryside, which rang to the sound of their bugles. Mary was elated. 'For isn't it me own country I've returned to!' Gentian's first move was to hire a room at a hostelry, order hot water and towels, wash herself from head to foot and put on clean under-clothes. She felt as if the smell of the ship's quarters would cling to her for ever. The money she had brought with her, safely stowed—with some gold pieces, as once before, sewn into her underclothes—would have to last heaven knew how long, but to be clean again was an extravagance she would not deny herself. She would also spend something on supplementing the rations. Adam would be glad of some variety, and since the women were allowed only half-rations, the amount for Gentian, although a small eater, was just adequate and the con-tents most unpalatable. They both should have a little luxury, for they might soon be at sea again and facing a long voyage. She tried not to think of that.

Nights were the worst time. She was thankful for Adam's rough gallantry and Mary's kindness, and at least felt safe, crammed in between his broad back and her ample hips. But she could not move an inch to change her position on the hard boards, and all around were the smells of tar, tobacco and unwashed bodies, while snoring, muttering and an occasional nightmare cry went on all night. Sleep for her was never more than a fitful doze. Daytime was a little better, for they were divided into three shifts, each spending four hours on deck; it was a blessed relief from the foul atmosphere below.

She was careful always to keep in a group of women. When, as happened once or twice, she caught a glimpse of Charles, she was able to make sure he did not see her. If he did, he would if possible find some way to send her back. At Cork, she saw him several times disembarking with the riflemen for drill, but avoided any confrontation. Once we are on the high seas, she told herself, and bound for America, it won't matter, he can't send me back then.

The stay at Cork was a delightful interlude for the freedom it provided. The women had plenty to do —they washed and sewed for themselves and their men, and most of them did what they could to keep themselves and their quarters clean—but they were able to go ashore, to walk up and down the quays and streets, and if they had money to spare they shopped for provisions, needles and thread, soap and suchlike basic necessities. They expected to stay only for a day or two. To their surprise, four days passed; a week; and still there was no sign of sailing orders. They discussed it among themselves, but with unconcern; they would enjoy shore leave while they could, sooner or later the fleet would sail again. The ships lay at anchor for a whole six weeks.

Then, suddenly, they were given orders. There was all the business and bustle of getting the last fresh supplies on board, and of herding the men and women like cattle into their cramped quarters, from where they could hear above them the thud of bare feet, the shouting of orders and all the rattle and clatter of preparing to leave port. And so, on a fair July day, they put to sea, bound, not for America, but for Portugal.

Portugal! The word passed from mouth to mouth like an incantation—and they all knew what it meant. Napoleon's armies were occupying the Peninsula, holding Portugal and Spain in subjection, and it was to be the lot of the British troops to dislodge them.

'It won't be easy,' the wise ones said. 'The Froggies have had nothing but victory on land for years.' But they all agreed that 'Nosey was the man to do it.' They had heard that Sir Arthur Wellesley was to be in command, and that he was ahead of them aboard a fast frigate.

Gentian congratulated herself that it would be a much shorter passage to Portugal than it would have been to America. She refused to look into the future, to the possibilities of marches, of battles, of danger, wounds or death. But she soon considered that nothing the future might hold could be worse than the present. The weather became rough; the ship was tossed about frighteningly; a high majority of those on board were seasick. In the crowded quarters the most elementary sanitary arrangements were almost impossible, the state of the between-decks was indescribable and the stench appalling. She was a good sailor, and believed that if she could stay above decks in the fresh air she might not succumb, and since so many were prostrate below, she was usually able to spend more than her allotted four hours in the open. Not that being on deck was an undiluted pleasure: the sea was so rough that she had continuously to cling to something—anything—for support, and it was only too easy to lose one's footing on decks insufficiently cleaned from grease and kitchen refuse. Sometimes everyone was ordered below for safety.

One day, feeling distinctly queasy but determined not to go back to the hell below decks until obliged, she was clutching the rail and trying to decide whether it was better to look down at the rolling sea or out over the swaying ship when she saw an officer in rifle green making his way along the deck. He raised his head into the wind, and she saw it was Charles. At the same moment his eyes fell on her, he checked, and gazed incredulously.

He made his way to where she stood. There was no

one near by, and he came close, stared at her and spoke, almost shouting over the wind, his voice hoarse with amazement and shock. 'Gentian! In God's name, what are you doing here? How did you . . .'

'I drew lots, and got "To-Go".'

'You *drew* . . . ?'

'As Adam Brenzett's wife.'

For a long moment he was silent, his eyes burning at her under his black brows, his face fixed, darkened. Then, '*Brenzett's* wife! I thought you loved *me*!' The words were wrenched from him like a cry of pain.

'I *do*! I'm not his wife—it was the only way.'

'Are you mad? You gave him a husband's rights—for *this*?'

'*No!* I gave him nothing! It was the only way I could stay near you. He agreed, for he never thought I'd win in the draw. But I did, and he has protected me, he is the best of friends, no more.'

Slowly the agony in his face eased. They were standing a little apart, careful not to touch, as if each knew that physical contact would release a torrent of emotion. Then the ship gave a sudden lurch and she was thrown against him. At once his arm was round her, his face pressed to hers, and passion and desire swept over them. He held her as the ship wallowed in the trough of the wave, and she felt that they were drowning together in an ocean of frustrated love.

'You've been on board since we left Deal, and I never knew,' he muttered hoarsely. 'Come to me now.'

'I cannot, Charles.'

'Why not? You must leave that hell-hole! You *must* come.'

'And make Adam look like a cuckold before his companions?'

'Oh, God!'

'And you—how would you appear? An officer

stealing the wife of a private soldier? The men would lose all respect . . .'

'Don't, Gentian! Yes, I know you're right, but you can't stay there. I've seen the conditions.'

'It's rough, and crowded, but I'm safe with Adam and Mary.'

She dragged herself away from him. She had been in his arms too long. He looked at her, eyes blazing with desire, but made no move to touch her.

'Then how long will it be before we can be together?'

'We must wait till this is over. Meantime . . .'

'*Meantime!* Meantime I'll know you are suffering every privation following the drum, and I'll be helpless, and longing for you, burning for you!'

'I would rather have it this way, than be sitting comfortably in England.'

'*I* would not! Wait—let me think.' He gave his head a shake as if to bring himself back to reality. 'You are a good sailor, it seems?'

'I've not been sick yet.'

'Well, there are three officers' wives on board. They are all sick. If you will nurse them, you can share their cabin. I'll arrange it.'

'But I belong below.'

'They will be thankful for your help, and if you let it be known you're being paid for your services, it will be understood, and it will not reflect on Brenzett.'

'Then it's possible . . .'

'I will see about it.'

'But you and I—we must be like strangers.'

'If you insist. For the time being, at least.'

'I'll do nothing to hurt Adam.'

'I'll not ask you to. He's a good fellow.'

'Goodbye, Charles,'

'Not goodbye—I'm superstitious—not goodbye!'

'It means "God be with you", my dear.' She turned

away before the tears filled her eyes.

Perhaps it is selfish, Gentian thought, to take this chance of release. But she could not resist it. There were no difficulties. When she told Mary Mulvany she had been offered money to nurse the officers' wives and stay with them, she answered,

'Sure, and wouldn't you be the fool to refuse? You'll be better off there, and the money will be useful to you and your man.'

Adam was plainly thankful that she could leave the common quarters, so, taking her bundle with her, she found her way to the small cabin that the three ladies were sharing. There were all too sick to question her as she attended them; they lay and accepted her ministrations with a sigh of relief or a whispered word of thanks. The ship continued rolling and pitching through the heavy seas for another week, and Gentian conscientiously did all she could for the sick women, although at times she felt far from well herself. Then, when she felt at the end of her endurance, the sea miraculously became calmer, the ship stopped behaving like a wild animal trying to shake itself free of all encumbrances and they rode the waves with a pleasant, predictable motion. The ladies recovered enough to sit up in their bunks, to sip at the light nourishment Gentian had brought them from the officers' cook, to look at her wanly but with dawning curiosity, and wonder how a young woman of a certain refinement could have been found among the soldiers' wives.

'You have looked after us so well,' said Mrs Braithwaite. 'What is your name?'

'Jenny, ma'am. Mrs Jenny Brenzett,' she lied.

'Who sent you here?' asked Mrs Canning.

'Major Claverton saw me on deck. He knew me—and my husband—in Hythe. He saw I wasn't sick, and asked if I was well enough to look after you.'

'How thoughtful of him. And so kind of you to agree,' said Mrs Barclay. She was considerably younger than the other two, and looked less sick and more curious.

'It helped me too, ma'am,' Gentian admitted. 'I was glad to escape from the conditions in the common quarters.'

Mrs Barclay shuddered. 'I've not seen it—but I've heard . . .'

'You do not look like a soldier's wife to me,' said Mrs Braithwaite. 'Not the type at all. You'll find it a hard life.'

'I shall manage,' said Gentian quietly.

'Well, Jenny,' interposed Mrs Canning, 'I'm sure we shall all be glad if you can stay and act as maid to us for the rest of the voyage.'

'That would suit me very well, ma'am,' Gentian answered, feeling she was already acting the part fate—or Charles—had bestowed on her.

As the ladies regained their strength, they began to be curious how a girl of Gentian's stamp came to be on board. She parried their questions with enough information, mixing truth with the necessary falsehoods. Her husband, a baker, had lost his business and joined the army as he could find no other work; she had not wanted to be parted from him, but neither of them realised conditions would be so hard for her. But she did not regret it, she said, she would hold her own.

In return, she gleaned some knowledge from the ladies. Most of the officers' wives who wished to follow their husbands were coming later, when a base had been established. The troops were to land on the coast near Lisbon and fight their way to the capital, where the ladies expected to stay during the campaign.

'Lisbon is an attractive city, so I'm told,' said Mrs Canning.

'I dare say it will be, once the French are driven out,' was Mrs Braithwaite's retort.

Gentian avoided Charles, but one day when she had just left the cabin, they came face to face. There was no one else in sight, and he swept her into his arms and kissed her.

'Gentian—my darling!' Then, 'There's not much time to talk. When we reach Portugal, you must go back. The ship will be nearly empty, and we can find a good excuse.'

'No, Charles, I'm not going back. I came to be near you.'

'But you can't be near me! Your reputation . . .'

She gave a shaky, teasing laugh. 'You've never bothered about my reputation before!'

'It's different now. I know you. I love you.'

For a moment she savoured the sweetness of his words, the grave but ardent look in his eyes.

'I shall be near enough to know what is happening to you.'

'But *you*—God knows what may be happening to you! If you won't return, you must stay behind with the ladies as their maid.'

'No! It is one thing to be a maid when we are on board ship, but once on land I must stay with Adam.'

'You *cannot*! Think of the conditions on the march.'

'If I've survived the conditions below decks, I'll survive them on the march. Don't you understand, Charles? Adam has been so good to me—like a brother. I'm thought to be his wife. If I leave him, it will shame him before all the men.'

'I don't care! I can only think of you.'

'I care! I'll stay with him, and be as near to you as I can.'

'My darling, no!'

They heard footsteps on the companionway. Charles

released her, and she fled. Further talk would have made no difference; she would not change her mind.

When the coast was sighted, the men were ordered to be ready to disembark, and on the beach at Mondego Bay on the first day of August the riflemen were the first to land. Gentian was alarmed to see the height of the waves which were roaring in surf on to the beach. The small boats had great difficulty in getting ashore; many of them came to grief and capsized in the great waves, flinging out the men into the boiling surf. The men were encumbered by their packs, and a number drowned. Gentian saw Charles get safely ashore in one of the first boats, and then, a little later, Adam also. She breathed more easily.

Much later, the women were taken off. It was terrifying to be in the frail boat as it reared up and then plummeted in the surf; she could think of nothing but clinging on for dear life until it grounded on the beach. The women dragged themselves in the wake of the men up the bare rocky shore; the sun was strong, the rocks burning hot to hands and feet as they scrambled up. Well, our shoes will soon dry, Gentian thought.

The men set up camp near the beach. There were many more troops to come, and it would take some days for them all to disembark.

'We'd best try to get a place to sleep among the baggage,' Mary said. 'There's no chance of making a shelter here—but not much need, it seems.'

After misty Ireland and then the turbulent seas this looked a charming place, open, sunny, with a sky of clearest blue over the turquoise sea behind them, and in front a smooth green landscape. Not far away a cluster of little white houses gave life to the pastoral scene. Boats were still bringing men ashore when a few figures appeared in the distance, coming from the houses. The local people, the women in bright dresses, the men in breeches and checked shirts, hurried towards them. They seemed to be shouting. Gentian felt a twinge of nervousness. Then, as they came nearer, she realised they were cheering.

It was a heartening welcome. They were ordinary, poor people, fisherfolk, she guessed, yet there was something noble in their behaviour. Every look, every gesture, was warm and friendly, and they had brought gifts, baskets of fruit and bunches of flowers, which they thrust on the British invaders, their hoped-for deliverers. They were small, wiry folk, dark of hair and complexion, some of them very handsome. I shall like the Portuguese, Gentian thought.

The next few days were full of suppressed excitement. The men were in a state of constant readiness, for Sir Arthur expected total efficiency. Gentian saw him more than once as he rode past on his horse checking the troops, she registered that he was very plainly dressed in dark clothes, but noticed no details for she could not take her eyes off his face. It was such an alert face, with the bright piercing gaze of a man who would miss nothing. The nose, not nearly as big as she had expected, was high-bridged, arched and strong—he's like an eagle, she thought—but his mouth was well shaped, uncompromising yet with kindness in its lines. His look and bearing spoke of great capability and confidence; she felt his magnetism and could understand why the men were ready to follow him unquestioningly.

She saw Charles often as he rode to and fro, and always he glanced to where she was, as if assuring himself that all was well with her, but he did not stop or speak. They must keep their distance.

On the tenth of August, with all the landings completed and the army organised, camp was struck and the troops were on the march. Many of them, like Adam, were unseasoned men, and the going was hard. They had full packs, a great load—as well as their knapsacks with greatcoat and blanket on top they carried three days' ration of ship's biscuits and beef, a water canteen, a rifle and eighty rounds of ball cartridge, plus, if they were craftsmen, the tools of their trade. Because of the size and position of their packs they could not march freely, and this discomfort was aggravated by the fact that most of the time they were marching with deep sand underfoot and a burning sun overhead. Gentian and Mary had been lucky enough to get places in an ox-wagon carrying baggage. They were thankful not to have to walk, and happily endured the jolting and the ear-piercing shrieks which continually rose from the ungreased axles of the cart. After twelve miles of slogging torment they reached a small town dominated by a fine castle—Leiria —where they encamped again. This time it was a brief camp, and they were soon off again along the coast road. Somewhere between the British troops and Lisbon there was a French force under Junot lying in wait for them, so they might meet advance posts at any time. Mary and Gentian from their perch on the baggage wagon kept a sharp look-out, and Mary was the one who noticed a detachment of the Rifles separating itself from the main body.

'They've sighted some Frenchies, I'll be bound!' she cried.

They could see the men making their way across open country, watched them manoeuvring for cover as they approached a windmill on some rising ground. From the distance if was not possible to see what was happening, but they distinctly heard firing, which continued and increased; they lost sight completely of the men, but more troops left the main body and they too disappeared over the low ridges from which the sound of sporadic firing continued.

'French outposts, I reckon.' Mary said. 'Let's hope

our boys don't chase 'em too far and meet a bigger force.'

Several hundred troops had been left behind at Leiria, with another commander, but they hoped to be able to hold their own with any force that might bar their way to Lisbon. When the main force halted and the women were able to mix with the troops and start cooking-fires, the skirmishers had not returned. Adam had been among them. Gentian was seized with anxiety, but told herself she must not lose her nerve over the first engagement, and tried to look unworried. That night she slept little, her nerves on edge, ears straining for the sound of returning troops. At dawn the camp awakened and fires were rekindled, and at last they saw soldiers streaming down the gentle green hills towards them.

Adam was there, dirty, dog-tired, but exultant, and he had a tale to tell. It was his first taste of action, and in his quiet country way he made the most of it.

'Drove the Froggies out, we did, and then set off after them. They led us a fine dance, and the lead was flying on both sides, and then bother me if we didn't come across their rearguard. It was getting a bit hot, I can tell 'ee, but lucky for us General Spencer came up with some men. We made a good fight of it till dark, then we all got away. Well, not quite all. One of our officers was killed and another wounded, and some of the men injured, I think.'

Gentian's heart gave a thud, and she felt sick. She shot a swift glance of terror at Adam. He caught her eye, understood, and gave her a smile and a slight shake of the head. Charles was safe.

The army pressed on towards a straggling white village, walled and with a castle soaring above it as at Leiria. In and about the village the army spent the night, and around the cooking-pots the gossip passed. The village was called Obidos; Sir Arthur was there, and from some vantage-point—the church tower, perhaps—he had seen French forces concentrated and apparently ready for battle. General opinion was that there would be an engagement soon. At present they outnumbered the French force and Sir Arthur would want to strike before French reinforcements arrived.

At dawn the next day, the seventeenth, the army marched out and deployed on the plain beyond the village. The French army, to the number of four thousand, was drawn up about eight miles away in front of the little hamlet of Roliça, which nestled comfortably in the middle of a wide valley encircled by mountains. The French did not stay there long. General Laborde was a seasoned soldier, and he realised that Wellesley's intention would probably be to send two columns right and left to make a pincer movement and cut him off, so he withdrew behind the village to a very strong position on high ground. Soon fighting commenced.

It was impossible for the women to follow the course of the battle. They saw a detachment of redcoats dash out from the British centre and fight their way up a gully, but they did not know until much later that this precipitate action by the colonel of the 29th had put the day in jeopardy. He and his men had been cut off behind the French lines; he had been killed and his men suffered very heavy casualties. This movement had forced a general advance, and the British troops had fought their way up the rugged mountainside. It was a desperate business, for the mountain was a mass of clefts, gullies and ravines, and the enemy were in a fine defensive position.

The women could hear the sounds of battle, the sharp crackle of musket and rifle fire, the heavy boom of guns, and acrid smoke drifted back to them, but they knew nothing about the action for some hours. They heard the sounds of battle die away, and waited, desperate for news—was it victory or defeat?

Then an old baggage-master appeared, and began to rouse his team. 'The French have retreated,' he said. 'Left three of their guns behind.'

The women moved forward. With anxious hearts they crossed the edge of the plain towards the battlefield of Roliça.

CHAPTER SIXTEEN

HUNDREDS OF WOMEN, a draggle-tail army, spread across the plain, moving forward in waves like sluggish water, covering the fields and flowing slowly to where the battle had been fought. Men were now coming down the mountainside, men with blackened faces, with uniforms dirty and dishevelled, torn and bloody. Further ahead, higher up the mountain, the picture grew more ugly. Now there were battered bodies of men and horse amid dropped weapons and equipment, a scattering at first, becoming thicker, and blanketing everything was the lingering smoke of the gunfire. Higher up in the gullies it lay like fog, and from its grey folds came chilling sounds, the groans and cries of the wounded and dying.

Gentian was desperate to find Charles and Adam, but in this piteous situation her own anxieties had to be pushed aside, she was faced with suffering on a tremendous scale. She saw a steady flow of soldiers making for an isolated farmhouse building, men helping their comrades towards it. Near her, one man alone with a leg soaked in blood was trying to hobble along with the aid of his musket.

'Lean on me,' she said, putting his other arm round her shoulders, and helped him towards the building. She thought she would collapse under his weight, but somehow carried on until, nearing the building, another soldier came to help and between them they got him into a large barn which was being used as a makeshift hospital station. Now she saw work she could do, and began to help the few orderlies to give the wounded some attention. An army surgeon came up, saw her sponging a man's wounds, gave her a nod, and she worked on.

Time passed, one hour—two—she did not know. The smell of blood and sweating bodies filled her nostrils, nauseating her. She was near to losing control. Outside, the air though full of gunsmoke might be less tainted, perhaps it would revive her enough to carry on. She got up from her knees, stiff with cramp, and picking her way through the men lying all over the floor she stood outside, leaning against the wall, shutting her eyes and breathing deeply. The air though smoke-laden was fresher than inside. She opened her eyes to see some wounded being brought into the farmyard. Those from the top of the mountain ridges, she supposed. It would be a long and difficult business to bring them down from there.

She looked across at the bearers. 'I fear there is no room inside,' she said, then gazed down compassionately at the nearest man they carried. She saw Adam's face. For a moment it swam before her eyes, dreadfully changed, waxen under the filth, eyes closed as if in death. She pulled herself together. 'Put him down here,' she said, and went into the building again to fetch a bowl and cloths.

She knelt beside Adam and began to sponge his face. She had the dreadful feeling that he was already dead; he had lost a lot of blood, for there was a gaping wound in his left side and his left arm was shot away. Someone had put a rough tourniquet high up on the shattered stump, but nothing more had been done. Now there was little more to do.

'He's for it, missus,' said one of the bearers.

He was just breathing, in quick shallow gasps drawn between pallid lips.

'Adam . . . Adam . . .' she murmured.

Slowly his eyes opened. 'Jenny . . . waited to see you . . . before . . .'

It was a whisper, little more than a breath, but she heard it.

'Don't talk, dear. I'm here.'

'I'm for it . . . Jenny . . .'

'No. Just hold on.' She held his face in her hands and bent close.

'Jenny . . . I'm going . . .'

She bent still closer, and put her lips to his. He smiled.

'Jenny . . .'

Then his eyes no longer looked at her, but stared without sight. He was dead, with her name on his lips and the kiss he never claimed in life on his cold mouth.

She knew he had loved her for years. She found that tears were streaming down her cheeks. She closed his eyes. There was nothing to cover his face. She got to her feet. 'I'll try to find room inside for the wounded,' she said to the bearers.

It was dark, and she had rejoined Mary. Pat was safe; they had got the cooking-pot on the fire, and Mary was trying to persuade her to eat.

'You must look after yourself, Jenny. If you don't, you won't keep up, and you must come with us as far as Lisbon. You'll be able to get a passage back to England there, I'll be bound.'

Gentian forced down a few mouthfuls. She would go beyond Lisbon. She would go wherever Charles might go. No matter if her stomach turned at the food—it was salt beef and biscuit stew, augmented with a few vegetables they had acquired—she would eat it and keep her strength. Now she could fix her mind on Charles—nothing but Charles. But she would remember Adam in her heart, for she had loved him like a brother. She sat staring into the fire, numb with sorrow.

She was hardly aware that a man had come across to their group and had sat down beside her. Now he spoke, and the tone of his voice jolted her into some sort of awareness. It was eager, ingratiating.

'Well, missus—what's your name? Jenny Brenzett, I reckon?' She remembered he had tried to talk to her before. She nodded, and wished he would go away. 'So you've lost your man, eh?' She nodded again. 'Well, then, you must see about getting another.'

Now she looked at him, amazed, affronted. He was a red-faced, coarse-looking rifleman with small pale blue eyes, bloodshot, which peered at her curiously, and a big loose mouth which breathed stale wine over her.

'Don't do for a woman to be on her own,' he went on. 'When you follow the drum and lose your man you take another, sharpish. It's only fair. With not enough women to go round, you're in demand, so you pick another partner and the rest know to keep their hands off.'

She looked at him in horrified disgust, and could not speak. He put out his hand and rested it on her thigh.

'Come along, girl—you're pretty—I'm offering for you! I reckon what you lack in size you'll make up for in looks.'

She pushed his hand away and scrambled to her feet. 'Leave me alone!'

He swore an oath. 'Not likely! Give some other chap the chance of getting you? No, I'm first—you'll settle for me!'

He seized her arm and swung her round to face him. She tried to struggle free but he caught her other arm and dragged her towards him. Instinctively she began to struggle, and heard Mary's voice crying,

'In the name of God, leave the girl alone! She's only just widowed, as you well know, you brute! Give her time!'

Now she was sobbing as she tried to fight him off and

Mary was tugging at his arm, but he still held her. Pat was scrambling to his feet.

Then another voice, a man's, broke in. 'What's going on here?'

It was a voice with authority—and it was Charles's. The man, still holding her by one arm, turned.

'I was just telling the girl she should find another man—sir.'

'Let her go!' Charles moved closer, staring at the man, his face black with anger. 'The women make their own arrangements in their own time, without coercion. Be off with you, and don't try that again!'

With a surly resentful look the man slouched off. Charles looked at her, his eyes now tender and anxious. He put his hand on her shoulder, and she felt it tremble.

'Mrs Brenzett, I believe you were widowed in the action?' His look belied the formality of his words. 'Please accept my sympathy. I came to see—forgive me if this is a bad time—but the surgeons will need extra help with the wounded. I heard you were a nurse. Will you assist them?'

'Yes, certainly I will. Do they need me now?'

'No, but if you would find me before we move out tomorrow, I will take you to the hospital wagons. Thank you.' He turned to Pat, who was standing near by with Mary. 'Rifleman Mulvany? Will you see that Mrs Brenzett is not troubled any more tonight?'

'I will do that, sir.'

They spent another night in the open, haunted by nightmare sounds, within earshot of the more comforting noises of tethered horses and mules. But it was better lying in the country than being below decks in the transport ship.

The next morning Gentian found Charles. Amid the bustle of assembly they could have no private conversation; Charles told her that provided she helped with

the wounded, she could, with the Surgeon-Major's
agreement, ride in a wagon with the wounded and
receive rations. But before he called an orderly to show
her where she was needed, he added, low and swiftly,
'Find me tonight, darling.'

She nodded, and went to tend the wounded, to help
settle them in the wagons. She knew Charles had
arranged this for her safety, and to bring her nearer to
him. She was glad of that, but she was just as pleased to
have the chance of being useful; she would not spare
herself. She took her place in the wagon. The army was
on the move again.

The French had retreated into the mountains, but
they were still a strong force, and there would be another
battle soon. In the meantime the British were marching
to the coast to cover the disembarkation of reinforcements. These were arriving at the mouth of the River
Maceira, nearer Lisbon than Mondego Bay where the
Rifles had landed.

The wagons rumbled, jolted and screeched their way
in the wake of the marching troops, and Gentian, sitting
among the wounded, did what she could for them.
Because of the movement there were wounds to be
rebandaged; she eased the position of some of the
soldiers and propped others more securely, she gave sips
of water from canteens, but to her nothing she could do
seemed enough. One young rifleman was so badly injured that every movement of the wagon was agony to
him, and for the last hours of the journey she sat most of
the time with his head and shoulders lying in her lap,
cushioning him as best she could from the worst of the
jolting.

The relief of coming to a halt did not mean the end of
her labours, and it was a long time before she felt she
could leave the men she had taken into her particular
charge. They had reached a village called Vimeiro,

which stood where a smaller river jointed the Maceira before it altered course and flowed through a gorge towards the sea. The houses lay at river level, surrounded by heights; a hill behind and ridges on the sides beyond the two river arms. The hills were clothed with scrub and pine trees. It was a charming and peaceful scene—but for how long? Gentian wondered. Charles, she discovered, had a billet in the village, and she soon found it. He was by the door as she came up; he took her by the hand and drew her inside. He looked down at her anxiously.

'When did you last eat?' he asked.

'I don't know . . . Oh, I had some bread at breakfast.'

'And it's nearly nightfall. Come.'

In the main room of the cottage an old woman was stirring a pot over a fire, and from it came a savoury smell. Charles with sign-language indicated that Gentian should be fed, and the woman nodded and gave her an earthenware bowl of stew with a wooden spoon and a hunk of dark bread. Gentian took it gratefully, but with a sign of doubt.

'It's all right,' Charles said. 'She's had rations from me, and we pay for anything extra—that's Wellesley's rule.'

Gentian ate thankfully; it was the best food she had had since leaving England. Charles hardly took his eyes off her, and when she had finished he said, 'And now I expect you would like a wash.'

She laughed ruefully. 'That should have come first, but I was so hungry.'

'And tired. No matter.'

Sign-language produced from the old woman a jug of water, a bowl, and, wonder of wonders, a coarse but clean linen towel. Charles took the articles through a door and Gentian followed. She knew the old woman had been eyeing her wedding ring and had accepted her as Charles's wife. The room was small and bare, with one little window, whitewashed walls and a stone floor like the main room. It held nothing but a bed, a stool, a shelf and a few pegs on one wall. On one peg was Charles's cloak and tunic on the shelf was a leather box—his toilet case—and his travelling-chest stood on the floor. Charles gave her some soap from his case, and left her.

The room was still suffused with summer heat although it was now evening. Gentian undressed and washed from head to toe; the water was cold, and all the more refreshing for that. She took a clean shift from her bundle and put it on, then unpinned her hair and combed it. Suddenly she felt not only physically clean but mentally free, loosed from the burdens of struggle and hardship. With Charles she felt secure. She was still combing her hair when Charles reappeared carrying a fat-bellied earthenware jug and two mugs of the same reddish pottery, which he placed on the shelf. She began to braid her hair.

'Leave it loose, sweetheart,' he said. 'I love to see you like that.'

He passed his hand over her hair. 'You are beautiful. Sit on the bed, dear, and drink this. You need it.'

He poured out two mugs of wine from the jug and took his place beside her. For a little while they drank slowly and in silence, savouring the sweetness of being together at last, while the wine revived them. I am entitled to be here, she thought; by the unwritten customs of campaigning I can take any protection I choose. But that is not important, what matters is that we want and need each other.

In those peaceful moments, sipping the strong red wine, Gentian looked at Charles, reminding herself of every feature, every line in his face, and saw his emotion shining in his eyes. Her tiredness, her sorrow had dropped away form her, and she was beginning to live again. The fact that they had not even touched hands somehow intensified the feelings of love and longing that surged between them.

He was the first to speak. 'Is that better, darling?'

It touched her to hear how naturally the endearment slipped from his lips.

'Much better.'

'You will stay with me now,' he said. She smiled and nodded. 'That is,' he went on, 'until we reach Lisbon. Then I will make arrangements for you.'

'We shall see.'

'You'll stay there. Let's not argue. For a while we can live from day to day, together.'

'That's all I want, Charles.'

'And all I want is you.'

She looked at him, and felt his love surge out and envelop her like a cloak. She turned to him and his arms enfolded her. The need each for the other, so long denied, was overwhelming them. With his cheek warm on hers he murmured, 'Now, darling, whatever happens, you are mine.'

Her heart leapt, her pulses raced. She nodded, unable to speak. His lips were roving over her face, her hair, brushing her brow and cheeks and neck, finding her mouth and taking it with soft gentle kisses. His hands were gentle too, caressing her throat and shoulders. His kisses strengthened in intensity as passion fought against restraint. It quickened the longing within her, so that emotion so long denied rose and overwhelmed her with its force. Her body cried for love as much as her heart had yearned for it.

With unhurried movements, each one a caress, he showed her how desire led naturally towards fulfilment. She let him teach her all she needed to know, giving her body to him without embarrassment, trusting him utterly. She gloried in his maleness, in his brown lean torso, his crisp dark hair which smelt of smoke, the roughness of his cheek and chin against her face. As passion grew she felt the rapture of union surging within her till ecstasy reached a peak of unbelievable delight. There was no holding back, she was his.

The next morning, without complaint, they returned to reality. Nothing could take from them the knowledge that in the simple room of the humble cottage they had achieved a union, not only of the body but of the heart and spirit, and from now on everything was changed for them. At last, in the face of anything the world might do, they belonged to each other in a bond which was indissoluble.

So Charles went to organise his troops, and she returned to nurse the wounded. She could not help thinking that Adam had given his life for her as much as for this unhappy country. She would always be in his debt; he had loved her, he had protected her, and asked for nothing. She knew under what danger she had been in the camp, not from the majority of the soldiers who treated with respect all women except the prostitute camp-followers, but from the few who were brutal, lecherous and uncontrolled. Adam by his very presence had protected her. He had been happy to serve her, knowing that she loved Charles.

But there was no time for personal thoughts nor for indulgence in sorrow or regret, there was work to do. Gentian was shocked by the lack of facilities for caring for the wounded—surely they deserved better than this?—and Roliça, she was told, had only been a small battle. So what was to come? So by day she tended the wounded, at night she lay in Charles's arms. She tasted purgatory and paradise. In a couple of days, on the twentieth, the last reinforcements came ashore.

'That's the last of the landings,' Charles told her.

'We're now raised to seventeen thousand men. But that's not much more than half of the French, if you include Junot's troops, which, thank God, are miles away. And a sloop, the *Brazen*, has brought General Sir Harry Burrard, who, rumour has it, is to supersede Wellesley. Seniority counts above ability, you see. It will be a bad day for us if we lose Sir Arthur. Let's hope General Burrard agrees that Wellesley should lead us at once to outflank Junot.'

But Junot was already on the march. In the small hours of the morning the word reached Wellesley, who at once went up the ridge above the camp to watch for the French. At nine o'clock they were sighted, coming, not from the south as expected, but from the east. Gentian, from her post in the village, thought everything was in confusion, but the movement was done in masterly order, and the troops were settled in their positions before the great French army came into view of the naked eye.

The women were supposed to keep with the baggage wagons or in the village. Some of them, Gentian among them, managed to find a spot at the end of the main street from where they could look up the small river valley between the rising ground. In the distance a great cloud of dust foreshadowed the army of the French. They waited and watched, too keyed up to talk, knowing that the terrible event of battle was in the making. It was a bright day, the sun shining out of a clear blue sky, and already warm. Soon they saw flashes of light among the huge dust-cloud as the sun glanced off the steel of weapons and the gold of the standards of the Imperial Eagles, piercing the thick haze lifted by marching feet. How long . . . How long? Gentian wondered.

Now the bulk of the French were facing the British troops on the hill, but a tell-tale cloud showed where others were moving out towards the rest of the British force which was massed on the ridge on the other side of the river. It concerned Gentian that although most of the British troops were concealed behind the crest of the hill, there was a thick line of riflemen posted at the foot where they would meet the first French onslaught. Was Charles there? She could not tell, but her heart thudded with apprehension as the French made their first attack.

In front of the main body came a mass of *tirailleurs*, their swift darting skirmishes intended to demoralise the troops and make them an easy prey for the solid mass of Grenadiers following behind. But the British riflemen were prepared for these tactics and were their match, taking on the *tirailleurs* with quick, steady, destructive fire; there was a thunder from the cannon behind them, balls ploughed through the Grenadiers and then the red coats of the British infantry appeared from behind the crest. Steadily, inexorably the two long lines, company after company, rained their alternating fire into the massed ranks of the Grenadiers.

The smoke from rifles, muskets, and cannon now hung over everything and it was impossible to see what was happening, only the confused noises of the battle pierced the white fog and reached the ears of the women who waited. To Gentian there was no such thing as time, just a suspension of all reckoning, an agony of dread which stretched into infinity. The sounds of fighting grew nearer; the area of conflict had spread and was spilling around the side of the hill next to the village.

Some women were shouting, 'Back! Into the houses!' and she went with the rush down the main street. Without ceremony, the women pushed their way into the buildings where the Portuguese inhabitants had stayed in fearful expectancy. Some doors were barred and Gentian fled on past one which remained tight shut, to find the next was opened for her and then barred again.

The sounds of fighting were just outside the village now. Almost at once it raged down the street, the sound of shots being followed by the clash of hand-to-hand fighting, shouts, yells, the screams of wounded men and the frantic neighing of horses. In the room where she had taken refuge the sounds echoed and rang, an old man stood to one side of the window, gazing impassively out, an old woman stared at nothing, crossing herself repeatedly, her lips moving in soundless prayer. When a young girl looking distracted burst into wild sobs, Gentian put her arms around her and held her close. After some time the noises receded, and died away.

When they dared to open the door the street was like a picture from hell. It was scattered down its length with dead and wounded men and horses, the beaten earth spattered with equipment and splashed with pools of blood. There were no signs of fighting on the hill, where the French were in full retreat. Mechanically Gentian took her watch from her pocket. Unbelievably it was not yet one o'clock. Only three hours. And still she must wait.

She moved in a kind of trance. How much time had now passed she did not dare to know. She paid no attention to what was being said around her. It had been a victory. General Burrard had arrived from the *Brazen* part way through the action, but had allowed Wellesley to continue directing the battle. Then, with the day won, he had refused to let Wellesley advance and pursue, to rout the French and clear the way to Lisbon. He insisted on waiting for the reinforcements under Sir John Moore, to Sir Arthur's evident disgust.

'And Nosey had to give in to the old fool! What else will he have to agree to!'

It meant nothing to Gentian. She had left the village and hurried to where the troops were having roll-call. When she found the Rifles, to her the green uniforms looked much fewer than before, and scan them as thoroughly as her apprehension dared she could not see Charles among them. So she stumbled on towards the hill. I should have stopped to ask, she thought. But she would not go back now.

The evidence of battle grew thicker. At the foot of the hill and up the slopes the ground was strewn with wounded and dead, and the smoke was lying so thick that it was difficult to distinguish anyone or anything more than a few yards away. Trying desperately to keep in control, not to burst into sobs of fear and horror, she picked her way, her feet slipping on the trampled, bloodsoaked turf. A man loomed out of the smoke, a man she recognised. She caught him by the sleeve.

'Sergeant—you're Sergeant Webb?'

The blackened face turned to her. 'Yes, missus.'

He was one of Charles's men.

'Major Claverton—do you know . . . ?'

The man shook his head. 'I'm looking for him. Saw him go down. Horse shot from under him. I reckon he caught it too. Didn't see him get up—but I was busy at the time.'

Terror struck Gentian. 'Where was it?'

'Not easy to say. Somewhere on this slope—I reckon a bit further along.'

She joined him in the gruesome search. They were not alone; by now there were men seeking for wounded and bearing them away, farriers ending the lives of wounded horses, and a scarecrow band, both men and women, turning over bodies and looting from the dead. Gentian fought the sickness rising within her, she even ignored the wounded, leaving them to the orderlies' help, concentrating every scrap of strength she possessed to search for Charles, dead or alive. Please God, not dead! But hope was ebbing fast.

'Here, missus!'

She heard the shout, and stumbled to where Sergeant Webb was stooping over a body. She dropped to her knees. It was Charles.

CHAPTER SEVENTEEN

WEBB WAS RAISING Charles in his arms. As he did so, Charles's eyes flickered open and he muttered, 'I'm not dead yet! Take your hands off me . . . Oh, it's you, Sergeant.'

Gentian could see beneath the grime of battle an even darker bruise on the side of his forehead, and, much worse, that his left sleeve was tattered and soaked with blood. She lifted the shredded cloth. He was still looking at Webb.

'What the hell am I doing here? Where's the fighting?' he asked.

'The fight's over, sir—and won. Your horse was shot from under you—you've been unconscious.'

Charles muttered a curse, then turned his head and his eyes fell on Gentian. 'You here! For God's sake!'

'Charles, let me look at your arm.'

'Can't move the damn thing.' A spasm crossed his face. 'Funny—I felt nothing at the time, but now it's hurting confoundedly.'

It was still bleeding, and he had already lost too much blood, she thought. But only emergency measures could be taken here. Without more ado she lifted her skirt, picked up a bayonet which lay near by and cut into her petticoat. She could then tear off a wide strip, and with a piece of this she improvised a tourniquet around his upper arm, with the rest she made a sling to cradle the arm against his chest.

'Now, Sergeant, can we get him down to the dressing-station?'

'Can you walk, sir?' he asked.

'Yes, I'm all right, man.'

He was far from all right, Gentian thought, and was thankful to see that Webb at once put Charles's right arm over his shoulders and supported him. They began to pick their way down the hill.

She could see that under the dirt of battle Charles's face was white and drawn with pain. But there was no question of waiting for help from the orderlies, who had far too much to do with the crippled and unconscious to carry a man capable of moving himself with assistance. If the way up had seemed long, the way back seemed interminable and like a continual nightmare. In the aftermath of battle, the ground littered with bodies and the shards of war, they walked through swirling acrid smoke which caused a preternatural darkness around them. When they at last reached the bottom of the hill and turned into the main street, conditions were little better.

Gentian stopped an orderly. 'Where are the surgeons?'

'In the churchyard, missus,' was the reply.

'Convenient,' Charles remarked ironically.

The churchyard was one of the few open spaces. The wounded were lying in ranks beside the graves, wherever room could be found for them. Two large tables had been brought there, and surgeons were already at work. Gentian, in control till then, suddenly sickened. She could see a surgeon, with hands and arms covered in blood to the elbows, ripping at the uniform of a man on the table. With a gesture to his assistants to hold the patient in position, he raised a kind of cleaver and hacked off the limb. The leg was thrown aside on a heap of severed limbs, the man was lifted down and another put in his place. It was like watching a butcher at the block. But these were men being hacked about in this shambles. How many of them would survive such treatment she could not guess.

A surgeon who was inspecting the wounded had almost reached them. She undid the sling and exposed Charles's arm. He gave it a cursory inspection.

'Amputation,' he said, and gestured to the tables.

Charles's brows drew together in a black line, and his mouth set. 'No,' he said.

The surgeon halted and stared down at him. 'Come, man, your arm's useless. If it's not amputated, you will die of gangrene.'

'Then I'll die. You'll not take off my arm.'

'See sense, Major.'

'No.'

The surgeon's face was grim.

'I've no time to argue with you. If you continue obstinate, I wash my hands of you.' He walked on.

Charles turned to her. 'Gentian, I won't agree. If I die, I die.'

'Don't think of dying,' she said swiftly. 'I'll do what I can.' She turned to Webb. 'Sergeant, we must take him to his billet. Then I'll try to dress his arm.'

'Right, missus. You tell me what you need, and I'll get it.'

Webb was as good as his word. While Gentian settled Charles and began to cleanse the wound, Webb went out and returned with dressings and splints. She had no time to question her ability but must do what she could, even if she could not save the arm. The surgeon thought it impossible, and perhaps Charles would develop gangrene and die; but what were his chances of surviving such brutal surgery? Some men lived after amputation, many did not. Such thoughts were in the back of her mind but she forced herself to be dispassionate, to attend to the injury as if it were a technical exercise. She could not be sure how badly the bones were shattered, how injured the muscles and blood vessels, she could only do her best to help nature's own efforts to repair the injury. From the mass of torn and bloody flesh she could see loose splinters of bone protruding; she picked them out, and prayed enough would remain for the bones to knit. Webb was at her elbow.

'Webb, we have got to straighten the arm. You must pull it into shape, and hold it while I bandage it into position. Charles, this will be very painful.'

He nodded. 'Carry on.'

Gentian gritted her teeth and began. There was no way she could spare Charles the agony; if she could save his arm and if it were not to be permanently deformed, the bones must be pulled into alignment, and it was already some hours since it had been broken. Webb was an intelligent man who responded quickly to her instructions, and at last it was done. Gentian sank back with a sigh, and found that she was bathed in a cold sweat. Charles lay with eyes closed. Had he fainted with the pain? It would not be surprising. She wiped his face, and his eyes opened.

'Is that it?' he asked. 'Well, we all need a drink. There's some brandy on the shelf.'

Webb, besides being an invaluable source of dressings and supplies—Gentian never asked how he came by what he brought—was also a mine of information. Vimeiro had been a resounding victory, but it was said that Wellesley, superseded by an elder and over-cautious man, robbed of the chance of following up the victory by pursuing and routing the French, was now being obliged to agree to a truce.

'A truce! When we gave the Frogs a thrashing! We don't need a truce to get them out of Lisbon—out of Portugal, for that matter!'

He talked to her of Charles. 'He's a fine man, and a fine officer. The men would follow him anywhere. You should have seen him when we were catching the worst of the French fire. Cool as a cucumber—held the men together, then at the right moment, let us get at them. You've got to save him, missus.'

'Oh, Webb, I pray that I can. But I'm not an expert in wounds—I am a herbal healer.'

'I reckon you'll do it, missus, better than those fellows with their choppers!'

Charles was still suffering to some extent from the effects of the blow that had knocked him unconscious, besides that of his shattered arm and the loss of blood, but Gentian had a hard job to convince him that his injuries demanded rest. He was fit for light duties, he said. Only a visit from his commanding officer won from him a grudging assent to rest until the army moved on.

Some hours later there were sounds of horsemen outside, and a knock at the door. Gentian saw against the light the figure of a man in dark clothes with close-cropped hair. As he moved in, to her amazement she recognised the alert and brilliant eyes, the high-bridged nose, the firm but kindly mouth of Sir Arthur Wellesley.

'Major Claverton's here, eh?' he said without preamble.

'In here, Sir Arthur.' She indicated the door.

'Don't get up, man. I hear you refused to let the surgeon lop off your arm. Can't say I blame you. How is it?'

'Too early to say, sir.'

'Hmmm. Well, blood is getting to the fingers, that's something. I liked the way you handled your men in the fight. I've plenty of brave officers, but not so many that are cool-headed as well.'

'Thank you, sir.'

'That arm of yours. If it doesn't mend well enough for you to return to active service, we'll find something for you. Posts crop up on my staff from time to time.' Sir Arthur brushed aside Charles's stunned words of gratitude. 'In any case, that arm will need time—so you had best return to England from Lisbon. The lady with you—Mrs Claverton?'

'No. Mrs Clark.'

'Hmmm. Who set your arm?'

'Mrs Clark, sir. She has been nursing the men since Roliça.'

'Then my advice to you is to engage her as your nurse and she can travel with you to England. Good day to you, Major.'

Gentian rejoined Charles to find him still looking slightly dazed. 'That was Wellesley! He said . . .'

'I heard everything. Oh, Charles, he noticed you in the battle!'

'Lucky for me! Cool-headed, he said! I know he's suffered from impetuous cavalry officers who dash on after a charge and then have to be rescued from behind enemy lines. It happened at Roliça—and nearly happened here.'

'He might take you on his staff.'

'Don't count on it. He sometimes has to take what he's given. But if he did, it would almost compensate if I should lose the arm. And he noticed you—had heard about you, I shouldn't wonder. But I don't need Wellesley to tell me how to keep you with me. You're mine, my darling, and I'll never let you go.'

A man can say that, Gentian thought, yet fate may decree otherwise. But she would not consider it; that was for the future, and she was concerned only with the present. She thanked Sir Arthur in her heart, for he had dispelled Charles's despondency and given him hope. That was enough for now.

Meanwhile the wounded were languishing in the extreme August heat, there were difficulties about burying the dead, the smell of corruption hung over the village, and the vultures came down from the mountains. It was a relief to everyone when a couple of days later they had marching orders.

'We're on our way to Lisbon, Mrs Clark,' Webb told her.

Gentian wanted Charles to ride in a hospital wagon, but he would have none of it. He had lost one horse, but Webb had been looking after his remounts, and he would ride. There was no arguing with him, all she could do was to make the arm as immobile as possible in the sling, and leave Webb to help him to mount. The men cheered as he joined them, and she took her place in one of the hospital wagons. When they camped that night he was exhausted but cheerful. Two more days on the march, and they reached Lisbon, to camp outside the walls.

Row after row of tents, pitched with military precision and amazing swiftness, made a city of canvas. Beyond could be seen the houses, white-walled, pink-roofed, clustering together at the mouth of the Tagus, while on the hill above, St George's Castle stood, the Portuguese standard once more flying from the battlements.

Charles was not so well. The days of riding had exhausted him, and Gentian believed he was starting a fever. Her love for him seemed to produce in her a strength, an energy, a persistence she did not know she possessed. She obtained permission from his commanding officer to find a billet for him in the town and for Webb to be his official batman, and with the sergeant as escort, she set forth.

Had her errand not been so urgent she would have enjoyed to the full the apparent normality of life around her. People were going about their daily business, untroubled, cheerful and carefree now they were released from French domination; there were men leading donkeys laden with produce, girls in bright dresses and shawls carrying earthenware pitchers, barefoot women from the port balancing on their heads large shallow baskets full of gleaming silver fish. She listened to the voices; the language was soft, full of slurs and diphthongs, she still knew only a few words. To make herself understood she had to use French—though she was always careful to make it plain that she was English—for many of the Portuguese had picked up some French while the enemy were in occupation.

But on her first outing she was concerned only to find a good comfortable place where Charles could stay, and this, by sheer persistence, she eventually achieved. The resourceful Webb hired a little carriage, and between them they moved Charles and settled him in a clean bed, with more comfort and convenience than had been available at any time during the campaign. And not a moment too soon, she thought; the fever was getting worse. Because such medicines as she had brought with her were all used up, she would have to find an apothecary and somehow get help to nurse him. She looked at him as he lay with flushed face, his head turning spasmodically on the pillow. Had she waited so long for his love, had she come so far with him only to see him die?

'Gentian . . .' He muttered her name, his eyes opened and searched for her.

'I'm here, Charles.' She knelt beside him and placed her hand on his brow.

'My darling . . . don't leave me! What years we have wasted!'

'Don't think of it. We are together now—I won't leave you.'

'Divorce . . . when I get back . . . I'll try for divorce.'

'Don't worry about it, dear. It doesn't matter.'

'It . . . matters. Can't have you . . . despised . . . Should be my wife.'

'All in good time. It doesn't matter now.'

'Wife . . . never had a wife . . . only a selfish bitch!'

'Hush, darling.'

'Bitch! I've had cause . . . but she's clever! Must find proof . . . for she'll not let me go.'

'Don't think about it now, Charles.'

'Children . . . no children . . . never wanted hers. Can't bear to touch her . . . but Gentian's . . . our children . . .'

Gentian realised he was no longer aware of her presence, but was lost in the gnawing pain and regrets of the past as the fever mounted within him. She must get help, and quickly.

She found that close by there was an order of monks who ran a hospice, and they agreed that one of their number would visit Charles. To her joy she discovered that the monks used herbal remedies, so she understood their preparations and their methods. After a few anxious days the fever began to diminish. Fray Anselmo approved of her treatment; what she had done to the arm was good, he said, but it was so badly damaged that he could not say with any certainty whether Charles would be able to use it again. Still, there was hope, and the herbal salves he provided would help to make it clean and healthy; for the rest they must wait and pray.

Gentian did not leave Charles until she was sure the fever was controlled, then she gave herself the pleasure of finding fresh clothes for herself. She had been able to bring so little with her that everything was in a sorry state. She still had most of her gold pieces, so she spent some in re-equipping herself. This was not merely selfish; she knew her morale would be stronger and her chances improved when she paid a visit to Military Headquarters, where she must go to arrange their passage home. She wished to look like a respectable woman, not a draggle-tail camp-follower.

Charles was well enough to understand where she was

going, and why, and fretted that he was not fit to arrange matters himself.

'Maybe it is as well,' she consoled him. 'If you could go, they might not consider the matter urgent, and the sooner you get home the better.'

She set off on foot, as she knew where to go. The city was surprisingly handsome, beautifully planned with fine buildings and tree-lined avenues. She passed the Opera House in a fine square, at the end of a straight street leading from it was another even finer square, in the centre of which stood a fine equestrian statue in weathered-green bronze. By now she knew that most of the city had been rebuilt in the previous century after a disastrous earthquake, but this morning she had no mind for such matters; the interview was the only thing of any importance.

After a considerable wait at Headquarters, she was shown into a room where she found herself facing an elderly colonel whose bewhiskered face with its antagonistic expression was a physical manifestation of his prickly attitude. The interview started on a bad footing. In the first few moments he established that she was not Major Claverton's wife, and stated bluntly that he disapproved of officers being accompanied by any less formal attachments.

'My *attachment* to Major Claverton is as a nurse,' she explained. That was half true, and would serve her best. 'My husband was killed at Roliça, and I have been nursing the wounded. At Vimeiro, Major Claverton needed attention. He has now engaged me as his nurse, which is why he wishes me to accompany him.'

'And so, no doubt, do you. Who was your husband?'

'Rifleman Brenzett.'

'I thought your name was Clark?'

'It was.'

'A rifleman, eh? And you change your name at the

drop of a hat. I can see it would be very much to your advantage to attach yourself to a major—in any capacity.'

His manner was openly insulting, but Gentian tried to stifle her anger. 'It is the Major's welfare that is to be considered, not mine.'

'If he's fit to return, I do not see that he needs a nurse.'

'He is weak from fever. His wounded arm needs regular attention, and with only one usable arm he needs help.'

'Which will be better provided by a male orderly.'

Was there no moving him?

'There is something else. If he did not need all my time, I would be willing to help nurse other men who needed attention. I have experience.'

'I am sure. But what sort of experience?' His sneering inference was obvious.

'I am a herbalist, used to treating illness and accidents. I have been attending the wounded, as I said, since Roliça.'

'A *herbalist*! That is quackery!'

'It is a natural science, and effective healing.'

'In plain words, you have no abilities other than that of any woman who can claim she can nurse. I do not doubt your talents in other respects. But since there will be a surgeon and orderlies on board to attend to the wounded, Major Claverton has no official need of you. Good day.'

'I am not asking for favours, Colonel. I am able to pay for my passage.'

He brushed that aside. 'Payment does not enter into it. It is a matter of accommodation. We have more wounded than the transports can manage.'

That might or might not be true, but there was no way she could argue with it. She had but one more shot. 'Sir

Arthur Wellesley assured Major Claverton that if he engaged a nurse she would be allowed to accompany him.'

'Sir Arthur Wellesley, eh?' His lip curled. Here is a man, she thought, with no capacity for warfare, who resents the success of a younger man in the field. She would get nothing from this jealous, embittered colonel. 'Sir Arthur Wellesley is no longer in command,' he said with open satisfaction. 'He is returning to England. In any case, the allocation of places in the return transports would not be his business. No, Mrs . . . Brenzett . . . Clark—what ever you call yourself—you really must understand that I am in charge of this affair, and I say you would be taking a place which could be filled by an injured man. I will arrange for Major Claverton's repatriation, but you will have to wait. Since you can pay, you may be able to make private arrangements. If not, you are at liberty to come and see me again when passages have been provided for all the wounded. That, of course, will take time, and should there be another battle . . . well . . .' He spread his hands. 'I advise you, as I said, to make private arrangements.'

'I see. Then may I settle the passage for Major Claverton—now?'

Muttering under his breath, the colonel shuffled about in the papers and books on his desk. Eventually, with a vicious stab of his pen into the inkwell, he made an entry, and filled in a form which he passed to her.

'See that he's there. There will be no other notification. Good day.'

Gentian left the room, frustration and fury boiling within her. Must everything and everybody conspire to separate her from Charles? She knew there was nothing she could do but accept the situation, just as she had had to swallow the colonel's insults. Charles must not know, not even that she could not sail with him. Time enough for that later. In his condition, the longer she kept it from him the better.

Still upset and angry, she made her way out of Military Headquarters, and was crossing the entrance hall when she saw a familiar figure. It was Mrs Braithwaite, who recognised her at once.

'Jenny! What are you doing here?'

Gentian remembered with pleasure her kindness on the voyage out. 'Mrs Braithwaite! I have been trying to arrange return passages for Major Claverton and myself.'

'Oh, the Major! How is he?'

'His condition is not good. He has had a fever, but that is improving now.'

'But, of course, his arm . . . Poor man! And have you fixed passages?'

'For the Major, yes. I had hoped to go as his nurse.'

'You . . . But, my dear—your husband? Has anything happened . . . ?'

'He was killed at Roliça.'

'Oh, you poor creature! Of course you wish to return. Do I understand you were refused?'

'Yes, although I have been nursing since Roliça, and would . . .'

She had not the heart to continue. Mrs Braithwaite's mouth pursed, and her eyes glittered.

'That Colonel Brant, I'll be bound! The petty tyrant! When does the Major sail?' Gentian passed her the form. 'That's official. Good! Now Colonel Braithwaite can get me a list of the ladies sailing on that ship. I am sure there will be one who would like to take you as her maid. I will find one, and we will arrange it between us. Tell me where you are staying, and you will hear from me.'

'You are so kind—but are you sure? It is a great deal of trouble.'

'No trouble at all. Leave it to me.'

Gentian felt dazed at her possible good fortune, yet she did not dare to count on it. How could Mrs Braithwaite—even with the assistance of her husband—persuade Colonel Brant to include a lady's maid when he had refused a nurse? Yet somehow she did, for a few days later a sailing pass arrived for her.

Charles, unfit as he was, was not concerned about himself. Constantly he thought of her. His mind was preoccupied with the need for a divorce. Charity would do everything possible to avoid it, he said, but somehow evidence must be obtained, and he must make Gentian his legal wife. At times she wondered whether he saw the possibility of death and was desperate to make proper provision for her.

At last the sailing date came, and they boarded. Charles was taken to the cabin he was sharing, Gentian found her way to Mrs Cumming's cabin. They had met once by Mrs Braithwaite's arrangement, and Mrs Cumming was pathetically glad to see her again. She was a young woman, little older than Gentian; her husband, a young lieutenant, had like Adam been killed at Roliça. She treated Gentian more as a new and sympathetic friend than as a servant.

The three-week passage was mercifully smoother than the outgoing one had been. Gentian divided her time between attending to Mrs Cumming and caring for Charles and the other three officers in his cabin. She worked hard, and in more leisured moments she read to them, wrote letters for them, played chess with them. Only rarely was she alone with Charles. But she found the passage enjoyable, feeling a wonderful sense of freedom, revelling in the open sea and sky.

They reached England on a cool October day. They had anchored overnight in Plymouth roads, and disembarked early with a rising sun struggling to disperse with its pale rays the morning mist which blurred the outlines of the buildings and made the horizon indistinct and grey. Charles had gained strength on the voyage, and had made what plans he could. Duty would oblige him to go to his home in Sussex and to see his father who lived near by; after that he must see the surgeons in an army hospital, for their report would decide his immediate future in the army. But to him only two things mattered: Gentian, and the possibility of divorce. Reluctantly he conceded that she could not stay with him, although he intended to tell his father his reason for wanting a divorce; he was not going to conceal that his love for Gentian was the spur. Charity's behaviour in the past during his absences had given him cause and the law was heavily on the side of the husband; though he himself in the past had not been blameless, if proof could be obtained, she might not contest.

The fact that he might be compelled to go into hospital for an indefinite period, rather than any regard for convention, had made him decide he would not be able to keep Gentian with him. It would be more practical for her to wait for news of him elsewhere, and what better place than the Homewoods' cottage in Hythe, where she would be loved and cared for? They could travel a good part of the way together.

From the quay Charles had their baggage taken to an inn where they ordered breakfast in a private room, while the landlord sent a boy to enquire about hiring a chaise. Breakfast was ample and the coffee good; a feeling of comfort stole over them. Charles laid his hand on Gentian's and voiced her own thoughts.

'We're back in England, dearest. A little patience and things will go our way.' He smiled into her eyes. 'I don't intend to lose you again.'

There was a knock on the door, and the landlord appeared.

'Major Claverton, sir, there's someone asking for you. Name of Brewer.'

'Brewer?' He turned to Gentian. 'My father has a servant of that name . . .' He broke off. 'Show him in.'

They exchanged looks of surprise and apprehension.

'My father must have been told I am returning wounded. He may have sent a coach.'

It was the most likely explanation. A middle-aged man in plain dark clothes came in.

'So it is you, Brewer!' Charles exclaimed. 'What are you doing here? Is my father well?'

The man gave a respectful bow.

'His Grace heard you were due in this week, sir, and sent me with the coach and a letter for you.' He paused and cleared his throat uncertainly. 'I am happy to find you reasonably well in spite of your injury, sir, for I was told to use my discretion whether I gave you the letter at once.' He drew a sealed letter from an inside pocket. 'I fear it is bad news, sir.'

Charles shot him a sharp glance and took the letter. Brewer stood looking at nothing with the impersonal stare of the well-trained servant; Gentian gazed at Charles, wondering what unwelcome information was in store for him. His father was apparently well—so his brother, perhaps? With his one good hand Charles broke the seal and unfolded the sheet. She saw his brows draw together as he scanned it, and then he looked fixedly at it for a few moments, taking in the contents.

'Thank you, Brewer,' he said quietly. 'I'll see you outside in a few minutes.'

The man bowed and left them.

'What is it, Charles?' Gentian asked softly.

His face changed from a forced impassivity, twisting into anger and despair as he crushed the letter in his hand. Then, 'Read it,' he said, and thrust the crumpled sheet towards her.

Her heart was sinking with apprehension; she had felt it on Brewer's arrival, and now it deepened as she smoothed out the page and read what it contained. The Earl had not wasted words.

> My dear Charles,
>   This is not the sort of letter with which I care to greet you on your return. I can only trust that you will be well enough to stand the shock. The fact is that a week ago your wife met with a riding accident. You know that she does not spare her horses, and there is no doubt she asked too much of the poor beast that fell with her. The upshot of it is that she is gravely injured. I have one of the best surgeons from London in attendance, but he'll commit himself to nothing save that he believes she will live. It seems that she has broken her back, and may never walk again.

Gentian looked at Charles, her eyes wide with horror. 'How dreadful! You will go to her at once!' He nodded. 'And don't worry about me. I'll make my own way to Kent.'

This shook him out of his thoughts. 'You'll do no such thing! We will go together as far as possible, and when we have to separate I'll leave you where you can catch a post-chaise. It will take no longer.'

Gentian said no more. At that time there was nothing to be said. He did not love Charity, in fact he detested her, conventional expressions of sympathy would ring false; but that did not make it any less of a tragedy, and Charles owed Charity the duty of a husband.

They said very little until they had been more than half an hour in the carriage, rattling along the road from the south. They were travelling as fast as was possible, and their haste was plain, other vehicles gave way to the coroneted carriage with liveried coachman and a sober-suited servant beside him. Inside on the dark red cushions Charles and Gentian began to realise the implications of the news, but did not discuss them. There was no point in talking about a situation so dependent on matters outside themselves. When they spoke, it was solely of immediate things, of subjects under their control.

'I shall see how things are when I get home,' Charles told her. 'As long as Charity has the best attention, my presence will not, I think, be necessary for long. I shall go for treatment for this arm as planned. It is in everyone's interest for me to get as fit as I can, as soon as possible.'

'Yes, Charles. You should not delay. And I shall be with the Homewoods, so you need have no worries for me. We shall write to each other.'

'Darling, I shall live for your letters!'

They relapsed into silence. Each knew what the other was thinking. Charity's appalling accident did not affect herself alone. It laid waste Charles's plans to free himself by divorce—how could he cast off a woman who might never walk again? He had put up with her infidelity before; to divorce her for it now would be the action of a blackguard, however little affection there was between them. Their marriage, an act of folly, doomed from the start, must remain, a millstone round his neck which he would never now be able to shift.

As they rattled on, Gentian took Charles's hand in hers and rested her head on his shoulder. He bent to kiss her hair, and so, in silence, each tried to comfort the other by their presence. They said their farewells in the carriage, before Charles left her. A few words passed between them; assurances that they would keep in touch by letter, and simple expressions of love. It was pointless to speak of the future; it looked barren, empty.

Gentian went on by post-chaise to Hythe, where the warmth of her reunion with the Homewoods comforted her temporarily. There was a great deal to talk about, experiences and news to be exchanged, and to slip back into the old way of life was balm to her tormented mind. As the days passed she tried to school herself into an attitude of peace. But it was not the peace of contentment, it was an acceptance of a miserable reality.

She could not understand why Charles did not write. For a month she waited for a letter, but still nothing came. He must be in hospital by now, he could write from there. Had he decided that with Charity crippled he must give up all plans for their future, and was putting off the pain of telling her? Or had he had a relapse, and was too ill to write?

Still she waited, than at long last a letter arrived that Charles had written from hospital. She opened it with a heavy-beating heart.

My dearest,

Forgive me that I have not written before. I have not felt settled enough till now to do justice to a letter to you, nor in the circumstances would it have been seemly. Charity is dead; she died the day before I reached home. Death is never a matter for rejoicing, but for her it was a release; for me, I admit, a relief. Having settled affairs at home I then went into hospital, where, as you see, they are keeping me for lengthy treatment. That, I suppose, is as well—it prevents me from flouting all conventions and rushing to you.

The doctors said my arm had been saved by a miracle. I told them that you were the miracle —their colleagues would have chopped it off. They looked a little sourly at that. I am getting back some use of it, and hope for more, but I think it will depend more on my own efforts than on any skill they possess. I am impatient to be discharged from this place so that I can come to you, and in good time make you my wife. Perhaps it is as well that they will not let me leave just yet, for I know that when I see you I shall want to marry you in what would be called indecent haste! We have waited too long already.

Meanwhile there is something you can be thinking about. You will realise that Charity's money has come to me. I have never taken it and never shall. It has occurred to me that I can use it for a fund to help private soldiers wounded in action or ill as a result of service. There seems to be no provision for them, and many are in great want and suffering. A small hospital might be established; you will know more about what is needed than I do. It is something we could do together, in remembrance of our good friend Adam.

And so, my darling, at last we can look forward. Please God that I may soon be with you.

She finished reading the letter and sat holding it, feeling peace and contentment flowing through her. She knew in her heart that the years of waiting had not been entirely wasted; she and Charles now understood and loved each other as they never would have done if she had gone to him a frightened servant seeking a refuge, to give him physical pleasure. It would never have been more than that. Time and experience had altered both of them for the better, and had shown them the fulness of love.

Charles came to her on a March morning that gave the first promise of spring. She had been out walking in the

country. There were black buds on the ash-twigs, a few
hazel catkins, and a pale primrose. Soon there would be
herbs for the gathering. When she left the lanes and
entered Hythe she decided to walk home by the shore
path. After weeks of rain the horizon was clear at last,
the cool blustery air seemed almost tremulous in the pale
sunshine. The sea was grey-green and full of movement,
the sky tinged with delicate blue and brushed with a
sweep of light cloud. The break and suck of the waves on
the shore echoed in her ears as she walked above,
holding her shawl round her against the snatch of the
breeze. Both beach and path were deserted.

'Gentian . . . Gentian!'

At first she thought she was imagining the sound of her
name, called distantly in Charles's voice as she had
heard it so long ago in this same place when she had
walked away from him, renouncing her love. At the
memory of it tears started to her eyes.

'Gentian . . .'

It was louder. It was real. She turned in swift amazement to see a dark figure—Charles—hurrying towards
her, hand outstretched. She gave a gasp of delight and
began to run.

She saw him take his left hand out of the sling he wore,
so that when he reached her he could clasp both her
hands in his. The left was weak—but he could use it. She
looked up at him, the happiness in her eyes meeting the
triumph in his own. Then he flung his arm about her,
holding her crushed to him, gazing down at her, then
taking her mouth with kisses that claimed back all the
months of separation. She clung to him, feeling the
warmth of his body against hers, and in the same moment love woke the springs of passion in her so that she
felt her life beginning anew.

'My darling,' he murmured. 'Don't cry.' His lips
kissed away her tears. 'We are together at last, my love,'

he went on. 'What's past is past. We shall only count the future now.'

'Charles—dearest Charles—is the waiting really over?'

'Quite over. Today we make a fresh start.'

'How strange it will be—a different life . . .'

She spoke seriously, and he looked down at her, teasing her into a smile.

'You're not nervous, after waiting so long? What do you see in the future, my little white witch?'

Her eyes gave back to him the look of love. 'Only you, Charles. Only you.'

And that was all she needed to see, for now he was all her world.

Mills & Boon

JAN 1988 HARDBACK TITLES

ROMANCE

Dark Desiring *Jacqueline Baird*	2852	0 263 11625 5
My Brother's Keeper *Emma Goldrick*	2853	0 263 11626 3
Dark Lucifer *Stephanie Howard*	2854	0 263 11627 1
Tarik's Mountain *Dana James*	2855	0 263 11628 X
Payment in Love *Penny Jordan*	2856	0 263 11629 8
Takeover *Madeleine Ker*	2857	0 263 11630 1
Rider of the Hills *Miriam Macgregor*	2858	0 263 11631 X
Close Collaboration *Leigh Michaels*	2859	0 263 11632 8
A Golden Touch *Mary Moore*	2860	0 263 11633 6
Heart's Treasure *Annabel Murray*	2861	0 263 11634 4
The Course of True Love *Betty Neels*	2862	0 263 11635 2
A Question of Pride *Michelle Reid*	2863	0 263 11636 0
Fortunes of Love *Jessica Steele*	2864	0 263 11637 9
Mistaken Wedding *Sally Wentworth*	2865	0 263 11638 7
Another Eden *Nicola West*	2866	0 263 11639 5
Savage Hunger *Sara Wood*	2867	0 263 11640 9

MASQUERADE HISTORICAL ROMANCE

The Warlock's Wench *Evelyn S. Armstrong*	M183	0 263 11714 6
No Place for a Lady *Ann Hulme*	M184	0 263 11715 4

TEMPTATION

As Time Goes By *Vicki Lewis Thompson*	0 263 11734 0
The Family Way *Jayne Ann Krentz*	0 263 11735 9

DOCTOR NURSE ROMANCE

New England Nurse *Helen Upshall*	D101	0 263 11716 2
The Surgeon She Married *Elizabeth Harrison*	D102	0 263 11717 0

LARGE PRINT

The Bride Said No *Charlotte Lamb*	169	0 263 11683 2
One in a Million *Sandra Field*	170	0 263 11684 0
A Lasting Kind of Love *Catherine Spencer*	171	0 263 11685 9